TOUCHED
BY YOU

TOUCHED BY YOU

Elle Wright

Kensington Publishing Corp.
www.kensingtonbooks.com

DAFINA BOOKS are published by

Kensington Publishing Corp.
119 West 40th Street
New York, NY 10018

All Kensington Titles, Imprints, and Distributed Lines are available at special quantity discounts for bulk purchases for sales promotions, premiums, fund-raising, and educational or institutional use. Special book excerpts or customized printings can also be created to fit specific needs. For details, write or phone the office of the Kensington special sales manager: Kensington Publishing Corp., 119 West 40th Street, New York, NY 10018, attn: Special Sales Department, Phone: 1-800-221-2647.

Dafina and the Dafina logo Reg. U.S. Pat. & TM Off.

ISBN-13: 978-1-4967-1600-2
ISBN-10: 1-4967-1600-0
First Kensington Mass Market Edition: June 2018

eISBN-13: 978-1-4967-1601-9
eISBN-10: 1-4967-1601-9
First Kensington Electronic Edition: June 2018

10 9 8 7 6 5 4 3 2 1

Printed in the United States of America

To my mother, Regina,
I still can't believe you're not here physically
to take this journey with me.
I want to do things that continue to make you smile,
so I hope you're smiling now.
I feel so blessed to have had you for as long as I did.
You are missed. Love you forever.

Chapter 1

The ground was wet. Cold.

But Carter Marshall couldn't bring himself to move, to walk away. He clutched the weathered copper ornament in his hands. It was the only thing he had left of his old life, the only tangible reminder that they both existed. Everything else was gone, charred beyond repair.

"I'm not sure how to do this," he mumbled to himself. He knew he had to let the anger go now. It had consumed him, filled him to capacity and pushed him to keep going. He wondered what would take its place, or if he'd even be able to let go of the hate he had in his heart for the man who had taken away everything.

The rain pounded on his head, drizzled down his face. It had been an hour since he'd arrived, but he couldn't bring himself to complete his task. Instead, he'd sat there, his expensive Tom Ford suit soaked and his Cole Haan shoes muddy. Nothing mattered anymore. Not his wealth, not his name, not his work. Everything that he'd once held dear seemed like a curse now.

"I'm sorry," he muttered. "I'm sorry I wasn't there. I was too obsessed with work, too driven, too focused on my damn money. I thought if I just worked hard enough, I could give you the life you deserved. I only wanted to make you happy."

His eyes welled with fresh tears. As if he hadn't cried enough already. The loss of his beautiful wife and daughter had devastated him to his core, weakened him. Even now, almost two years later, he could still smell the gasoline, taste the smoke in the air, hear the screams of the neighbors as the fire burned. He recalled the determination on the firemen's faces as they worked to put the blaze out, and he remembered the exact moment they all realized that it was too late.

You're the best part of my day, my hero.

Her words still haunted him. *Her hero.* His wife of three years, his college sweetheart, had told him he was her hero. Only he didn't feel heroic. What was the opposite of hero? Coward. Loser. Nobody.

Instead of being home with his wife and new-born daughter, he'd been working. Late. It seemed his work had eclipsed everything in his life, despite his denials. Krys had told him time and time again to live a little, to enjoy life. But the lure of the prestige, the money, the connections that his business guaranteed was important to him. He'd worked too hard, too long to let it go. He'd been distracted, meetings all day and projects to finish. When the phone rang, he'd moved it to voicemail with a little text that said, **Give me a minute.**

To think that was the last thing Krys heard from

him . . . He'd been so busy he couldn't even pick up the phone and answer. Was she scared? According to the arson investigators, the fire had started around seven o'clock. The call from her came through a little after seven. What if that one phone call could have changed something? Countless hours in therapy, numerous assurances that he couldn't have known, did nothing to quell the guilt he felt every time he looked at her response to his text. The worse part was that he hadn't even seen her response until hours later, after he'd been ushered from the scene of the crime. It read, I love you. Always remember.

Even in her last minutes, she'd been thinking of him. And he'd been thinking of his next project, his next dollar. *What good is all the money in the world without her, without them?*

Closing his eyes, he willed himself to move, to do what he came to do.

He scanned the area around him. It was *their* spot. Krys had insisted they visit as often as possible since it was the place where he'd proposed.

Today would have been their wedding anniversary. Remembering her beautiful face on the day he made her his wife made his heart ache. Krys was beautiful, in a classic "Clair Huxtable" kind of way. She was a good woman, believed that taking care of the home, being a wife and mother was the best job in the world. They'd been so young, so full of hope.

People had questioned him about the choice to marry so soon after college graduation, for even being with the same woman for so long. Even his best friend and business partner, Martin Sullivan, had been wary. And he'd known Krys for as long as he'd known Martin. Carter couldn't explain it, though. He wasn't an impulsive person. Everything Carter had done in life had been carefully planned. It was the reason he and Martin had been so successful. Neither of them played around when it came to business.

Marrying Krys, though, was his destiny. At least, he'd thought so at the time. She'd supported him through some of the worst times of his life—the death of his youngest sister and his grandmother and his parents' subsequent divorce. Krys never wavered, never wanted him to be anybody but himself. She'd never complained when he traveled for work or forgot to take the trash out. She was perfect, and he didn't deserve her. He'd broken the promise to love and to cherish, to have her and to honor her. If he had, he would have answered her call. He should have been there. Especially since she'd always been there for him. Krys had given him the best gift he could ever have—her heart, her body, her soul. He'd promised to protect her, to be there for her. *Except I wasn't, not when she needed me the most.*

Time hadn't made this wound better, hadn't healed him like they told him it would. He'd started to resent them—his parents, his friends, his employees . . . everyone. The questions were becoming unbearable. The sad looks infuriated him. Most of all, when people told him *It will be okay,* he wanted to slap them. Because he was not okay, and wasn't sure he would ever be okay again. He knew he had to try, though. For them. For Krys and for his baby girl, Chloe.

Carter closed his eyes and inhaled the wet, night

air. It was too late to be the father Chloe needed. She wasn't even a year old. He'd never heard her say "Da Da" or had the pleasure of watching her toddle into his waiting arms for the first time. *It's not fair.*

The tears fell freely down his cheeks and his stomach lurched into his chest. *I failed.* Carter looked down at the glass Christmas ornament in his hand. It was shaped like a heart, personalized with their names and their wedding date. Krys had purchased it for their first Christmas as a married couple. Sighing heavily, Carter dropped the ornament into the small hole he'd dug, next to the tree where he'd dropped on one knee and proposed to his first love, his only love.

"I made them pay, Krys."

Within days after the fire, the Detroit Police Department had arrested the young men that were responsible. But pressure from city officials had them backtracking on the investigation. Of course they did, because one of the men, the main culprit, was the college-aged son of one of the most influential business owners in the city.

The McKnight family was well-known in the Detroit area. Carter had effectively launched a smear campaign, blasted them on every social media site. Through his own computer skills and those of his partner, they'd crippled the McKnight business. Revenge was best served with a depleted bank account. A guilty verdict wasn't enough for him. He'd just been awarded a settlement in the civil lawsuit he'd brought against the city and the family for hampering the investigation.

Money wasn't his motive, though. He wanted

them to lose everything, just like he had. Those young men had destroyed his life on a whim, because of a bet. They'd targeted his house because it was on the corner lot in a mostly African American neighborhood—because they could.

"I donated most of the money to the burn unit at Children's Hospital and set up a foundation to help burn victims and families who've lost everything to a fire."

It would never bring them back. He knew that, and he'd certainly paid the price of the personal vendetta he'd waged against the culprits, with his family and his work. The criminal and civil trials had taken a lot out of him. Now, it was time for him to let the anger go, let them go. That was the hard part.

He covered the glass ornament with mud and stood to his full height. By all rights, he should be celebrating. He'd won. His mother had set up a family dinner, and his brothers had mentioned a hookup he had no intention of taking advantage of. What would be the purpose? Sex? Because that's all it would be. He was empty, a void that would never be filled.

"Everyone wants me to move on, but how? Is it even okay to love someone else?"

And now he was officially crazy, talking to the night air, to Krys like she could actually answer. At the same time, if he had a sign, maybe he could let go fully. His wife and child died, but his love never would. That much was certain. *I don't have room for anyone else.*

"I love you. Take care of each other."

Sighing, he made his way back to his car and, after one last glance at the tree, sped off.

A houseful of people awaited him when he arrived at his mother's place about an hour later. There were old friends, cousins, and more cousins. The smell of fried chicken wafted to his nose, and his stomach growled.

"Carter, get your butt in here."

Iris Johnston was a loud, formidable woman. She pulled him into her strong arms and squeezed tightly. Carter wasn't an overemotional person, rarely gave out hugs, but he couldn't help but wrap his arms around her plump waist and relax into her embrace.

"Ma, I thought it was only going to be family." He pulled back and kissed his mother on her cheek. "You promised not to make a big deal about this."

Iris shrugged and gestured to the table of food in the corner. "Eat. You deserve this. You've had a tough few years."

His stepfather, Chris, joined them and patted him on the shoulder. "She's right, Carter. Have a seat and relax yourself. This is the least we could do for you."

Carter walked through the house, greeting the people who'd turned out for him. One by one, they hugged him, gave him sad glances before they offered more congrats and condolences. *Shit.* It was like Krys and Chloe had just died. His thoughts flashed back to all the food his mother insisted be dropped off to the house, all the stares.

When he finally made it to the kitchen, he grinned at the sight of his brothers.

"Carter, I'm glad you're finally here," Kendall said, giving him a quick man-hug. "Mom has been worrying the shit out of us." Kendall was the baby brother, and officially a college graduate as of two months ago. It had been a happy day when he'd walked across the stage, because they all thought he wouldn't make it.

"Yeah, man. She was a nightmare." His brother, Marvin, leaned against the sink. Carter reached out and clasped his hand in their signature handshake. Marvin was the middle son, the lawyer of the family.

"Well, I'm here. Not sure how much longer, though. I told her I didn't want a party."

"Baby brother, if you leave, we're all going to have to pay for it." Carter turned to see his older sister, Aisha, standing behind him. "And let me tell you, I'm sick of y'all fools leaving me behind to clean up your messes."

Carter pulled his sister into a tight hug. "I'm sorry, sis. But you know crowds are not my thing. I'm getting antsy just listening to the chatter."

Aisha's expression softened, her brown eyes wide with unshed tears. "I know. But you have to start living again. You know Krys would want that." She rubbed his cheek. "You can't die with her. You're still here for a reason."

Carter blinked and prayed for an intervention, anything to stop the pain in his sister's eyes. She was worried about him. Being the oldest of five siblings, Aisha had been a sponge her whole life, taking on their emotions like they were her own.

"I don't want to talk about this," Carter said, leaning down and kissing his sister on the forehead. "Where's the food?"

Aisha's shoulders fell, and she nodded. "I'll fix you a plate."

Moments later, he was sitting at the small table in

the kitchen, eating while the party roared on in the other room. Aisha sat across from him, watching him eat.

"I've been calling you. When are you going to come back to the office?" she asked. Aisha worked as the chief financial officer of Marshall and Sullivan Software Consulting Inc. She basically kept the company up and running while he and Martin traveled the world. His sister had been calling him for weeks, every single day. "Martin needs you back in the office."

Carter knew he'd been a lousy business partner. Martin had basically picked up all the slack in the last two years. It wasn't right for him to continue this way. And with his best friend recently tying the knot, Carter wanted to be able to step up again to let him be a happy newlywed. "I know, Aisha. I plan to go back soon."

"Soon? The office has been inundated with calls, requests for proposals. You're on the verge of something bigger than you ever dreamed, especially with the Wellspring offer. Don't give it all up."

"Aisha, please shut up!" he snapped. His sister's mouth closed in a tight line, and he immediately regretted his outburst. "I'm sorry. It's just . . ." *Forget it.* She wouldn't understand. Work was the last thing he wanted to do, because work was what he'd allowed to get between him and his wife for too long.

"I get it," his sister said, picking at the table with her thumbnail. "You're hurting, and I don't want to take that away from you."

He was such an asshole. Aisha had only been trying to help, to take care of him like she'd always

done. It wasn't her fault he was incapable of being
social. He had never really been the type of person
that enjoyed being around a lot of people. Carter
had always been more solitary, preferring to be by
himself than go to the club.

"I didn't mean to yell." He dropped his fork on
his plate. "But Krys is gone, Aisha. She's dead, and
so is my baby girl. It takes a huge effort for me to
get out of the damn bed in the morning. I just . . .
I need some time."

"I know Krys is gone, Booch. I get it."

Carter rolled his eyes at the use of his childhood
nickname. Only a few people still used it, but it
always reminded him of being a kid. He wasn't a
child anymore. He wasn't going to conform to everyone's ideas on how he should handle his grief.
Shit, he was the one that had to go home every night
to an empty house, an empty life.

"No, you don't get it, Aisha." Carter pushed away
from the table and stood, pacing the floor. "Please
stop pretending you do." He pointed at his chest
and whirled around to face her. "I'm the one that
has to deal with the fact that some ignorant prick
decided to set fire to my freakin' house. With *my*
family inside. I'm the one that has to look at myself
in the mirror every day, knowing that my wife was
scared and needed someone to talk to her and I
didn't answer the phone."

"You can't be everywhere at once, Booch. You
were working. Krys understood that about you."

"How do you know what Krys understood?" The
anger that rose up in him was irrational and di-
rected solely at the one person who didn't deserve
it. "She needed me." Bile rushed up his throat and

he fought to control it from coming out, spewing over his mother's hardwood floor.

Aisha stood and approached him, fire in her brown eyes. She gripped his chin and twisted it downward to meet her gaze. "You want to know how I know? Krys called me."

Carter's eyes widened. "What?"

"I didn't want to tell you because I knew it wouldn't help you at the time. You had the trial and then the lawsuit. It was keeping you going. Now that it's over, I need you to hear me, Carter."

He swallowed roughly, clenched his hands into fists.

She sighed. "Krys called me that night. She knew she wasn't going to make it." His sister's eyes filled with tears. "She needed to talk about some things. One thing she made sure she said was that she loved you. Carter, she loved you. Everything about you. But she knew you. She knew that you'd let her death consume you, she knew you'd let this ruin you. Your wife, my sister-in-law, wanted to be sure that you didn't. She wanted you to live, to have a life even though she wasn't here. She made me promise to tell you when the time was right. I'm telling you now."

Exhausted and emotional, Carter gave in, letting the tears that had filled his eyes spill. He fell back into the chair. His head bowed, he whispered, "I don't know how to do this, Aisha. How can I live without her?"

Aisha pulled a chair in front of him and sat down, tilting her head to meet his gaze. "It won't be easy. But you have to. You deserve to live. That's what she wanted for you. God didn't keep you here so that you can die a slow death, in your grief."

"What else did she say?" His voice cracked. "Was she scared?"

Shaking her head, his sister squeezed is knee. "Krys cried, but not because she was scared for herself. She didn't want Chloe, your baby girl, to suffer. She was scared for you, for the family she'd leave behind. I, on the other hand, was hysterical with tears."

Knowing that Krys wasn't scared for herself didn't surprise Carter. His wife was never scared. It was something he'd always loved about her. During labor, she'd refused to take pain meds. But she'd squeezed the shit out of his hand. So bad, he'd needed it iced afterward. "I can imagine you bawling. You're such a big baby."

"Hey, I'm still the oldest."

The room descended into silence as they sat there. Finally, he said, "I miss her." The admission was probably obvious to his sister, but it was the first time he'd said it out loud to anyone. It was like he'd been walking in a haze, refusing to show anyone that he was affected. Only the people closest to him could tell, and that was because they knew his routine, his personality. Everything about him had changed that October night.

Aisha pulled him into a strong hug. "I know."

They stayed like that for what felt like an eternity, him being held by his big sister. They'd grown up, but remained close. As children, they were joined at the hip. Only two years apart, Aisha had dragged him everywhere with her, to all the parties. She'd been taking care of him since they were toddlers, when she would sneak him cookies under the kitchen table.

When he pulled away, he brushed her tears away. "Thank you," he mouthed.

She gave him a wobbly smile. "Always."

"What's going on at work?"

"So much. Martin is handling everything, but I don't want him to get burned out. He's finally settled with Ryleigh and they're happy. They deserve some time to just be newlyweds. Traveling to Wellspring, Michigan, is not ideal for him right now."

Carter thought about Aisha's plea. She was definitely right. Martin did deserve to enjoy his new marriage. And he had to step up and let him.

"Who was scheduled to go with Martin to Wellspring?" Carter was so out of touch he couldn't even remember the Wellspring project particulars.

"Walt." Walter Hunt was the new software engineer they'd hired a few months ago. "He's not strong enough to handle point on this project. Handling a project of this magnitude is too much for him."

Carter rolled his eyes. Parker Wells Sr., president of Wellspring Water Corporation, had hired Marshall and Sullivan because they were the best in the state, and they'd designed an excellent Enterprise Resource Planning system. And his sister was a big part of that. *Aisha is right. This is too big a job to trust to anyone other than me or Martin.*

"So what are you going to do?" Aisha asked, a mixture of worry and challenge lining her face. "Someone is supposed to be in Wellspring on Monday to meet with the players. We've pushed the date back already. If we don't do this—"

"Calm down, Aisha." Carter had the perfect solution—one that would give him time and space from the emotions that surrounded him in Detroit. "I'll go. I'll head the project myself. And I'll leave in the morning."

Carter and Aisha talked for several more minutes, working out the details of his trip. Aisha also gave him updates on a few other issues with the company. He would leave first thing in the morning and drive to Wellspring, which was approximately a three-hour drive from Detroit. A hotel had already been booked for Martin, so Aisha was charged with switching the reservations to Carter's name.

"Aisha?"

His sister turned toward the door. "Hey, girl!" Aisha stood and hugged the woman who'd interrupted their conversation. "Long time, no see. Carter, remember Ayanna? We went to high school together."

Carter smiled at the woman. He definitely remembered Ayanna. The woman standing before him, with her light skin and light eyes, was still as beautiful as he remembered. Instead of the trademark braids she'd rocked in high school, her hair was wavy and flowing down her back. But the attraction he once had to her was long gone.

Ayanna was also his "first." And judging by the way Aisha was singing her friend's praises, his sister didn't know. There were rules, after all. Back then, Aisha had banned him from ogling her friends. Little did she know or even realize, her friends weren't exactly shy when it came to him. Carter might have been a one-woman man when he met Krys, but he hadn't always been that way.

Aisha was yapping away, catching up with her friend. And Ayanna was checking him out. The heat in her eyes told him exactly what she was thinking.

"How have you been, Carter?" Ayanna asked, batting her long lashes. "You've been in my prayers."

"I'm good. And you?"

"I've been enjoying life." Ayanna inched closer to him and wrapped her arms around him in a tight hug.

Carter inhaled Ayanna's scent. She still smelled the same. It would be so easy to take it to the next level. The look in the woman's eyes when she pulled back and shot him a sexy grin was an invitation. Any other man would have run with it. All Carter felt was cold. But this could be what he needed to move on. He just wasn't sure he believed that.

"I didn't know you were coming," he said, wondering if Ayanna was the "hookup" his brothers had told him about. Only Marvin knew of their dalliance all those years ago.

Ayanna folded her arms over her breasts. "I actually was in the neighborhood, saw the cars and decided to stop. Your mother sent me in here to give you best wishes."

Aisha piped up. "You should totally stay. There is plenty of food, and we'll be playing cards later. It'll be good to catch up."

"I'd love to," Ayanna said. "It's a shame that we grew up together and barely see each other."

Detroit was a large city, with a population of almost seven hundred thousand people. Plenty of people he'd grown up with still lived in the city, but seemed so far away. Many of the kids he went to school with had left, though. Some had moved to the suburbs, and others had left Michigan altogether.

Growing up in Detroit was a good experience for Carter. His parents both worked good jobs, and their neighborhood was a safe haven for him. Everyone knew each other and looked out for each other. He remembered block parties and going to the skating rink with friends. No matter what the outside world thought of his city, it was his home. Although he'd had plenty of offers from different companies, he'd never considered moving. It helped that Krys was also from Detroit. They'd actually grown up fifteen miles away from each other, but had never met.

Thinking of Krys brought him back from the walk down memory lane. Even if Ayanna was giving him "the eye," he had no business even considering it. Especially today.

Taking a deep breath, Carter grabbed his still-full plate and tossed it in the waste bin. "I'm going to go out and talk to Mom before I leave," he announced to the two women. "I'll call you in the morning, Aisha—before I leave."

Even if he hadn't believed it was a good idea before, he was sure that taking on this project was the perfect solution—a new town, a new opportunity where no one knew him. Wellspring might be the welcome change of pace he needed.

Chapter 2

Brooklyn Wells hated charity functions. *But I love chocolate,* she thought.

She snatched a chocolate éclair from the tray as the waiter passed her, and stuffed it into her mouth. Moaning in delight, she chewed the piece of heaven as if it was the last one she'd ever eat. Damn, that was good.

"If you don't slow down, you're going to turn into an éclair, Brooklyn."

Rolling her eyes, Brooklyn assessed her stepmother as she walked by with a wealthy benefactor. The sound of her fake, monotone laugh echoed in the massive ballroom. The woman was as stiff as a board. Or was it boring as a stiff? She snickered to herself. It wasn't funny, but she'd been forced to amuse herself all night. Between countless handshakes, fake smiles, and polite nods, she'd had enough. But her father, the almighty, had mandated that she attend—for the family. Never mind that the charity was in the top twenty-five of America's worst charities. Despite her countless emails

and pleas to donate to a more deserving charity—
one that didn't line its executives' pockets with cash
and one *not* connected to her father—her domi-
neering father dismissed her requests and told her
she'd better "shut up and show up."

"Can I talk to you?"

Sighing heavily, Brooklyn looked at her ex. Sterling King used to send a shiver up her spine with
one look from his startling gray eyes. But the puppy-
dog look he was sporting at that very moment only
made her want to shove him into the tray of caviar
right behind him.

"I have nothing to say to you," she hissed. "We've
been through this so many times, Sterling. If you—"

Her words were cut off by his hands pressing
urgently against her back as he guided her toward
the back of the room, away from the stares of Wellspring society.

When they were tucked away from the crowd,
behind a pillar, she jerked out of his hold. "What
are you doing?" She folded her arms across her
chest. "I told you I didn't want to t—"

Before she could finish her thought, he was on
his knees. In his hand was a box holding a solitaire
marquise-cut diamond. Absolutely stunning. But
not her style.

"Brooklyn, I love you. Will you marry me?"

She glanced behind her, hoping her father
wasn't lurking in the shadows. It would be just like
Parker Sr. to have planned this entire thing. For all
she knew, he'd purchased the ring himself. Her
father had been trying to get her to marry Sterling
since she'd graduated from college. Something
about building an alliance between the King and

Wells family. Brooklyn could care less about the business and her father's interests, so she hadn't intended to follow her father's directive when it came to Sterling and marriage.

"Um . . ." It wasn't like her to be rendered speechless. But she couldn't seem to find the words—well, the one word she needed to say. "I-I have to . . . pee." She turned on her heels and dashed through the ballroom without a backward glance.

Brooklyn breezed past a group of investors, lifted a glass of champagne from a moving tray, and headed straight to the private bathroom in the hallway. Once inside, she locked the door and gulped down the sparkling drink.

Gazing at herself in the mirror, she turned on the water and pulled out her cell phone. When her brother picked up, she whispered, "Parker?"

"Sis, where are you? Didn't I just see you?"

"I need you," she pleaded.

"What is that in the background? Water? Where are you?"

"I'm in the private bathroom."

"Um, you're crazy. Why are you calling me from the bathroom?"

Brooklyn knew he was on his way to her. After their mother died, her older brother took care of her when her father never bothered. He took her everywhere with him, introduced her to all of his friends. He'd threatened all his fellow football teammates with bodily harm if they even dared to approach her. So, she ended up with twenty brothers and no boyfriends.

Even now, as adults, she recognized that they didn't have the same philosophy in life. Parker was all about the family business and name, being the guaranteed Wells heir, and she couldn't care less about her trust fund or the perks her last name provided. But she never doubted her brother would be there for her, no questions asked. She heard him greet someone, excuse himself from another person, then . . . There was a knock on the door.

She rushed to the door, unlocked it, and swung it open, pulling him inside with her.

"What the . . . ?" he said, brushing off his charcoal-gray designer suit and straightening his tie. Parker crossed his arms over his chest. "You've really flipped out this time, sis. Why are you holed up in the bathroom?"

"Sterling proposed," she blurted out.

Instead of the fury she'd half expected in her brother's eyes, she was shocked to see the light of amusement in his brown orbs.

"Are you . . . Parker, did you hear what I said?"

Then, a smirk? Her dear brother thought her predicament was funny.

Clearing his throat, he said, "Sis, calm down." He gripped her shoulders and squeezed. "You had to know this was coming sooner or later."

"Sterling and I haven't been together in years!" she yelled. "I can't even stand him, let alone want to marry him. What was he thinking?"

Although she and Sterling had grown up in the same circles, and were great childhood friends, their attempt at a relationship went up in flames after three months. Unfortunately, his handsome—almost perfect—face and physique weren't enough to keep her interest. Not only was he as boring as glue, he was horrible in the sack. As if that wasn't bad enough, his incessant need to call her "Brooksie-lynsie" made her want to throw up. God, she hated stupid pet names with a white-hot passion.

"You know this is all Senior, right?" Parker told her. Her father had insisted that they call him "Senior" instead of Dad, although Brooklyn was the only one that could get away with calling him Daddy at times. She guessed it had a lot to do with her father's need to be superior to everyone else in the world. "Just tell that idiot hell no, and keep it moving. This isn't the end of the world." Her older brother barked out a laugh. "I can't believe you locked yourself in a bathroom. Get it together." He shook her gently for emphasis. He wiped the corner of her eye with his thumb. "Fix your face, baby sis. You are looking rough."

"You get on my nerves." She pouted, turning to the mirror and pulling out her compact. She eyed her brother through the mirror. "I panicked, okay? I'm allowed to panic. We can't all maintain control like you, big brother."

Parker stared at her and gave her a small smile. "You remind me of Mom."

Averting her gaze, she busied herself with her makeup. "I can't add tears to this night, Parker." She missed her mother, Maria, with everything in her. Her mother had been dead for fourteen years, but the grief was still just under the surface. Especially since her death was so tragic. "Let's just concentrate on getting me through the night without killing Sterling."

He placed a kiss on the top of her head. Her

brother had more than a few inches on her in height, but he never made her feel small, like some of the other people in town. "Point taken. Stay clear of Sterling for the night. We can't have a scene. But tomorrow, make it clear that you'll never be Mrs. King. No matter how our father has conspired with his father to make it happen."

Her father had been cultivating a business relationship with Sterling's family for years. When Sterling's father was elected to the state senate, Brooklyn's father practically salivated with glee. Although Brooklyn wasn't involved in the daily business of the family company, she knew her father thought that having political allies would further strengthen his hold on the town and the state. For years now, Senior had been attempting to buy land in several counties to tap into the springs, and expand the company. It was obvious Senior had something up his sleeve, but Brooklyn would not be a pawn in any game her father wanted to play.

Parker picked up her empty champagne flute and opened the door. He held the glass up to her. "You need another of these. And go find that man with the chocolate puff things you love so much. It's going to be okay."

She waved at her brother as he strutted out of the small bathroom and followed him a few minutes later. Spotting a cute server with tray full of those yummy chocolate eclairs, she grabbed one and smiled at him as he strolled by. When he returned her smile with one of his own and a wink, she averted her gaze and pretended to look for someone in the crowd. She was not in the mood to be propositioned or hit on.

"And please try not to get drunk tonight, Brooklyn." Senior's fifth wife stopped right in front of her and scowled. "This is a charity event, not a Super Bowl party."

"Leave me the hell alone," Brooklyn muttered under her breath.

"I heard you," Patricia hissed with a hard roll of her eyes. The woman, barely ten years older than Brooklyn, smoothed a hand over her messed-up blond wig.

"I'm sure you did. Did I stutter?" Brooklyn said between clenched teeth.

"Look, I'm not playing with you," Patricia snapped. "Be good."

"You are not my mother, so stop acting like it."

"Well, I married your father."

"So did his last few wives, before he dumped them."

Patricia grumbled incoherently before she stomped off, probably in search of Brooklyn's father. At any minute, Senior would come over and berate her for daring to talk to his child bride that way.

Shrugging, Brooklyn scanned the room, looking for her brother. Parker was standing with one of her father's board members. They were talking in hushed tones, probably about some business deal. Parker was always talking about business, always trying to please their father. For the life of her, she couldn't understand why. It's not like he didn't loathe him as much as she did. Unlike her, though, Parker thrived on business and he was good at what he did. One day, he'd run the company—Wellspring Water Corporation.

The music faded and the chatter dimmed. Parker Sr. approached the podium, Patricia close to his side and . . . Sterling right behind him. Dread coated her insides as she watched the trio on the stage. *What the hell is going on?* When she met Parker's concerned gaze across the room, she guessed he felt she same way.

"Hello, ladies and gentlemen," her father's baritone voice greeted over the microphone. "I'm so glad that you've joined us tonight. We're on target to meet our fundraising goal for such a worthwhile organization. But I hope you don't mind me taking a few minutes to make an announcement and a toast. The servers will be around to make sure your glasses are filled."

With a smile, Brooklyn took the offered glass of champagne from a short server and waited for her father to speak again. Something told her that what was coming next was a game changer.

With his glass held high, her father smiled and wrapped his arm around Sterling. "I've watched this young man grow into quite a remarkable young man, capable of greatness."

Brooklyn gulped down her champagne.

"I want to congratulate him and my beautiful daughter on their engagement."

Brooklyn choked on the champagne and it sprayed out on the woman in front of her.

"Congratulations, baby girl," her father announced before turning to Sterling. "You will be a fine addition to the Wells family, son."

She glared at her father, standing in front of

the crowded room with a satisfied Sterling. That son of a—

"Brooklyn, cóme here," her father commanded from the stage.

Before she could stop herself, she shouted, "Hell, no!"

Gasps from the crowd filled her ears as her gaze met her brother's across the room. Parker started toward her, but she backed away. Out of the corner of her eye, she saw appalled older women frowning at her. But she couldn't care. She didn't care.

I have to get out of here. But her legs didn't seem to want to work right. As she stumbled toward the door, as if she was stepping in quicksand, she tried to block out the loud whispers from the guests. Focused straight ahead, she finally took off at a sprint, intent on getting as far away as possible. Vaguely, she heard Parker calling her name, but if she stopped to look at him or speak to him, she'd never make it out of there.

The cold, bitter temperatures smacked her in the face when she made it outside. She hugged herself, rubbing her arms. Glancing back to see if anyone followed her, she shuffled down the street. Her dress was long, her toes were bare, and the snow was coming down, but she had to keep going. To where, she didn't know.

Grabbing her phone, she tried to dial her friend Nicole. No answer. She typed a quick 911 text to her friend. Distracted, she started across the street. She heard the blaring horn before she saw the truck heading straight for her. She tried to run, but slipped and fell on her side. Opening her mouth to

scream, she frantically searched for someone. The
street was empty. Bracing herself for the impact,
she prayed for mercy and forgiveness for being
such a bitch sometimes.

Only there was no pain. Instead she felt like she
was wrapped in a warm, heavenly cocoon surrounded by trees and ginger and . . . Gain detergent?
Was she in heaven?

"Are you okay?"

Her eyes popped open and she was met with
beautiful, brown, unfamiliar ones staring back at
her. Her mouth fell open when she realized that
she wasn't sitting at the Lord's feet. She was still,
in fact, outside in the brittle Michigan cold, lying
underneath a stranger. She bucked up and the man
stood to his full height.

She peered up at him and back at his waiting
hand. Sliding her hand into his, she let him pull
her to her feet.

"Are you okay?" he repeated, surveying her face
with a worried expression. "You were . . . I thought
that truck was going to . . . I picked you up and
pulled you out of the way, but slipped on ice and
we both went down."

"It's . . . okay." Suddenly, she felt warm again and
it wasn't because the man had taken his own coat
off and wrapped it around her shoulders. She had
a strong feeling it had something to do with the
man himself standing before her. Brooklyn had
never seen him before, but she was immediately
intrigued by him. Maybe it was because he'd
saved her life? Or maybe it was because he was
fine as hell. Either way, she wanted to find out more
about him.

He swayed back and forth on his feet and scanned the immediate area. "Do you need me to call anyone?" he asked, shoving his hands into his pockets.

She shook her head and waved a hand in dismissal. "No, I'm just going to head over to my friend's place. It's right around the corner. I'm . . . I can't thank you enough for saving my life. I thought for sure that truck was going to take me out."

"No worries." His full lips held her attention as he asked her . . . Lord, she didn't even hear what he'd said. Was it weird that she was focused on some strange man's mouth after she'd barely escaped death?

Shaking herself from her haze, she asked, "What did you say?"

He chuckled. "Just that I'm glad you're okay."

"I'm sure I have a few scrapes and bruises from the fall. But I feel okay."

"Good to hear," he said, glancing at his watch.

"Thanks again. I wasn't paying attention. I was distracted," she babbled on as she brushed the snow off her dress. "I don't know what got into me. It's just . . . I was trying to get as far away as I could, but I didn't bring my coat, and Nicole didn't answer her . . ." The rest of her sentence died on her lips when she looked up and realized she was talking to herself. The mystery man was gone.

Chapter 3

"Do you have anything to say for yourself?"

Brooklyn sighed heavily. She'd listened to her father go on and on about how she'd embarrassed him in front of the entire town, made a mockery of the Wells name, and she was so close to telling him to go to hell.

She scanned the massive home office, remembered how she used to run the halls searching for hiding spaces. More times than not, she'd find herself hidden behind the heavy curtains or beneath the oak desk in the center of the room. The house had been through many transformations—usually with the addition of a new wife—but the office hadn't changed much. Brooklyn never knew why Senior had refused to update it. It still had the drab beige walls, wood paneling, and tall bookshelves. The same lamp stood in the corner, even though it hadn't worked in fifteen years. Lining the walls were paintings of Wellspring in various stages, from the first building erected on the vast expanse of land to the huge corporation that it was now. In the middle was a huge oil painting of her great-grandfather, the founder of Wellspring Water.

Wellspring Water was a top bottled water company worldwide, with several brands of spring water, mineral water, distilled water, sparkling and flavored water, and now iced teas. The company's top brand, its namesake Wellspring Spring Water, was sourced from natural springs in and around the Wellspring area. The Wells family was powerful, with production sites in twenty countries. Water was big business, and worth billions of dollars, and Senior had made it his life's mission to corner the market.

Brooklyn hugged herself. As dark and cold as the space was, she wondered how it was ever comforting to her. When she was a small child, she'd loved to visit the office because it smelled like her dad. He was her world back then. No matter what was wrong, he'd always made it better. Her gaze passed over the large eleven-by-fourteen picture of his current wife, and she remembered why that had all changed. Sadness shot through her at the memory of her mother and her tragic death. Life was never the same after that cold day in November, right before Thanksgiving.

Brooklyn couldn't help but resent Senior for being her only surviving parent because he hadn't acted like a loving parent during that time. Instead of supporting them through their mother's death, he'd pushed them off on nannies. From the moment the casket was lowered into the ground, the loving father she'd cherished ceased to exist. In front of her was the man he'd become—cold, calculating, and distant.

"Brooklyn!" he blared, startling her out of her thoughts.

She looked up at her father, who was now standing, leaning over his desk. His hands were balled up into fists as he glared at her, almost like she was his enemy. It wasn't the first time he'd made her feel like that, and it wouldn't be the last. Things had changed between them a long time ago, and he was no longer her hero.

She stood to her feet and yanked her purse off the desk. "Senior, I got it," she hissed. "You're disappointed in me for not marrying a man I can't stand because that's what *you* want me to do. You've basically farmed me out to the highest bidder."

"Watch your tone, Brooklyn," he said between clenched teeth. It was the same tone he used to intimidate business rivals, which infuriated her even more.

"No, you watch *your* tone," she snapped. Brooklyn had no idea where all this false bravado was coming from, but she'd run with it even if her knees felt like they'd give out on her any minute. "You'd rather I forget every ambition, every hope for my life, as long as it suits Wellspring Water. And I'm not going to do it. I can't do it."

"You will do what I tell you," he ordered.

She frowned, determined not to let a single tear fall. "Marrying Sterling would be hell on earth for me. Why can't you see that?"

"It doesn't matter," he said, matter-of-factly. "We've already discussed this. As far as I'm concerned, this conversation is over. If you want to continue living in this house, off of *my* money, you will do as you're told. Period."

Brooklyn thought about her father's threat. Knowing Senior, he'd meant every word. It was further confirmation that their relationship would never be repaired. After her mother had died, she'd rebelled, tested him in everything she'd done, got into trouble several times. When he was fed up, he'd shipped her out of the state to a prominent boarding and day school in Wellesley, Massachusetts.

A devastated Brooklyn had retreated into herself. Not only had she lost her mother, but her father had shipped her off like she was expendable, away from her brothers and Nicole. It was torture. But what he'd originally meant for punishment had turned out to be a blessing. Brooklyn slowly realized she loved it in the Boston area. She'd made wonderful friends, focused on her studies, and thrived away from Senior. She'd spent three years at her boarding school before her father yanked her out of the school to return home for no obvious reason other than he could.

Because of her father's ire, she'd been forced to finish high school in Wellspring. And even then, she hadn't let him deter her. Brooklyn wanted to make a difference. She didn't want to sit up on high and look down her nose at the people who needed help the most. She wanted to do the dirty work, the types of things no one else would do, and she would do that regardless of what her father said. If that meant she had to move out, so be it.

Brooklyn never had any intention of staying with her father long-term anyway. The only reason she even lived in *his* house was because she'd been saving to purchase her own home. Staying in the family home had been a convenient way to stack her money, since her father still controlled her access to her trust fund.

Still, it felt like her father had just backhanded her. The mere fact that he was threatening to throw *her* away if she didn't marry Sterling wasn't lost on her. And even though it wasn't a surprise, it still stung because it had effectively destroyed the tiny thread of hope that her real dad was hiding somewhere in the man standing before her.

Brooklyn gripped her clutch in her hand, closed her eyes tight. Damn that tear that slipped down her cheek. She wiped it away and turned on her heels. Stalking to the door, she swung it open. "Well, I guess I'm moving out," she said, slamming the door behind her.

A few hours later, Brooklyn walked into the same hotel she'd left the night before. This time, she had three suitcases full of clothes, a duffel bag, and her purse.

"I don't know why you decided to move out before you found a place to stay," Nicole said with a sigh, shifting the garment bag from her left shoulder to her right.

Brooklyn gave her best friend a side-eyed glance. "Shut it. I had no choice. I'm not marrying Sterling. I had to get the hell out of there."

Brooklyn and Nicole dragged her things to the front desk. After a few minutes, Nicole handed her the room key.

"Thanks," Brooklyn said, with a sad smile.

Nicole nodded and started toward the elevator. Once they lugged her things to room 305, her friend turned to her. "Are you sure you want to do this?"

Without answering, Brooklyn opened the door and stepped into the suite.

"Brooklyn, this is crazy. You can't live here."

"I can, and I will. At least until I find a place." Brooklyn pushed a suitcase into the closet and dropped the duffel bag on the bed.

"Your father owns the hotel. I wouldn't put it past him to have them kick you out. He's done it before."

"Don't remind me," Brooklyn said, plopping down on the bed. She eyed her friend as she hung up the garment bag and walked over to stand in front of her. "Besides, that's why we got the room in your name. Thank you, by the way."

"You're welcome." Nicole smoothed a hand over her auburn hair. "Hun, I know you're upset, but I need you stop reacting and start planning."

Brooklyn rubbed her friend's growing stomach. "Like you did?" she said, arching a brow at her very pregnant friend.

"Hey, I planned to get married and have kids." Her friend planted a hand on her hip as if she were upset. The gleam in her big, doe eyes told Brooklyn that she wasn't mad at the dig. "Yes, the pregnancy came before the marriage, but the baby will be born to happily married parents."

Brooklyn smiled at the first friend she'd ever had. Nicole had been there for Brooklyn since she got glue stuck in her hair in Ms. Brown's first-grade classroom. And she'd happily returned the favor when Kyle Wilson hit her friend in the head with a flying kickball. Brooklyn chuckled to herself as she remembered beating Kyle with her Trapper

Keeper. Who knew, twenty years later, Kyle and Nicole would be married and expecting their first child.

The road to marriage for Nicole and Kyle wasn't easy though. Brooklyn remembered the panic that accompanied the positive pregnancy test only two months before Nicole's planned wedding. Between Nicole's erratic mood swings and her very religious family, Brooklyn had worried that her friend's dream church wedding wouldn't happen. It was Brooklyn that approached Pastor Locke, Nicole's father, and begged him to allow the ceremony to go on. Her friend was the most beautiful bride she'd ever seen.

"You'd better be happy. I'm sure I could find that old binder and smack the shit out of Kyle again." The two lifelong friends laughed as they both fell back on the mattress. As Brooklyn peered up at the trace ceiling, she thought about what had just happened with her father. A lump formed in her throat and the tears finally fell unchecked.

Nicole rolled over and pulled Brooklyn into her arms, rubbing her back gently. "It's going to be okay, hun. You'll see."

"I think I hate him," she cried into her friend's cashmere sweater. It wasn't true, of course. She didn't hate him, even though she wished she could, more often than not. "I'm not sure why I thought I could stay there and avoid him meddling in my life." Brooklyn had chosen to stay in the pool house rather than the main house when she'd moved back home. It had been her failed attempt at a little privacy. "And despite how he's treated me, Parker, and Bryson, I still find myself missing the father he was when I was a kid. Even though I know that man doesn't exist anymore. To think, he's willing to barter with my life for business . . . How could he do this to me?"

"I don't know." Nicole's voice was thick with emotion and Brooklyn didn't need to see her friend's face to know that she was crying with her.

"It's like he's selling cattle or something, like I'm just a means to an end to him. It's always about Wellspring Water, never about me."

"Have you called Parker?"

Shaking her head, Brooklyn said, "No. He'd just try to ride in on his horse and save me. He has too much to lose. I can't involve him."

"I'm sure he wants to be involved. He loves you, Brooklyn."

"I know, but he's positioning himself as Dad's successor. If he aligns himself with me, it could ruin that. He's worked so hard to gain his trust."

"Okay, well I'm here," Nicole said. "I'll stay with you tonight."

"No," she mumbled, rubbing her face. "You're a newlywed, Nic. And your due date is next month. Go home to your husband."

"I don't know why you didn't come stay with us." Her friend squeezed her arm to get her attention. "We have plenty of room. I'd just hate it if your father pulled some stunt on you in the middle of the night."

Brooklyn knew Nicole had a reason to be worried. One holiday, Brooklyn had returned home for a visit and had promptly made an enemy out of Senior's fourth wife. When wife number four had accused her of stealing a fur coat, her father had taken the lying woman's side. Brooklyn couldn't stand to be around that woman, so she'd booked a room at the hotel, only to be kicked out of her room on her father's orders—at two o'clock in the morning, with subzero temperatures outside. Nicole and Kyle had come to get her and spent the whole night consoling her.

"I'll be fine," Brooklyn assured her. "I'll sleep it off and figure out what to do in the morning."

Her friend didn't look convinced. "Okay, but I'm only a phone call away. I'll come right over if you need me."

Brooklyn shot her friend a watery smile. "I know, and I love you for it." She pushed herself up on her elbows. "It sucks having a father who doesn't care about my feelings. It's like I don't have any parents."

It was a hard lesson to learn, but Brooklyn realized she'd lost both of her parents that night. Senior could not be trusted to be the father she needed. He'd shown her time and time again that she didn't rate with him.

Brooklyn remembered going to him, after her mother's funeral, because she'd needed his comfort. The warm hug she'd been seeking would never come because she'd walked in on him getting serviced by one of his mistresses in her mother's bedroom. And he'd had the nerve to get mad at her for interrupting. She never looked at him the same again after that, and he didn't care. He hadn't even run after her when she'd bolted from the house that night.

Instead, he'd ordered them all to suck in their emotions and see to the many guests that had come calling once news of her mother's death spread through their quaint town. They never spoke of the incident again, but Brooklyn had yearned for a conversation. Because despite what he'd done, she needed him. He was her father, and she'd just lost her beloved mother. Through the years, she wanted to love him again, so he could help her get through the grief. She'd dreamed of the day he'd apologize for being absent, cold. But that apology never came, and soon her longing was replaced with ire. Still, she wondered if she'd ever be able to turn him away if he came to her, begging for forgiveness.

"Where'd you go?" Nicole nudged her gently, shaking her from her thoughts.

Sighing heavily, Brooklyn shrugged. "Nowhere." She stood up and walked to the mirror, grimacing at her haggard reflection. Her hair was a hot mess, and who in the world let her out of the house without her foundation and lip gloss?

Nicole stood up and inched closer to her. "How about we get a pint?"

Brooklyn arched a brow at her friend. "Kyle is not going to kill me for letting his pregnant wife get smashed."

Nicole giggled. "No, silly. A pint of ice cream."

Brooklyn barked out a laugh. "Well, how about you get the ice cream, and I get some food? I'm starving."

"Room service?"

"Let's go out and grab something. It's a nice day out. Snow storms one day, blue sky the next. That's Michigan in a nutshell."

Brooklyn busied herself by unpacking some of

her suitcases. "I don't know what I was thinking, grabbing this dress." She held up the long maxi dress with the bright orange lines in it so Nicole could get a look, before she balled it up and threw it on the floor. "This needs to go in the trash."

"Girl, please. You should have never bought that dress in the first place. I worry about your style sometimes."

"Says the person who only wears black, brown, and navy blue. You need some color in your life."

"You know what you need?" Nicole asked. "You need to go out on a date, meet someone. You know, enjoy your twenties."

Dating was the last thing on Brooklyn's mind. "No, Nic. You're not hooking me up with Kyle's friend. It's just not going to happen."

Nicole's eyes widened. "Brooklyn, he's a nice guy. And hot."

Brooklyn giggled. Nicole was not slick. She had been trying to hook Brooklyn up with one of her husband's friends for weeks. From the picture, the guy was good looking and all, but Brooklyn just wasn't interested.

"Fine. I'll shut up about him." Her friend gasped. "Speaking of hot guys, tell me more about the man who saved your life."

Brooklyn had given Nicole the quick version of her run-in with the mystery man the night before. Hunching her shoulders, she said, "What's there to tell? He pushed me out of the way of an oncoming car, and he smelled so good, Nic. You know what the smell of laundry detergent does to me."

"Girl, bye. You and your Gain detergent. I've

never met anyone this obsessed with detergent and other cleaning solutions."

"Hey, I consider it a good sign when any man smells like clean laundry. It means he at least washes his clothes."

"Or his mama does."

Brooklyn laughed. "Stop. He didn't look like the type to live with his mother."

"A lot of men don't look like the type, but they are."

"I don't know," Brooklyn said with a shrug. "I just didn't get that vibe from him. Not that it matters anyway. He disappeared into thin air after I thanked him."

"I still can't believe that someone saved your life and you didn't get his name or anything."

"Well, he was probably just passing through on his way to Kalamazoo or something. He did his good deed for the holiday season and left."

"You don't believe that," Nicole said. "Besides, if he's a visitor, he could be staying here. I mean, he was outside of the hotel in a snow storm. And this is the best hotel in good ol' Wellspring."

The sarcasm in her friend's voice made her smile. "If you hate it here, why did you stay?"

Nicole had been talking about leaving Wellspring since eighth grade. Brooklyn had listened to countless lectures on how it was a stupid town with stupid people and nobody cool would ever come there. "Aside from the obvious?" Nicole rubbed her hand over her full belly. "Someone had to stay and keep an eye on you.

"I call BS because I didn't even live in town when

you could have left for Houston, like you wanted. Just go ahead and admit you love this ol' town."

"Whatever. Anyway, let's go find the mystery guy." Grabbing her hand, Nicole pulled Brooklyn out of the room.

Down in the lobby, Nicole marched to the front desk and rang the bell. Her friend had shared her plan of asking the front desk staffer if they'd had any men check in that fit the description of her stranger, as if she'd already staked some claim to the man. Brooklyn wanted no part of the "mystery-man hunt." Although it was quite possible that the stranger was staying at Wells Hotel, if he was visiting.

Brooklyn's gaze zeroed in on the hotel café, which was situated to the left of the front desk. The smell of coffee and bread wafted to her nose and she decided she'd grab something to eat there. She gestured toward the café and told Nicole she'd be over there and walked over. The place was busy, but not overcrowded which was perfect. There was no line at the counter and she walked right up. Smiling at the barista, she eyed the sandwiches in the glass case and placed an order for one and a bottle of water. She scanned the small area for a table, and froze. Mr. Tall, Dark, and Fine as hell was there, sitting in a cozy corner booth.

Nicole walked up behind her. "What did you order, Brooklyn? I think I'm hungry now, too."

Brooklyn heard Nicole place a complicated order, and tugged on her friend's sleeve, unable to articulate. Her friend, who was still talking to the barista about extra tomatoes and heavy mayo, swatted at her.

"Nicole," she muttered. "Nicole."

"What?" Nicole hissed.

"Look."

"What?" Nicole asked with a frown on her flawless skin. "What am I looking at? Can't you see I'm trying to get some information?"

"It's him."

Nicole whirled around. "Where?"

Brooklyn pulled her closer. "Shhh. He's over there in the booth."

"Oh my God!" Nicole breathed. "He *is* hot."

"Tell me about it."

As if on cue, the man raised his head and their eyes met across the room. She swayed on her feet and absently tucked a strand of hair behind her ear. Before she could stop herself, she waved at him. *I'm such a dork.*

"Go talk to him," Nicole murmured.

"I . . . Okay." Brooklyn had never been nervous about talking to men. But there was something about him that made her palms sweat and her mind cloudy. Not one to back down from a challenge, she started toward him.

A hand around her arm stopped her in her tracks. Next thing she knew she was face-to-face with Sterling. "Brooklyn!" he shouted.

Somebody kill me now.

"Brooklyn, what is your problem?"

You. She glanced back at the booth. Mystery man was gone. Rolling her eyes, she said, "Sterling, we have nothing to talk about. Now, excuse me."

His grip on her tightened.

"Let me go."

"I think we have unfinished business," he murmured. "You owe me a conversation."

"I don't owe you anything." She yanked her arm out of his grasp. In the process, she lost her footing and tumbled backward into a hard wall. With arms. Quickly realizing she had fallen into someone, she jolted up. "Oh my God, I'm so . . ." The word *sorry* died on her lips when she found herself face-to-face—again—with the man who had saved her life.

Chapter 4

Carter hadn't come to Wellspring to be a knight in shining armor. The days of him being someone's protector were long over. *Because I suck at it.* Yet, he'd found himself rising to his feet all the same when he noticed the man grab her. Before he could even reason with himself, he was over there, standing like a menacing hitman ready to pounce on a mark.

He glanced down at the woman in question. "Are you good?"

The woman blinked up at him. "Um, I . . ." She nodded furiously. "I'm good."

Carter glared at the man. "Not that you deserve a warning, but I don't take kindly to men who think it's cool to manhandle a woman. Keep your hands to yourself."

Nothing infuriated him worse than a bully. Especially a man bullying a woman. He'd watched his father berate his mother for years, abuse her physically and emotionally. There was only one word for a man that put his hands on a woman—*coward*.

"Please, it's okay." The woman placed a hand on his wrist, and he gently pulled it out of her grasp, ignoring the spark that passed between them. "Sterling is just mad that I turned down his proposal in front of the entire town."

Carter's eyes flashed to the woman. She was no pushover, judging by her stance and the fire in her light brown eyes. Swallowing, he nodded. "Good."

He started to walk away, but her hand on his back stopped him in his tracks. "Wait."

"Really, Brooklyn?" Sterling shouted. "You owe me an explanation."

So her name is Brooklyn.

"I don't owe you anything, Sterling. You ambushed me in a room full of people. We're not even a couple. But you and my father don't care about what I want. So I don't care about your pride. Leave me the hell alone."

"You know I can't do that."

Carter turned to face the bully. He gave the man the once-over and cracked his knuckles. A fight would definitely release the tension in his shoulders, and it would make him feel better. Only problem was, this wasn't the "D," and he didn't know anybody in town that could vouch for his character if he got arrested for pummeling the bastard.

He didn't know what it was about the other man that made him itch to teach him a lesson. Carter had learned a long time ago to never judge a book by its cover. Black men had it tough already, especially in the current political climate. Yet, he'd immediately realized he didn't like the man. Maybe it was the way the guy had strolled into the café like he owned the place. For all Carter knew, this

Sterling guy could be the owner. But he didn't think so. The man had money, that much was obvious, considering he was wearing an Armani suit—albeit one similar to one Carter owned himself . . . last year.

Carter let his gaze travel over Brooklyn quickly before turning his attention back to the other man. *I should just walk away. This isn't my battle.*

Brooklyn turned her back on Sterling to face him, holding her hand out. "I'm Brooklyn, by the way."

He reluctantly took her hand and gave it a quick shake. "Carter."

"Nice to meet you. This is my friend Nicole." She gestured to the very pregnant woman standing behind her. He shook the other woman's hand as well. Carter didn't bother addressing Sterling. "I wanted to thank you for saving my life. I wasn't paying attention."

Carter couldn't help but smile. Brooklyn was unbothered by the man looming behind her, shooting them death glares. *I like her.* The thought made him take a step back. "No need to thank me. I'm glad I was there."

"I'd like to do something for you." She giggled softly, ducked her head before meeting his gaze again. "Have you visited Wellspring before? Maybe I can show you around? Wellspring isn't big, but there are a lot of things to do."

"Like what?" He hadn't meant it to come out that way, like he was better than the town and its people. Wellspring seemed quaint, quiet. When he'd arrived, he'd noticed the storefront businesses lining the main road. It appeared that the town's mayor had done a good job of luring business owners to the town, judging by the new construction in the downtown area. Compared to Detroit, though, it left a lot to be desired.

"Well, there's the new Walmart. We could always walk around there. And the drive-in. We have all the new movies." Brooklyn's eyes flashed with amusement, before rolling her eyes. "I'm kidding. Well-spring might not be Detroit, or even Grand Rapids, but we're nice people and we know how to have a good time."

Curiosity made him want to say yes. But he didn't leave his friends and family behind for this. He was supposed to be concentrating on his business. Still, he was conflicted, torn between the need for peace in his life and the desire to get to know this woman standing before him. It was the first time since Krys died that he'd actually been genuinely intrigued by a woman, and he didn't even know her.

Averting his gaze, he sighed. "Thanks for the offer, but I'm going to have to decline. I have work to do."

"What do you do for a living?" Sterling asked.

Carter had met men like Sterling before, entitled men who looked down on people who actually had to work for a living. "If I thought it was any of your business, I don't even think I'd tell you then."

"Ouch," Brooklyn murmured.

"I'm not even sure why you're still standing here." Carter folded his arms over his chest.

"Do you know who I am?" The other man stepped closer, still behind Brooklyn though. *Little punk, hiding behind a woman.*

Carter narrowed his gaze on the man, satisfied when Sterling retreated back a step. "I believe the question is, do I care who you are? Obviously, she doesn't want you around. Yet, you're still here."

"Damn," Nicole mumbled. "I think that would be your cue to leave, Sterling."

Carter didn't know why he was engaging. It wouldn't bode well for his company to get involved in the local drama. Brooklyn, a woman he'd just met, was not worth his reputation. Hell, what if she was the mayor's daughter or something? She had trouble written all over her tight body. *What does her body have to do with anything?* Nothing, that's what. And he needed to stay away from trouble. As it was, they'd drawn the attention of a few patrons seated in the café.

After Krys and Chloe died, he'd shut down, preferring to be alone rather than surrounded by people. He'd reasoned that it was better that way because there always seemed to be an underlying tension in his body that made him feel hostile, and he hadn't wanted to do or say anything he would regret later. He didn't drink hard alcohol, or even coffee, because it affected his mood. So he'd spent some time in the gym, taking his frustrations out on a punching bag. Boxing had become his escape, and a way to release the tension.

"Sterling, please just go," Brooklyn said. "We've said all we need to say, and you're causing a scene. You know how the gossips are in this town."

That seemed to get the man's attention. Finally. "Fine. I'll go, but this isn't over." Sterling exited the café, bumping into innocent people on the way out.

Another threat. It took every ounce of discipline Carter had not to follow that asshole out into the street and kick the shit out of him. "Does he always threaten you like that?"

"No. Like I said, I hurt his pride. He'll be alright."

Something told him that Brooklyn was withholding important information about Sterling and his motives. Something also told him that the other man was not going to give up. And it would be best if he stayed the hell away from him while he was in town.

"Coffee?" she asked, drawing his attention back to her. "At least let me buy you a cup?"

He glanced over at Nicole before looking at Brooklyn again. *Say no.* But he couldn't, not yet, not when she was looking at him with those big, expressive eyes. "I am looking for something other than pastry or sandwiches to eat. Maybe you could help me with that?"

Brooklyn swayed on her feet. In the light of day, Carter was even more handsome than she remembered. He was built like a wall, tall and hard in all the right places. There was an edge to him. Instinctively, she knew he had a story. He was running from something, or someone. Memories? Or a past that had forced him to leave his life behind to start anew? Maybe both.

But there was something about Carter that made her want to know more. His name alone was so masculine, strong. The way he'd stepped in and basically threatened Sterling with bodily harm had her tingling in places that hadn't been used in months. No, she wasn't going to think about her drought. It was unproductive.

The intensity in his stare pinned her to her spot, held her in a trance. This wasn't her, all shy and tongue-tied. *Say something, damn it.*

"What type of food are you looking for?" Nicole said from behind her, pinching her back like an old church mother would for not paying attention to the "word from the Lord."

Next thing she knew, Brooklyn was pushed forward, nearly falling into Carter's arms. Again. She braced herself on . . . his chest. She tugged at her shirt. "I'm sorry," she murmured, shooting Nicole a glare out of the corner of her eye. "There is a Panera Bread and you could always go to McDonald's or Jimmy John's."

I'm such an idiot. He was probably from a big city, where there was a Panera or Jimmy John's and the like on every corner. And those weren't the type of restaurants that set Wellspring apart from the average city. Since he was visiting, she'd direct him to Wellspring's best.

"If breakfast is what you're looking for," she continued, "the Bee's Knees has the best western omelet this side of the state. But if you have a taste for lunch, I'd recommend Margie's Soup Kitchen for lighter fare. I enjoy the chicken and rice. On brisk days like this, it's packed, but I know the owner."

"The Bee's Knees?" he asked, a frown lining his forehead. "Is that like a diner?"

Nodding, she babbled on, aware of the stares

from townspeople entering the café. "It is. I eat there almost every day, sometimes twice a day. It's close to my job, and the prices are reasonable. And they have really good chocolate cake. It's my favorite. Oh, and—" An elbow in her back stopped her from revealing a bunch more information that he didn't ask for. *Like he cares if you enjoy the chocolate and caramel brownies that Dee makes every Tuesday.*

Carter tensed visibly, almost as if he had to work extra hard to not flee from the awkwardness. "Thanks for the information," he offered stiffly. She watched him glance at his watch and mutter something under his breath. "I better go."

Brooklyn turned just in time to see him practically run out of the café. *Well, that was . . . mortifying.* She caught Nicole's wide-eyed glance out of the corner of her eye. "Don't say anything."

"What the hell was that?" Nicole said, her arms outstretched. "And what did you do with my best friend?"

Pushing past Nicole, Brooklyn gestured to the barista. "Shut up. I was just . . ." Hell, she didn't even know what she was doing. The stranger with the most soulful eyes she'd ever seen had just brushed her off. In the middle of the café. "I don't want to talk about this." Brooklyn decided to forgo the water she'd ordered and instead settled on a frozen double caramel cocoa latte, extra whipped cream.

"This is nuts. Since when do you get all nervous when it comes to men?"

"Have you seen him?"

"Yes, and he's fine as hell. And you just let him slip right through your fingers."

It was probably a good thing she did. She had to focus on finding a place to stay, not some brooding stranger. "Nicole, I need you to focus. I have things to do."

"No, don't turn this around on me because you choked."

Her best friend, the traitor, barked out an amused laugh. Brooklyn ignored her and paid for her order. Mumbling a string of curses, she pulled out her phone and busied herself checking her calendar.

A few minutes later, they were walking arm in arm down Main Street toward the downtown court-yard to eat their lunch on one of the benches and people watch.

"All jokes aside, did you see how he turned me down cold?" Brooklyn asked, sipping on her latte. "Maybe he has a girlfriend?"

"You never know. Men are full of it."

"Says the happily married pregnant woman," Brooklyn muttered.

"Ha ha." Nicole bumped her shoulder as they walked. "Or maybe he turned you down because you were a babbling fool?"

Her best friend burst out in a fit of laughter, drawing a reluctant chuckle from Brooklyn. Nicole was right, she had been off her game. But next time she saw Mr. Tall, Dark, and Brooding, she wouldn't be.

Carter hurried down the street, his mission clear. Food. *And get far away from Brooklyn.* His phone buzzed in his pocket and he picked it up. "What's up, Aisha?"

His sister's calm voice carried over the receiver. "How's everything going?"

"I'm good. On my way to find something to eat."

"This won't take long."

Carter snickered. Aisha was about their business at all times of the day. His sister had never married, nor seemed inclined to be attached to a long-term partner. *Maybe she has the right idea.*

"Martin will call you later this evening so you can go over the game plan for the initial meeting. Your rental will be ready next Friday, possibly sooner."

Aisha explained that the company provided housing for however long it was needed. It was a nice touch when trying to lure prospective consultants to such a remote area.

"Thanks, sis. How many rooms?"

"Two. Apparently, the place is new construction with stunning views and an indoor/outdoor pool for residents. There is also a small gym in the clubhouse, but an even bigger one about a mile away."

Aisha had obviously bought into the hype. She seemed more excited than anybody about the project in Wellspring.

"Where is it?" he asked. The hotel he was in was nice, but he'd prefer to have a private entrance and a kitchen so he could cook his own meals.

"It's about ten minutes from the downtown area. According to the map, it is about five miles from the expressway and twenty from Wellspring Water, so you'll have a bit of a commute. But you don't like to be too close to work anyway, so it works."

His sister knew him well. Carter had never been too keen on living close to the office, preferring a commute to gather his thoughts before and after work. He did his best thinking in the car. The drive to Wellspring had been therapeutic for him, leaving the city behind for fresh air and open space.

"You're set to meet with Parker Wells Sr. and Parker Wells Jr. Monday morning at ten o'clock. Martin is available to conference in as well."

"Perfect," he said.

It felt good to be working again, better than he'd hoped. With Martin conferencing in, he'd have a chance to observe while Martin talked. They were a true tag team. Where he fell short, Martin excelled. And vice versa. Normally, they worked alongside their client company's employees for a few weeks, getting to know them without revealing their true mission. It gave them a chance to observe the dynamics between employees and management. Upper management was often not aware of the actual day-to-day work and the needs of the employees. It helped to delve into the organizational culture to figure out what employees needed to be effective and efficient.

"Have you met anyone yet?"

His sister's question caught him off guard, because he'd managed to get through the entire conversation without thinking about Brooklyn— *until now. Thanks a lot, Aisha.* Clearing his throat, he mumbled that he'd only met a few people in passing.

"Liar," his sister said. "Spill."

"Aisha, it's nothing. I have to go." He glanced up

and found himself standing at the Bee's Knees. He scanned the immediate area, half expecting to see Brooklyn somewhere around since she'd mentioned she worked close to the place. She wasn't there, which was supposed to be a good thing. "I just found a spot to eat."

He walked in and was immediately greeted by an older man, probably in his late sixties. "How ya doin', young man?"

"I gotta go, Aisha. I'll call you later." Carter hung up and shook the man's waiting hand. "I'm doing okay."

"Table for one?"

Carter nodded. "That would be good."

The man hobbled over to a corner booth and gestured for Carter to take a seat. "You must be the new guy in town." *This damn town is small as hell.* "Word has it you're from the big city."

Feeling a little uncomfortable about revealing too much, Carter simply nodded.

"My wife delivers pastry over to the hotel café and the ladies are talking about a handsome stranger," the older man clarified. "You'll find that word gets around fast in this town."

"Yes, I'm in town for work. I was told you had the best western omelet this side of Michigan."

The man perked up then, swung the towel in his hand. "I do. My wife was born and raised in Colorado. She grew up on what they called Denver sandwiches. The Denver, or western omelet, derived from that sandwich. One day of the year, we have a Denver sandwich day. People come from the surrounding area for it."

The man went on to tell the story of how he'd

met his wife one day while traveling to California. He'd stopped off in Colorado to see the sights and happened upon her working as a cook in a diner. They'd hit it off and he asked her to marry him before the week was out. Back then, it wasn't uncommon for men and women to marry quickly.

"How did you end up in Michigan?"

"Family. I grew up in Wellspring. My grandfather was the first mayor of the city, one of the founding fathers along with the Wells family. The name's Clark. William Clark."

Carter clasped William's hand again. "Carter Marshall."

"My wife, Dee, is in the back, bothering the cooks. I swear, she needs to sit down somewhere. But I'll see to it she makes you a nice western omelet. The first one is on the house."

"Thank you, sir." Carter smiled at the older man. He kind of reminded him of his grandfather.

"Where are you staying, son?"

"I'm over at the Wells Hotel."

Mr. Clark snorted. "Pretty highbrow, huh? Not sure why he built that eyesore in a town known for its natural beauty. Always trying to do it bigger and better than everyone else."

Carter had the feeling there was an unpleasant history between Mr. Clark and Mr. Wells. He couldn't help but wonder about it. "Do you know Parker Wells Sr.?"

"Do I know him?" The man finally slid into the booth across from him, making himself right at home. "Everybody knows Senior. I went to school with his father. My father and his grandfather were best buddies as kids. All of that changed when

Wellspring Water started buying up all the land.
He's tried to buy mine right out from under me
many times, but I refuse to sell. My granddaughter
is friends with his youngest son, so I try to be nice,
but he can shove his Wellspring Water up his ass."

Carter barked out a laugh. Mr. Clark had laid it
all out there for him, and now he couldn't wait to
finally meet Parker Wells Sr. He always did like a
challenge.

"There is a lot more to Wellspring than that
damn corporation," Mr. Clark continued. "I hope
you get a chance to visit some of our landmarks.
Not too many mostly black towns in this country.
We made it work back in a time when it was hard
for us to even find gainful employment."

Being from the city wasn't much better for finding
employment back in the day. It just so happened
that the boom of the automobile industry in Detroit had paved the way for many people of color to
find work and earn a livable wage. The opportunity
was there for many to take advantage and make
good lives for themselves working the assembly line.

He suspected Wellspring had a very similar story,
with Wellspring Water being the main corporation
in town. Carter made a mental note to do a little research into the town's origins when he was settled
into his rental house.

An hour later, Carter had finished the best
omelet he'd ever eaten, full of juicy ham, cheese,
onions, and bell peppers. As a result of his eyes
being bigger than his stomach, he wanted to go to
sleep. But he had a lot to do, including making his
way over to his temporary residence to scout out
the area.

"Did you enjoy it?" Mr. Clark asked, approaching him with a grin on his bearded face.

"I did. Please give your wife my thanks."

"She ran out the back door, probably in a rush to go gossip with the church ladies." The old man laughed. "I tell ya . . . women." He shook his head, amusement lining his features.

"Well, she really did make me a believer in the wonders of the western omelet. Tell me, where can I buy groceries? I'm moving into a rental house about ten minutes away from here next week."

"Oh, you must be moving into those new condos coming up. They're real nice. Plenty of space, I heard. Tried to get my wife to consider downsizing."

Carter felt a sense of relief at the man's obvious admiration for the neighborhood. For some reason, he trusted the man's opinion, which didn't come easy to him. "That's good to know."

"If you're going to be living there, you'll be pretty close to the Walmart. We fought tooth and nail to keep that store out of here, but in the end, it turned out to be good for the local economy. Well, except for Mr. Mays, who ran the small market round the corner."

Standing, Carter stretched and dropped a tip on the table, only to have his money pushed right back into his hand.

"Your money is no good here today, son." Mr. Clark shot him a scolding look. "It was a pleasure to meet you."

"Thank you, Mr. Clark."

"Call me Will. Mr. Clark was my father's name."

"Thanks, Will."

"If you should find your way back over this way

for dinner, our special is fried catfish with coleslaw and home fries. One of our best days of the week."

Carter nodded before saying his goodbyes. Fried catfish and home fries? He just might get used to this town.

Chapter 5

Monday morning, Carter allowed himself extra time to take the scenic route to Wellspring Water Corporation Headquarters. The run he'd taken through the downtown area had worked wonders, and he felt centered. He'd spent the weekend preparing for his meeting and avoiding Brooklyn.

Despite the fact that he'd tiptoed through the hotel, hoping he wouldn't see her, he'd actually seen the woman every day since he'd arrived—even though she hadn't necessarily seen him. They bumped into each other at the lobby store Saturday afternoon, and she'd shot him a wide smile, waving on her way out. On Sunday morning, he'd seen her in the lobby, in her pajamas, laughing with the hotel front desk employee and a few hotel guests. Sunday night, he'd watched as she ate at the hotel restaurant with her friend Nicole and a man who he assumed was Nicole's husband. Throughout their dinner, many people had walked over to her table and greeted them. As far as he could tell, she was well-known and well liked in the community.

He understood why, too. She was personable, and always seemed to be laughing. It was hard not to be affected by her. He'd noticed that she was a hugger. She'd hugged every single person that approached her, and he was baffled by the fact that they were genuine hugs.

He'd also taken the opportunity to do a little exploring of the town. With a population of approximately six thousand people, he was amazed that the town was as progressive as it was. There were several historic buildings in the downtown area, but there were also several modern attractions as well. He'd half expected to come to a ghost town. But Wellspring was anything but.

There were several subdivisions that housed single family homes as well as condominium communities and apartment complexes. The city had four elementary schools, two middle schools, and one high school. Walker Park was a focal point and bordered the man-made Wellspring Lake. According to Mr. Clark, the park hosted several festivals throughout the summer and put on a light show at Christmas.

It was easy to see how Wellspring Water had impacted the city. He'd met several people who worked for the corporation and others who worked servicing the company and its employees. If something were to ever happen to the business, or if they chose to relocate out of the city, the effects would be devastating.

Wellspring Water had attracted business to the area. Although it was primarily a bottled water company, they'd diversified in recent years, delving into several industries. They'd made the news recently, donating a significant amount of bottled water every month to Flint, Michigan, which was going through a water crisis that had put thousands of lives in danger.

As he pulled into the company parking lot, he eyed the grand building in front of him. The glass structure was nestled in an expanse of tall trees, but it was still visible from the highway. The front of the grounds boasted a reflecting pool surrounded by lush landscaping.

He had to admit, he was impressed. The slate floors in the reception area and the wall of water in the lobby were brilliant focal points. The high-tech design and amenities would put many businesses to shame. WWCH was miles ahead of the competition.

The first floor was busy with activity as employees scurried through the doors and rushed off to their jobs. Carter approached the receptionist and gave her his name. It only took a few minutes for another woman to escort him to the executive conference room.

When he was ushered into the room, he was immediately greeted by a man his age. "I'm Parker Wells Jr." The man held out a hand and Carter shook it. "Welcome to Wellspring Water Corporation."

Carter introduced himself and the two took their seats. "You have an impressive building here."

"The recent reorganization allowed us to make much needed changes. The original headquarters was attached to the main warehouse, and wasn't conducive to our mission. There was a need for separation, and I think we're better for it."

"I'd say it was a worthy investment." Opening

his briefcase, Carter pulled out his laptop. "My business partner will join us via conference call. Will your father be joining us today?"

Carter caught the tick in the other man's jaw at the mention of his father. "My father had to leave town for a few days. I'll be your point of contact on this project," Parker Jr. replied. "And I'm available to assist in any capacity."

After a few minutes, Martin called in and the two went through the project schedule, giving Parker an overview followed by the details and metrics they would be compiling. Carter explained their process of shadowing employees as they complete their day-to-day tasks. Once the system was implemented, they'd begin testing prior to launch.

Parker had a wealth of knowledge about the business, and was willing to listen and contribute. The goal was to bring Wellspring Water into a new era, one strengthened by the use of data to improve their operation. Carter was excited about the possibilities.

The meeting ended on time, and Parker showed Carter to the office he'd be occupying. "Please let me know what you need to get started. We want to be sure you have everything you need. Once you decide to bring your team out, they will be housed in the area right outside your office."

Carter walked around the office before stopping to stare out at the view of the river. "Excellent." He'd lived in Michigan all his life, but had not made it a point to actually explore the different counties. After a few days in Wellspring, he viewed his state in a new light and made a mental note to visit other areas.

As they walked toward the bank of elevators, Parker greeted employees. Carter studied their interactions, noting the sincere admiration on many of the people's faces when talking with Parker. He briefly wondered if they'd have the same reaction to Parker Sr.

"How are you enjoying Wellspring?" Parker asked.

"I haven't had much of a chance to see the town. I arrived late Thursday night. Thank you for arranging for a rental, by the way."

"It's no problem. You're going to be here a while, and hotel life is not what's up."

Carter's business was based on being able to travel to different locations, nationally and internationally. Prior to the fire, he'd spent a lot of time in the airport and on airplanes. He hated living out of a suitcase. Temporary housing was an amazing benefit of any job, especially one lasting longer than a few weeks.

"Do you shoot pool?" Parker asked.

Carter grinned. "I don't think anybody in this town wants to see me on that pool table." He'd learned from the best, his mother. She was a bona fide hustler and had made hundreds of dollars off fools who assumed they couldn't be smacked down by a woman.

"Ah, I sense a challenge."

"If you're ready to lose, I'm ready to school you." Carter didn't make it a point to get loose with clients, but he had a good feeling about Parker.

"Brook's Pub has four-dollar pitchers on Thursdays. Me and a few others go down there to shoot pool after work. Why don't you come out? It would be a good opportunity to meet some of our employees."

Carter agreed to join Parker and his crew, and ended the meeting with another handshake before leaving. He picked up this phone on his way to the car and punched in a number. "What's up? We need to talk."

Brooklyn tossed her bag onto a barstool at the hotel café and ordered a double latte. After her morning, she needed to skip the coffee and head straight to the bar. If she wasn't convinced she'd come off as paranoid, she would have accused the hotel valet of deliberately messing with her car. Because she'd rushed to her car, late to work, to find that she had not one, but four flat tires.

She'd spent the morning arguing with Sheriff Walker about not doing anything to deserve it. Brooklyn could admit that she was a little—or a lot—feisty. Yes, she had a touch of road rage and could be a little rude in the morning. But other than her penchant for being brutally honest, she'd done nothing to deserve vandalism as extreme as flattening her tires.

It wasn't the sheriff's fault, though. He'd watched Brooklyn grow up and knew she had never shied away from a good conflict, but that was back in her wayward teenage years, when she was a grieving, troubled child who'd spent far too much time with her brother and his football teammates. Yes, Brooklyn had been the ultimate tomboy and an honorable member of the "guy crew."

Nicole wobbled into the café and sat down,

groaning as if she was in tremendous pain. "What's up? You rang?"

"I did. I figured since the doctor took you off work, we could hang out together, since work is obviously a bust for me."

Her best friend hissed out a ragged breath, followed by another two deep breaths.

Frowning, Brooklyn assessed Nicole. "Are you okay?"

"Hell. No." Nicole rubbed her stomach. "This baby is like a freakin' horror movie in my stomach, always moving around and kicking me. The other day, I was sitting perfectly still and the baby kicked so hard, my boob jumped up."

Unable to hold her laughter, Brooklyn dropped her head onto the table and giggled. "You're crazy, Nic. That's impossible."

"No joke. Ask Kyle." Nicole ordered a passion-fruit tea when the barista approached them. "He got a real kick out of it. I'm so ready for this to be over."

"Girl, you better enjoy sleep while you can get it."

"Whatever. I just keep praying my stomach bounces back. I still have a lot of bikini years ahead of me." Nicole tapped the table. "Anyway, other than your car woes, how are you? I'm sorry I haven't been by to see you. I've been sleeping and eating. That's the only thing I can do with this bowling ball in my stomach."

Brooklyn wished she knew the answer to that. Staying in the hotel wasn't optimal for her. The rooms were immaculate, but she liked to sleep in her own bed. "It's okay. I've been searching for places. I even put an offer on a house."

Her friend's eyes went wide. "Really? That is a big step, Brooklyn."

Shrugging, Brooklyn said, "It was, but I didn't get the house."

"Not that I'm trying to get rid of you, but have you considered just moving back to Boston? You love it there. Or moving south? You won't have to see Wellspring Water everywhere. You could drink Nestle or Smart Water."

Brooklyn giggled. "Not really, not right now. I love my work at the clinic. Besides, moving south was never an option. That was your thing. I love the change in the seasons."

"Yuck. What I wouldn't do to be able to wake up to warm temperatures every day, and not just the sporadic days we have here."

"Anyway, I'm thinking I want a house near the river, with a wraparound porch and lots of greenery." Brooklyn loved to be outside, whether she was walking, riding her bike, or just sitting in the park and reading a book.

The barista, Harley, leaned over the counter. "Brooklyn, I hate to ask, but can you man the counter while I run to the restroom?"

Smiling at the young worker, Brooklyn nodded. It wasn't the first time Harley had asked her to pitch in. Her father did own the hotel, and Harley trusted Brooklyn. She walked behind the counter, grinning at Mr. Flankman, who sat at the bar, nursing a coffee.

"What do you think about a house on the lake?" she asked Nic, who was gulping down the rest of her tea.

"Expensive." Nicole burped. "And you're just

you. You don't need a house that big. Unless you're planning to get married and have babies like me."

Carter walked into the café at that moment, and headed straight to the corner booth he'd sat in each morning. Brooklyn wasn't sure if it was punishment, karma, or both, but it seemed like he'd been avoiding her. She'd seen him every day, but he'd barely spoken, and only waved once. She wondered what she'd done to turn him off.

"Nicole craned her neck to see what Brooklyn was looking at. "There's Mr. Hotness right now. Go talk to him."

"Again? He already turned me down for dinner once. What am I supposed to say?"

"Ask him what he wants to order, since you're filling in for Harley." Nicole wiggled her eyebrows. "You look hot today. He'll pay attention."

Brooklyn's gaze dropped down to her suit. She *did* look pretty damn good, with her favorite black pencil-skirt, wine-colored Bardot top, and pumps. Not to mention, her accessory game was on point. "Okay, you're right. I'm Ms. Hotness. He better recognize."

She grabbed a pad of paper and sauntered over to the booth. However, once she was right in front of him, a rush of nerves made her steps falter. He was reading his tablet, a frown fixed on his face.

This is it. Swallowing, she asked, "Can I get you something?"

His gaze flashed to hers, and he did a double take before meeting her eyes. "You . . . work here?"

"For about five minutes."

He scratched his temple. "For five minutes."

He'd repeated it as if he had to say it aloud to be sure he heard her correctly.

Brooklyn licked her lips. "I'm filling in for Harley."

"Okay." He stared at her.

Shifting under his silent assessment, she asked again, "So, can I get you anything?"

"Nothing for now, thank you."

Brooklyn let out a sigh, and gave a curt nod. "Fine." Grumbling a curse, she stalked back over to the bar and slammed that damn pad of paper down. "Do I have something stuck in my teeth, Nic?"

Her friend leaned in, squinting her eyes as if she were trying to see her teeth. "No."

"He's so standoffish." She smacked her hands down hard on her thighs as a wave of frustration took over. "I give up."

Nic turned to look over at the booth. Carter's head was down as he studied the tablet screen intently. "What did he say?"

"Basically, nothing. He hates me."

Nicole waved her off. "No, he doesn't. He doesn't know you enough to hate you."

"Whatever. You should have seen the way he was staring at me. Like I was disgusting or something."

Nicole rubbed her ever-growing belly again. "Maybe he's gay?"

Brooklyn tilted her head, watching the way he focused on whatever he was doing. He really was a beautiful man, long and lean with dark skin and full lips. Suddenly, she felt warm. Hot, really.

"Hello?" Nicole called, waving a hand in front of her.

She jerked back. "Sorry." She spared him one last

glance before topping off Mr. Flankman's mug. Now to the question at hand. *Is he gay?* Even though he hadn't spared her a second glance, she didn't think so. She couldn't explain it, but she would bet that Carter was a man who knew how to love a woman.

Carter tried to concentrate on his emails, but forcing his gaze from the attractive Brooklyn proved too difficult. He'd been shocked when she approached him, looking fine in her tight skirt and blouse. Her brown skin was glowing like a beacon of light in the dark. And her legs in those damn heels . . . Groaning, he swiped at his tablet.

There was nothing in particular he was searching for, he just had to keep himself busy. Because if he didn't, he'd probably give in to the impulse to look at her.

He wasn't an old man, but he acted like one. No woman since Krys had made him look twice—until now. The thought had thrown him off because it was unexpected. Most people would tell him he'd waited long enough to get back into the dating pool, but he didn't think he'd waited long enough. Yes, it had been two years, but the thought of seeing someone, of letting someone get close to him, felt like disrespect to Krys's memory. It was illogical, because he was a single man and *should* be going out with women.

He picked up his phone and dialed his sister.

"What's wrong?" Aisha asked. "Everything okay?"

"Damn, can't I call my sister?"

"Yes. It's just that . . . you never call anymore."

Carter felt like shit. He'd effectively pushed every-one he cared about away. "I know. I'm sorry." He'd treated them badly, with no apologies. But he hoped they would eventually forgive him.

"Don't apologize, baby brother. I love you regard-less of whether you call or not."

He chuckled. "I love you, too."

"How was the meeting this morning?"

Carter gave her the same update he'd given Martin when he talked to him a little while ago. He expected to be able to bring a team out after Easter.

"That's great. Meet any available women?"

He'd met a woman, alright. But he wasn't sure she was available. More importantly, he wasn't sure *he* was available.

"Aisha, am I ever going to be able to talk to you without you asking about my love life? You are my sister."

Aisha laughed. "Whatever. I'm just concerned."

"I know. But I'm okay." It wasn't an outright lie. He was okay. *Just a little tormented.*

"I may plan a visit down to see you. I could use a little getaway."

"Sounds like a plan."

He glanced up in time to see Brooklyn emerge from behind the bar with a pitcher of coffee. She walked over to an older gentleman. The man spoke to her with a wide smile, before she leaned down to place a kiss on his forehead. Then she filled up his mug.

"Carter?" Aisha called over the phone.

He shook himself out of his reverie. "I'm here."

"I was just reminding you to check the shared drive on the network. There are a few requests for proposals for you to review."

"Bet." He checked his watch. "I better get going. I'll check in later in the week."

He hung up the phone and stood, stuffing his tablet into his laptop bag. It was still early in the day. A late lunch would hit the spot. He headed toward the exit.

On his way out, he stole a glance at Brooklyn, who was now seated at the bar talking to the barista and Nicole. As if she sensed his presence, she turned and smiled before returning to the conversation. *Yep, I'm in trouble.*

Chapter 6

Brooklyn was going stir-crazy. She'd been stuck in her damn room for hours. Harley had called to warn her that her father was in the hotel. And since she didn't want him to see her, she'd holed up in her small-ass room for three hours. Three hours. It was Thursday night and her week had been one calamity after another. She'd planned to wind down with a few drinks at Brook's Pub. Instead, she was sprawled across the bed in her bra and panties, staring at the ceiling.

I'm such a dud. Brook's Pub was the Thursday night hangout for her age group. The fellas shot pool and drank beers, the women had shots and learned line dances. The music was loud and the food was good. And she was at home. Correction, she was at the stupid hotel.

Jumping up, she paced the room. *Why the hell do I let him control my life and my actions?* If she could figure that out, she would be one step closer to having the semblance of the life she'd always wanted for herself. An independent life. Yes, she'd made it a point to assert her own will for her life by leaving town multiple times. Yes, she defied her father by going into a field that he abhorred. Yes, she worked and made her own money, which was huge. Still, she needed access to her trust fund to live. And for that, she depended on Senior to give it to her.

It was time to make some lasting changes or she'd always be put in the same position—moving away every so often to prove a point, only to return because there was something that always brought her back to Wellspring. Safe to say she'd never return to her father's home, but she hoped she would be able to put down roots in her hometown.

Marrying Sterling was the last straw in her already tenuous relationship with her father. There was no way she was going to fall in line and marry a man that she couldn't stand. She'd suffocate slowly. Shaking her head out of those thoughts, she called the café.

"Is he still in the building?" she asked when Harley picked up.

"Yes. He's in the hotel restaurant."

"Fine." She slammed the phone down on the base. There was no way her father didn't know she was staying in the hotel. Where else would she go? Staying with Parker wasn't an option for her. She loved her brother, but he deserved to have a life.

Senior was probably doing this on purpose, dragging out his visit. Parker had told her about her father's surprise trip out of town earlier in the week. It had been a welcome reprieve for Brooklyn. She wished Senior would stay gone. Forever.

I'm still letting him control me. Brooklyn had waited

long enough. Her father wasn't going to keep her from living her life. Period. She pulled on her black skinny jeans, a black-and-white sheer blouse and a pair of high-heeled Mary Jane shoes. She twirled in the mirror once she was done. In a last-minute decision, she pulled her wig off and mussed her short hair. She'd wear it curly and natural.

With a burst of confidence, she tugged the door open and walked out with her head held high. On the first floor, though, she peeked around the corner like a thief. The coast was clear. She dashed through the lobby, throwing a hand over her face.

Home free, she walked out into the street. The temp was holding steady at fifty-five degrees. It was the perfect night for shenanigans and ice cream. Unfortunately, her partner-in-crime had turned down an invitation earlier, in favor of Netflix and ice cream with her husband.

Brooklyn was happy for Nic. Really, she was. But damn if she didn't need to make another friend. One who was single and ready to party. She was only twenty-six years old. She wasn't ready for Netflix and boring. She was ready for shots and table-top dancing. Throw in a little sex every now and then, she was living the life.

Brook's Pub was packed, standing room only. She stood on the tips of her toes and scanned the bar, hoping to spot Parker among the patrons. Brooklyn made her way over to the bar. Smacking a hand down on the bar, she shouted, "Juke, I need a shot over here."

The bartender, Juke, turned and winked at her. "You got it, Brooklyn."

Juke and Brooklyn had been friends for years, since they were students in Mr. Smith's seventh-grade science class. He was an imposing figure, a six-foot-one, brown-eyed block of muscle with tattoos covering his arms. But he was also the sweetest, most considerate person. And she loved the hell out of him.

When Juke bought the bar, he'd named it Brook's Pub. They were such good friends people had assumed he named it after her, and Juke had never corrected them. She figured it was probably because he was too manly to admit he'd named his bar after his dog. Juke returned, a full Kamikaze shot in hand. He slid it over to her and she took it, slamming the glass back on the bar.

"Thanks, Juke. Give me some love."

Juke reached out and pulled her to him for a quick hug. "I was wondering if you were going to come in here tonight. It's been crazy. Want another?" He motioned to the empty shot glass.

She nodded, before she leaned forward and kissed him on his cheek. He busied himself helping several customers before bringing her back another shot. "I almost didn't make it. Senior was at the hotel."

He frowned. "Hotel?"

"Oh, I forgot to tell you I moved out."

"When did this happen?"

Brooklyn made quick work of taking her shot. When he asked her if she wanted a refill, she shook her head. "Friday, man. Right after he and Sterling ambushed me. He wants me to marry Sterling."

He snorted. "Does he realize that you hate that fool?"

"He doesn't care. But I don't want to talk about that. Have you seen Parker?"

Juke pointed to the back of the building, where the pool tables were. "Over there."

She grinned. "Thank you. I'll call you this weekend. We can have breakfast. Love you, homey."

Brooklyn weaved through the crowd, waving at a few people as she went. She spotted Parker leaning against the pool table, lining up his shot. Then, she saw Carter. Stopping in her tracks, her gaze darted back and forth between her brother and the man who kept turning her down. *How does Parker know him?*

Judging by their interaction, she assumed they knew each other fairly well. Or at least had had a few conversations. Parker wasn't one to kick it with people he barely knew. She needed answers, but first . . .

Brooklyn bit down on her thumbnail as Carter leaned down, assessing the table, lining up his shot. When he finally made his move, the balls scattered over the table, three of them dropping into the holes. *He's good, but is he better than me?* Shooting pool with the guys as a teenager had been one of her favorite things to do. She'd spent a lot of time swindling men out of their money. She wondered if Carter would play her. Or would he make up an excuse and leave, as he'd been prone to do?

The man was obviously a pro. She noted his alignment, the way he addressed the ball, and how he stroked the cue. Just watching him made her hot all over, made her want to step into the line of fire and find out if he used that same precision when he stroked a woman. Carter took several turns before Parker was able to make his first move, and soon the game was over. Parker hadn't had a chance.

She froze when Parker pointed toward the bar, hoping like mad Carter hadn't seen her. Then her brother was advancing her way. Reaching out, she yanked him.

"Whoa," he said. When he realized it was her, he shouted, "Brooklyn!"

Slapping a hand over his mouth, she told him to shush. "Be quiet."

He pushed her hand away. "What are you doing?"

"How do you know Carter?"

"How do *you* know Carter?"

Brooklyn crossed her arms over her chest and threw her brother a look of disbelief. "Really?"

Parker laughed. "What?"

"Answer the damn question," she hissed.

Parker stepped back, rubbed a hand over his chin. "He's consulting on a Wellspring Water project," he said, with a shrug. "I invited him to hang out."

Carter works for Wellspring Water?

"Now, answer my question. How do you know him?"

Brooklyn stared out into the crowd. "The hotel. He's staying there, too."

Parker nodded. "Walk with me to the bar."

At the bar, Parker and Juke caught up for a bit while Brooklyn pondered the situation. Carter working for Wellspring Water presented a few problems. There was no way Senior wouldn't blow a gasket if she were to hook up with Carter. *Not that I have a chance in hell anyway.* And she and Parker had strict rules on dating one another's friends.

It niggled at her because, despite everything, she still wanted to know him. Her attraction to him only grew stronger. Each morning, she'd see him at the same corner booth, reading something on his tablet. He was quiet, intense. It had basically taken an act of God to prevent her from approaching him again, because *damn* . . . there was something about him. *I need to get out of here.*

Brooklyn patted Parker on the back. "I have to go."

He turned to her, tilting his head to the side as if trying to read her. "Everything okay?"

"Yep. Just tired." She gave her brother a quick hug. Juke lifted her up off her feet and gave her a kiss on the cheek. "See you guys soon." Soon she was out of the bar and into the fresh air. She lifted her head to the sky and inhaled. Without paying attention, she stepped off the small porch and ran right into Carter.

Carter gripped Brooklyn's hips to steady her. "Easy," he murmured.

Brooklyn looked up at him, her wide, doe eyes full of something he couldn't place. "I'm sorry. I guess we keep running into each other, huh?"

He hadn't expected her to come out so fast, or at all. He'd noticed her as soon as she'd walked in the place, watched her interaction with the bartender and Parker. While they were at the bar, he'd snuck out to get some fresh air. He needed a break from the music.

Brook's Pub was similar to so many in Detroit. It

was small, homey, and had a set of regulars that set the tone or vibe of the place. When he'd arrived earlier, he immediately liked the spot and would definitely return, eventually.

He smiled, unable to help himself. "I agree."

"I saw you playing pool." Brooklyn leaned forward and he could have sworn she'd just sniffed his shirt. "You're really good."

Carter realized he hadn't let her go yet, and dropped his hands quickly, then retreated back a step. She looked different, softer. She'd taken the wig off. Her hair was short, and framed her face well. He let his gaze travel over her.

Frowning, she asked, "What? Why are you looking at me like that?"

He caught himself. "Huh? What do you mean?"

"You're staring."

"I'm sorry, my mind was on something else," he lied. Carter couldn't think when she was so close to him. He'd managed to stay away from her for the most part.

Brooklyn swallowed visibly, and ducked her head. "Well, I'm going to go. See you around."

Carter scanned the area. While it didn't feel like there was a lot of crime in Wellspring, he didn't want her to take any chances. The hotel was five blocks south of the pub. "You're walking back to the hotel?"

"I am."

She started to walk away, and he fell into step beside her. "I'll walk with you."

Her gaze locked on his. "Okay."

They walked in silence at first. His thoughts were all over the place. The woman beside him was unlike any woman he'd ever met. He shouldn't want to be near her, to touch her even. But he did. It scared the shit out of him.

"What's your deal?"

Her voice was so soft he half wondered if he'd imagined it. She'd asked the same question he'd been asking himself since he'd arrived in town. What was his deal? This woman had thrown him for a loop, made him feel things he hadn't expected or even wanted to feel.

Glancing at her, he shrugged. "I'm not sure what you mean."

She looked at him like she didn't believe him. But she told him, "You saved my life. I mean, you literally saved my life. Yet, you refuse to let me do something for you, take you to dinner or even buy you coffee. I'm not sure what that is, and honestly, it grates."

"It's not you." He wanted to take the words back as soon as they hit the night air. It wasn't her fault he was incapable of letting himself go. He'd spent so much time grieving and seeking justice that he'd gotten used to the routine of shutting people out to accomplish his goals. And the way she made him feel . . . It had been a long time since he'd felt warmth instead of the cold that had taken over.

She shot him a look of disbelief. "Come on, you expect me to believe that? You literally shut down when I talk to you. You're giving me a complex."

They walked past the brightly lit ice cream stand. It was a small one, but still open and serving. There were several people milling around, some sitting at the tables in front and clusters of others standing off to the side.

"I'm going to stop." Brooklyn pointed over at the line and walked over to stand behind a couple.

Carter watched the man and the woman lean into each other, whispering to each other with secretive smiles. They were happy. "So that ice cream stand is open after ten o'clock?"

Brooklyn grinned. "Hell, yeah. This isn't just any ice cream. Jonah Wilder has the best soft serve around. He stays open late on Thursday, Friday, and Saturday. If you haven't guessed, Thursday nights are pretty busy around here."

"I noticed." Carter had seen the townspeople pile into Brook's Pub and it seemed there were more people strolling down Main Street than he had seen since he'd arrived. He wondered why. It was like that in college, but as he grew into an adult, Thursday nights were simply a preparation for Friday.

"Years ago, Wellspring Water Corp. was closed on Fridays. So Thursday was like our town's last day of the week. Even after the company changed their hours of operation, the folks in town had grown so accustomed to hanging out on Thursdays, it stuck."

She stepped up to the counter and smiled at the young lady behind it. "I'll have my usual," she said. Shooting him a side-eye glance, she asked, "Do you want something?" Carter opened his mouth to turn her down, but she forged ahead. "Please, let me do something for you. Haven't you ever heard the saying that giving is for the giver, not the receiver?"

Carter had heard the phrase, countless times from his mother. "I have."

"So, let me buy you a cone. You have to try it."

He hesitated, but reluctantly agreed, ordering a

small vanilla cone. When they received their ice cream, they started back toward the hotel. Brooklyn wasn't lying. He wasn't a person who ate a lot of sweets, but the ice cream was damn good.

"See," she said knowingly, dipping her spoon into the hot fudge sundae she'd ordered. "It's good, huh?"

He laughed. "It is. Thank you. So . . . Brook's Pub. Is there a connection there?"

She laughed. "I'd be lying if I said there was. No, the pub is not named for me. But a lot of people think it is, though, because me and Juke go way back."

Carter let out a breath he hadn't realized he was holding. It wasn't like him to feel jealous, but he'd recognized the feeling earlier when he'd seen Brooklyn interact with the other man. It had pushed him off his square because it was unexpected.

"Why?" she asked.

He shrugged. "I don't know. It just seemed like too much of a coincidence."

"That's fair," she said.

As they continued their walk, Brooklyn gave him a few tidbits about the town. He found himself wanting to ask about her, but he refrained. For now, it was nice to talk to her, to walk with her. It felt natural. Wellspring was a town full of rich history.

Once they arrived back at the hotel, Brooklyn tossed her empty cup into a trash can. "That hit the spot." They walked toward the bank of elevators, with her waving at the front desk attendant along the way. "Well, I enjoyed the walk." He followed her into the waiting elevator. "We should do it again sometime."

Carter nodded before he could even stop himself. "Okay."

The grin she graced him with then was nothing short of glorious. "Great." The elevator dinged on the third floor and she walked out. "Have a good night, Carter."

Chapter 7

Tucked into her favorite booth at the Bee's Knees, Brooklyn finished off her omelet and turned the page on her e-book. She was tired. It had been a long day already, and it was only eleven o'clock in the morning. She'd been up since five, yanked out of a dream about Carter and hot fudge by her ringing phone.

After she spent hours checking one of her clients into a rehab facility, she'd needed a break. She'd been slapped and bitten by the defiant teenager and drained by her antics. The girl had basically jumped on her mother, beating her like she was a stranger because the mother wouldn't hand over her purse. Instead of calling the police, the mother had called Brooklyn.

Unfortunately, Brooklyn wasn't new to this. Many teenagers in town were being introduced to drugs. In the past year, the rate of arrests for drug violations had increased five percent. It was disheartening to see the kids of people she knew overdose or even die from lack of education about the effects of drugs. Tie that in with the increasing homeless population, and she was a busy woman. But she wouldn't trade her job for the world. It wasn't lucrative, but it was rewarding.

Massaging her shoulder, Brooklyn swore at the tenderness there. She needed a vacation, though. A real one. *Or some hot sex on a platter.* Her muscles ached and her feet were sore, but it was all in a day's work. It had taken every last shred of energy she had to deal with the girl and the mother and the police, but it would be worth it in the end when the young girl made it out stronger and better.

One look at her when she entered the restaurant, and Will had given her an ice pack, a heating pad, a cup of coffee, and served up a hot omelet— all in the span of ten minutes. Will had history with her family, seeing as his grandfather was one of the founding fathers of the city. It was convoluted and tense, full of scandal and betrayal, but history all the same. He was like a great-uncle to her, and she'd spent a lot of time with him and Dee.

She was sure she looked a hot mess, but she couldn't bring herself to care at that point. If she could crawl into bed and sleep the rest of the day, that would be ideal, but she had to go back to work.

Sterling slid in across from her, interrupting her peace and quiet. Glaring at him, she hissed, "What do you want?"

Sterling looked her over with a critical eye. He'd always done that, and she hated it. "We need to talk."

"I don't believe there is anything to talk about. I'm trying to eat breakfast, by myself."

"Brooklyn, trust me, this is for your own good."

Leaning back against the seat, she crossed her arms over her chest. "What?"

"If we don't get married, it will be a problem. For your father and mine."

Curious, Brooklyn observed Sterling, the sweat on his brow and the clench in his jaw. "What are you talking about? I already told you I'm not marrying you."

"You know as well as I do what happens when our fathers don't get their way, and they've been banking on a marriage between us for years. I don't know what they have planned, but they're not going to take this lying down."

She wasn't in the mood to deal with Sterling and her father.

"Listen, I don't live with my father anymore. I moved out, so whatever he had planned is a moot point."

No, she wasn't stupid enough to actually believe that, but she also didn't have to say it out loud to Sterling either. Brooklyn had learned a long time ago that people who crossed Parker Wells Sr. never really recovered. All she had to do was look at her mother and the long string of wives who'd followed her to know that. But she'd actually seen him in action, seen the veiled threats to business associates and even employees. He was a controlling monster, no doubt.

"Brooklyn, you know you're not that naïve. My father is planning to visit you today, to convince you to make the right decision."

Well, then I'll just have to be somewhere else. "Good thing I won't be around today."

Sterling placed a hand on hers. "You're not thinking, Brooksielynsie."

She rolled her eyes. "What is there to think about, Sterling? I don't want to marry you. Nothing about this is appealing to me."

Sterling's head jerked back, and his mouth fell open. He pulled his hand away. "It's better than the alternative."

Leaning forward, palms flat on the table, she asked, "What do you know?"

He swallowed. "I saw you Thursday night on the strip with the new guy. Is that your man?"

"I barely know him. And you didn't answer the question."

Sterling let out an ugly, bitter laugh. "You like him, though."

He'd played her, and she'd let him. Coming into the restaurant acting anxious, scared even, had made her drop her guard a little. Never again. "Is there a point to this visit? How did you even know I was here? Have you been following me?"

"You do know he works for Wellspring Water?" he went on as if she hadn't even spoken. "I wonder how your father would feel about you spending time with the help."

Brooklyn gritted her teeth. Sterling was too self-important, too judgmental for Brooklyn to ever consider marrying him. He and people of his ilk made her sick to her stomach. They always seemed to have their noses turned up, thinking they're better than everyone else.

"Get the hell away from me," she ground out through clenched teeth. "I don't care if Obama told me the state of the union depended on me walking down the aisle. I'm not marrying you. Period."

Sterling stood, pushing her plate off the table. In a few moments, Will Clark was by her side, nose to nose with Sterling. "Get the hell out of my restaurant, King."

"What are you going to do about it, old man?"

"You'd be surprised." Will pointed at the door. "Get!"

Sterling glared at her, the chill in his eyes sending a shiver up her spine. "This is not done."

Then he stormed out of the restaurant.

Carter was officially moved in. He'd met a woman at the condo a few hours earlier and she'd given him the keys and other pertinent information about the subdivision. The spacious condo was move-in ready and fully furnished. There were balconies off of his kitchen and the master bedroom. Aisha hadn't been lying. The view of the Grand River was spectacular, peaceful.

The amenities in the neighborhood made the transition easier. There were walking trails, a park, and the indoor pool. The gym located in the clubhouse was small, but he'd definitely use it if he couldn't get to a larger gym. Located close were several restaurants and a Starbucks. He had everything he needed.

Glancing at his watch, he stepped back into the condo and headed toward the second bedroom, where he'd set up his home office. It didn't take him long to hook his computer and dual monitors up. It took a little longer than usual to set up the private network they used when they were working on a project, but he'd accomplished his goal and still made it to Walmart to grab a few items for the house and back in time. Martin would be calling in a little while so that they could discuss his first week on the project.

Carter logged into the computer and checked his email. After responding to a few, he heard the ringtone for the video conference.

Martin appeared on the screen a few seconds later. "What's up, man?"

"Nothing much. Just got moved in and everything. It's not too bad."

Ryleigh appeared behind Martin, waving at him. "Hey, Carter."

Carter waved back at her. "Hey, girl. You and Martin enjoying married life?"

His best friend's wife beamed, showing off the deep dimple in her cheek. "Immensely." She turned to Martin. "Babe, I have to run to the store, but dinner is ready when you are."

Carter groaned. "Aw, what did you cook?" Ryleigh was an excellent cook, and Carter had been blessed to be invited to dinner several times since the two became a couple.

"I made Martin's favorite, fettuccini alfredo with chicken and spinach."

"That sounds good." Carter couldn't help but envy his friend for being happy. He'd felt that way once before, and he missed it. Ryleigh was good for Martin. They fit together. His friend needed a woman that kept him on his toes. Before Ryleigh, Martin had been somewhat of a player, flitting from woman to woman. Ryleigh came along and threw Martin for a loop. "You'll have to come and visit so you can cook for me."

Martin laughed. "Good luck with that. Ryleigh is barely around enough to cook for me."

"Hey," Ryleigh said, smacking Martin's shoulder. "It's just been busy." She glanced at Carter and smiled. "Maybe we'll come visit in a few weeks. And I promise I'll cook for you."

Ryleigh said goodbye to him and Martin, and disappeared from view.

"So how was your first week?" Martin asked. "It's not too boring, is it?"

"Oh, it's boring. Definitely small-town living."

"Well, there are benefits to being in a small town, at least temporarily. Ryleigh grew up in one, and she is just now beginning to appreciate going home."

Ryleigh was from a small resort town in South Carolina. He'd yet to visit, but from everything Martin told him about Rosewood Heights, he would make a trip down there sooner rather than later.

"I'm sure Rosewood Heights is a big town compared to Wellspring," Carter said. "At least there are beaches, resorts, and Mama Lil's blueberry pancakes."

"Dog, you mean to tell me there isn't some diner there that has good food? You know those diner owners have the market cornered on good, greasy meals."

Carter thought about the omelet he'd had earlier in the day. He'd stopped at the Bee's Knees every day that week for breakfast or dinner. "Yeah, you're right. There's a joint here that I like. I almost overdosed on a western omelet earlier."

"See," Martin said, smacking his hands on his

desk. "I knew it. Eat more of those. Then, do some exploring."

"I'm actually considering a quick trip home tomorrow."

"What the hell for?"

"There are some things I want to take care of." Since the fire, Carter had purchased a condo in downtown Detroit. Carter never thought he'd want to move out of the city proper, but being in Wellspring made him rethink it. "I'm thinking of moving out of the city."

Martin sat back in his chair. "Really?"

"Yeah." Martin lived in Canton Township, which was about thirty miles outside of Detroit. His friend had often remarked how he loved the area because he had access to everything he needed. Carter didn't want to move to Canton, but he'd considered the town of Birmingham, which was on the north side of Detroit and not too far from his mother. "I think it's time to make some changes."

"Good. You need change in your life. You've been content to let it pass you by. And you don't need to come home to take care of business. That's what a phone and an internet connection are for."

Momentarily, his thoughts drifted back to Brooklyn. He'd seen her that morning as he was moving out of the hotel. She didn't stop to speak to him, though. Instead, she shot him one of her brilliant smiles and walked out.

"Martin, did you research the Wells family?"

Carter had been working at WWCH for a week, and had met many of the employees. They all seemed to enjoy working for Parker Jr., but when the subject of Parker Sr. came up, they all pretty much changed the subject.

Martin shot him a disbelieving look. "What? You do know who you're talking to? Of course, I researched the Wells family. I sent you a folder with everything you need to know about Wellspring Water Corp. last week."

"No, not the company." Carter didn't make it a priority to research the personal lives of their clients, but his talk with Mr. Clark and the reactions from Wellspring Water employees made him even more curious. "I'm talking about the Wells family."

"Since when do we dig that deep? Unless someone is threatening us. I know that Parker Wells Sr. has three kids and practically owns the town. It doesn't really matter what skeletons his family has hidden in its closet. Our job is to go in, help them develop and set up their ERP system, and get out of Dodge. That's it."

Sighing, Carter stared out the window. The sun was setting, signaling his long day was almost over. "You're right. Never mind."

For the next hour, they went over the project checklist Martin had created, discussing potential problems and ways Carter could keep them on schedule.

"I plan to make a trip that way next Friday," Martin told him. "I want to present our recommendations within the first three weeks, so I figured it would give me a chance to see how they're operating as well. I'll hold off on sending Philip and the team there until you give me the word. You'll be busy in meetings, conducting employee interviews for the time being."

"Sounds good." Carter knew that Martin loved this part of the business, meeting and working with the employees. If Martin hadn't married, he would be in Wellspring, probably enjoying the small-town life for the short period of time he'd be there. "I'll know more once I finish the interviews and meet Parker Sr. He's been out of office for the entire week."

"Definitely." Martin sat back in his chair. "Listen, man, I know we haven't talked about this, but I wanted to let you know that I hated missing the conclusion of the trial. But I'm glad it turned out the way it did."

Nodding, Carter tapped a thumb on the desk to a made-up beat that always seemed to calm his nerves. "I'm glad it's over. For what it's worth, I know I've let a lot of things slide. You picked up my slack and I appreciate it."

Carter meant it. Martin was more like a brother to him. They'd been best friends for years, grew into men together. They'd seen each other through some hard times, and he knew he could count on Martin to have his back.

"You know that's what we do," Martin said. "Aisha has been giving me plenty of updates. She also told me that you two talked about Krys."

"Tell Aisha she talks too much."

Martin laughed. "You know she's just concerned."

Carter couldn't be sure, but he'd always suspected Aisha had a thing for Martin. But his friend had never paid it any attention. *Or maybe he did?* "I know. We had a nice talk."

"She wants to see you happy. We all do."

"Things are not as bad today as they were yesterday. And I suspect tomorrow will be better than today. That's all I got."

"Maybe Mrs. Marshall is in Wellspring, Michigan."

Carter snorted. He might be attracted to Brooklyn, but no part of him was even considering marriage again to anyone. "Yeah, no. I'm not looking for another Mrs. Marshall." He'd already had one, and she was the best part of his life. And she was gone.

Chapter 8

The following Monday, Brooklyn awoke to a note under her door. She picked it up and cursed long and hard. It was an eviction notice. Dressing quickly, she rushed down to the lobby. Justine was behind the desk, and when she spotted Brooklyn, her face fell.

Before Brooklyn could say anything, Justine said, "I know. I tried to stop Tom from doing this." Tom was the hotel manager, and had been so for years. He'd watched Brooklyn and her brothers grow up with much of the townspeople. But like so many others, Tom was intimidated by Senior and would never stand up to her father. "Your father gave the order last night to remove you immediately, but I couldn't do that to you in the middle of the night."

Damn. Brooklyn closed her eyes, counted to ten. She hadn't had any luck with a place, and she'd run out of time. "Where am I supposed to go?"

It wasn't even really a question. Her father had effectively tied her hands. It was an attempt to force her back home, but she refused to give in. So, it was

either Nic's place or Parker's home. At least until
she could get her own. Briefly, she'd considered
renting an apartment but didn't want to sign a long
term lease if she planned on buying a home.

"I'm so sorry, Brooklyn," Justine said, a solemn
look on her face. "He wants the bill paid today, too."

"Fine." She texted Nicole to come pick her up.
"Do me a favor?"

"Anything," Justine said.

"Put a hold on housekeeping for my room. I
need some time to move my stuff out."

"No problem, Brooklyn."

Nicole rushed into the hotel lobby about twenty
minutes later, Kyle right behind her. "What's going
on, hun?"

Brooklyn hugged her friends. "Thanks for
coming. Senior is kicking me out of the hotel."

"What?" Nicole screeched. "I guess he didn't
waste any time once he got back to town, huh?"

"You know you can stay with us, right?" Kyle said.

"I know." Brooklyn dropped her gaze, hating the
burn of tears in her eyes. "This really sucks. You are
supposed to be preparing for my godchild, not
taking in a roommate. I just need to step up my
search for a place. I'm going to call the realtor
today. I would hate to do it, but I may have to rent
until I can find a house."

Nicole rubbed her back. "It'll be okay. In the
meantime, you'll stay with us."

A tear fell down her cheek and she wiped it away.
"Thank you," she whispered. "I have to get my stuff."

All three walked up to the desk. "Justine, I'm
going to come back in a couple of hours to get my

things, okay?" She handed the woman her debit card. "Use this for the incidentals."

Brooklyn had already reimbursed Nicole for the room, since it was on her credit card, but had incurred a few incidental charges for room service and movies. There were other hotels in town, but this one was convenient, walking distance to her job and close to everything.

"Brooklyn?" Justine said, a solemn look on her face. "Your card was declined."

Frowning, Brooklyn snatched the card away. "There must be a mistake. This is my bank account. Try it again." She handed Justine her card.

Nicole leaned forward. "Did the card expire?"

"No. I just used it last night."

Justine apologized. "It's still coming up as insufficient funds."

Kyle plopped a card down on the countertop. "Use mine."

Brooklyn unlocked her phone and opened up her mobile banking app, furiously typing in her username and password. What she saw made her stomach lurch into her chest. "Oh no," she whispered.

"What?" Nicole asked, concern in her eyes. "What happened?"

"I don't have any money. All of it is gone."

Brooklyn stormed into WWCH, or Wellspring Water Corporation Headquarters. She was livid, furious. After she'd rushed to the bank to check on her account, she'd been told that her accounts had been cleared out and frozen—by her father. It was her trust account, co-owned with her father, so there was no use in arguing with the bank manager. Senior had also closed her credit card account.

Backroom deals, corruption, lies, and scandal were all in a day's work for her father. Brooklyn knew this, and had anticipated a day like this once her father had started steering her toward Sterling King. She just hadn't expected the day to come so soon. She'd opened an account at a credit union in Kalamazoo once she was hired at the clinic. Since that time, she'd redirected her entire paycheck to that credit union. Brooklyn had a healthy stash of cash, but she needed a day or so to access it.

Brooklyn caught the elevator up to the twelfth floor, which housed the executive offices. Knowing the lengths her father had gone through made her want to confront him. And she would. He was going to know that he didn't break her resolve. She breezed through the suite, not stopping, even when his secretary tried to stop her.

Bursting through the frosted glass door, she yelled, "Senior, you can't do this to—" She paused, thrown off by the presence of her father's closest advisers.

"Get the hell out of here, Brooklyn," her father growled. "You know the rules."

"You froze my account, wiped me out. That was my money, trust or no. It's mine."

Senior motioned with one hand and the men in suits scattered out of the office like little mice running for cover. Leaning back in his chair, he crossed an ankle over his knee. "I can do whatever I please because I own this town. I control everything in your life, including your money. Oh, and don't bother trying to access your credit union money. I put a hold on that as well."

Brooklyn's gazed flashed to her father. "What you're doing is illegal. You don't have authorization to make changes on my personal account."

"Baby girl, you have no idea how much power I have. So listen up, when you disrespect me, you will be dealt with like anybody else."

The cold in his voice made her retreat back a step. Her chin trembled, and she fought to gain her courage back. "What would you have me do? Live on the street?"

"I wouldn't have you do anything of the sort. It's your decision. You defied me, Brooklyn Wells, and I won't have it."

She shuddered at her father's use of her full name. He only took that tone with her when he was sufficiently pissed at her antics. "I'm still your daughter."

"Then you better damn well act like it. You've done nothing but disrespect my wishes for years. I offered you a lucrative position in our company, but you chose to become a social worker, spending your days trolling the streets for addicts and homeless people. Instead of joining us at the boardroom table, you rebuffed me at every turn. Still, I let it go. But embarrassing me the way you did at my charity gala was unacceptable. And until you fall in line, you will have to make other arrangements for your living expenses. That includes living in the hotel. Oh, yes, I know your little friend put the reservation under her name. But as of today, neither of you are welcome there."

"I hate you," she hissed, hating that it came out as only a little more than a whisper.

Her father leaned in, tilting his ear toward her. "What's that? I didn't hear you, sweetheart."

Brooklyn wouldn't repeat herself because there was no use. Standing up straight, her shoulders and chin high, she met her father's murderous gaze with one of her own. "Just so you know. You can't control me, Senior. I won't marry Sterling because *you* want me to. And if that means that I have to make my own way, then that's what I'll do."

Her father stood slowly. His six-foot-three frame seemed to block out all the sun shining in. "Brooklyn, I won't tell you again. You will not ruin everything that I've worked for with your behavior."

"You and your plans can go to hell."

Brooklyn turned on wobbly feet and rushed out of the office, slamming the door behind her. She needed to talk to Parker. She rushed over to Parker's office, practically at a sprint, on the far side of the floor. Pushing the door open, she hurried in, shutting and locking the door behind her.

Leaning her forehead against the glass door, she took slow breaths in an effort to calm down.

"Brooklyn, what's wrong?" She turned to find her brother sitting at his desk, a quizzical look on his face. "Were you running?"

She dropped her purse to the floor and slid down the wall to join it. "I hate him," she whispered, burying her face in her drawn-up knees. The tears flowed then, and she cried.

"Sis, tell me what happened." Parker was in front of her, kneeling low, rubbing a hand over her back as she sobbed. "You're scaring me. Who do you hate?"

"I hate your father." She peered up at him then through her wet lashes. "He took my money, emptied out my bank account."

"Your trust account?"

"That and my hidden bank account. How did he manage to do that? Does he have people following me? Has he hacked into my computer or something?"

The vein that only popped out when Parker was upset was now in full view. He cursed, long and hard, then stood to his feet and paced the floor. "What happened, Brooklyn? What did you do?"

Her eyes jerked to his. "What did *I* do? He's the one who engineered this entire wedding plan. He promised a marriage to the King family, Parker. I'm nothing more than a means to an end for him. A business deal to further his interests for Wellspring Water. What did *I* do?"

Parker crouched down in front of her again. "I'm sorry. I didn't mean it like that."

Of all the people who should understand, her brother should. Their father had been controlling their lives since birth, making decisions about their future at every turn, without consulting them. Brooklyn knew that Parker had arranged to move to Los Angeles to get away from Wellspring, and had only stayed because of her and Bryson. He was a good big brother that way. But Bryson had left the first chance he got, off to parts unknown. She barely heard from him anymore. Even though she missed him, she wouldn't want him to come back to the prison she called their lives as the offspring of Parker Wells Sr.

"He told me I couldn't stay at the hotel anymore."

"You can stay with me, Brooklyn. I told you that from the beginning, and I'm sure Nicole did, too."

"Nicole is expecting a baby, due any day now. And I'm not going to come between you and Senior by moving in with you."

"I don't care about that. You're my sister, and I'm here for you."

"I care. And that's what matters." Besides, she'd claw her own eyes out if she walked in on Nic and Kyle doing it or something, or even worse? Parker and some woman getting it in. She'd been there and done that, and had the scars to prove it.

"Stop being so stubborn, Brooklyn. I'm not going to let you go to another hotel. I thought it was a bad idea in the first place. But you wouldn't listen."

"That's not the point. I shouldn't have to live with you or Nic. I have a job, my own money, and a plan to buy my own house. I don't want to depend on you or anybody else for support. You were able to move out, get your own place, and still have access to the trust. Why can't I be afforded that same right? Oh wait, I know why. Because I'm a woman and a means to an end for Senior."

Parker sighed. "I'll take care of it, Brooklyn. Don't worry."

"I don't need you to take care of it. I told you I don't want you to get in the middle of this. It's between me and Senior. He'll only come for you, and you have too much to lose right now."

Parker had plans. Their father would eventually have to retire, and Parker planned to take full advantage when he did. Wellspring Water needed to get out from under the Senior's influence, and Parker was in the perfect position to make lasting changes that would be good for the town and its people.

However, Brooklyn had seen the toll that stress had taken on her older brother. She worried that her father would corrupt Parker the longer he stayed under his father's thumb.

"Look, this conversation is done. I have a solution that doesn't involve you staying at my house. I have a place," her brother admitted, his voice quiet in his corner office. It had taken years for him to work his way up to the executive suite, because their father had always made things hard for him. "I purchased several units in one of the new subdivisions on the west side of town."

Surprised, she asked, "When did you do this? Does Senior know about it?"

He shook his head. "I bought it with cash, and registered it under an LLC. I thought it would be a good opportunity to expand my reach in this town and neighboring towns. I've also used it for contractors that are working with Wellspring on different projects, kind of like company housing."

"And you're sure Senior has no idea?"

"You know as well as I do that he doesn't care about shit like that."

Parker was right. Her father wouldn't care where the contractors stayed, he'd just be concerned with whether the work was getting done.

"My plan is to purchase other real estate in Wellspring and Grand Rapids," her brother continued. "It never hurts to have an additional stream of income."

"Parker, you're brilliant."

Her brother smiled. "This, I know. But you can stay there, rent-free. It will take a while for Senior to find you, and if he does, he can't do anything about it because I own it. Plain and simple. And don't worry about my relationship with Senior. You're more important to me than he is, and I've got your back."

But he will find me eventually. Brooklyn would be stupid to think this was the end of her problems with her father. His reach was long and his wrath was the stuff of legend. They weren't a crime family or anything, but she knew her father could be excessively ruthless to get what he wanted. What he was doing to her now was nothing compared to the way he'd abused her mother. Senior had treated her mother horribly in her last few months of life. Her mom had done a good job of hiding it, though. But shortly after she died, Brooklyn had stumbled upon her mother's journals. Within the pages, her mother had revealed her truth, had written about the threats from Senior if she left him, the abuse. It had made her sick to her stomach to think about it even now.

"I think I'm going to look into mom's death," Brooklyn announced. Her father's behavior toward her lately, had made her think of her mom even more.

Parker sighed. "Brooklyn, we've talked about this before. It was an accident. There was no foul play involved."

"But what if there was?"

"You're angry at Senior, and you have every right to be. But don't go drudging up mom's death. The police did their investigation then. It was a horrible accident, but that's all it was."

Brooklyn didn't want to go into all the reasons she'd suspected her father had something to do with her mother's death. Part of her wanted to agree with Parker, because if her suspicions were true, it would mean that her father had done the unthinkable. But she'd never been able to shake the thought that her mother's death was more than a tragic accident.

She pulled Parker into a hug, inhaling his clean scent. "Thank you, Parker. I love you."

He gripped the back of her head, tickling her scalp like he'd done when she was a little girl. "I love you, too. Listen, get yourself together. Meet me after work at the Bee's Knees, and I'll hand over the keys."

Nodding, she let her brother help her to her feet. "Thank you, again." She brushed off her pants and ran her fingers through her hair. "I better get to work."

"You need to take that damn wig off."

Brooklyn laughed. "Shut up."

"Seriously, Brooklyn. I understand why you wore it to the gala to please our father, but you moved out, baby sis. It doesn't matter what Senior thinks anymore."

Her father had made it clear that women with short hair were not attractive. When she'd done the big chop a few years ago, he'd lectured her for hours about being a lady and attracting the right kind of men. So, she'd bought a wig. Several, in fact.

"Okay, Parker. I'll take it off—as soon as I can get an appointment with Stacyee."

Stacyee was her stylist and had been since she was in high school. It was hard to get an appointment on the fly because Stacyee had amassed a clientele that kept her very comfortable. It helped that she was excellent at what she did and was worth the prices she charged.

Brooklyn and Parker shared another quick hug before she walked out of the office.

Chapter 9

A scream was about all Brooklyn had in her, and she let it out with gusto. Moving into her brother's condo had been a breeze, no hiccups. It was fully furnished and stocked with food, courtesy of Parker. Of course, she'd spent hours cleaning and washing clothes because she was obsessive about cleaning and loved the smell of detergent, bleach, and Pine Sol. But she was having the damnedest time hooking up the internet. And she needed to be able to connect. She had case files to access and reports to write.

She briefly considered kicking the damn laptop off the balcony and watching it crash to the ground. It was old, ancient really. And the fact that she'd put off purchasing another one while she had access to the family discount niggled at her.

Oh well, it'll be my first purchase with my own money. She wasn't spoiled, but she'd realized a hard truth when she was inconveniently tossed from her hotel room earlier . . . she was sheltered. No one had ever been mean to her, except for her father and her stepmothers. But because of her last name, no one in town had dared to treat her badly.

Well, today she'd been treated to one of the most humiliating incidents of her life, courtesy of Senior. If Parker hadn't come to her rescue, she would probably still be at the hotel living the same moment over and over again—or in jail for trespassing. Once she returned to the hotel to get her things, Justine was gone and her room was occupied by someone else.

Brooklyn knew the hotel manager Tom was only doing his job, but it infuriated her no less. They'd been told by Senior to toss her stuff in the trash, but Tom had taken pity on her and stored it in the basement.

Parker had found her in the hotel basement, tears in her eyes as she picked up a broken trinket her mother had given her. The hotel employee that transferred her items to the basement had inadvertently dropped a box and many of her personal things had tumbled out. The young guy had tried to glue it back together, but there was no use. The ceramic angel was destroyed.

Parker had taken one look at her, scooped her into his arms, and carried her to his car. Half an hour later, he'd gathered all of her things and stuffed them into his trunk and back seat. He'd offered to spend the night, help her get settled, but she'd rushed him off, intent on crying alone and trying to get some work done. *This damn internet.* She screamed again, not even caring if there were any neighbors.

Needing a break, she stepped out onto the balcony. Considering there had been a freakin' blizzard

a week earlier, the night breeze was soft against her
skin. It was a mild day in Wellspring, so she took
full advantage of it. She tilted her head up and inhaled the fresh scent of river water and wood. The
tears came then, just like she knew they would.
The helpless feeling in her gut wouldn't let her
rest. She was out of luck and there was nothing she
could do about it tonight. The knowledge that her
father had found her private account irritated her to
no end. She thought she had access to money, and
hated that she was essentially broke. And she hated
that Parker had to once again come to her rescue,
this time providing a place to live.

Parker had given up so much of his life for his
family, had always taken care of her, even when it
caused him personal hardship. When Brooklyn had
declared that she wasn't going to law school, as her
father intended, she'd been subjected to the lecture
of all lectures from her father. He'd threatened her,
pulled strings to prevent her finding a job. Parker
risked his own livelihood to stand up for her. And
he'd suffered greatly for it, being shunned and shut
out from the company as a result. He didn't say, but
Brooklyn suspected Parker had also endured phys-
ical abuse from their father in the past, because of
her and Bryson. The thought made her sick. But
Parker had never complained. And she loved him
for it. That's why she hadn't asked for help when
she'd first left the house. He'd done more than
enough for her.

"Lord, please don't let him be caught in the
middle of this," she prayed to the night air. She
wouldn't be able to forgive herself if her brother
had to suffer because of her. She buried her face in

her hands, a deep sob ripping from her throat.
"Please look out for him."

Parker didn't live in the family home, so there
was no chance of being kicked out. Her brother was
also over the age of thirty and had control of his
own trust now, so Senior couldn't threaten him
with that. But Parker had worked his way back into
the company after being shut out for a time. He'd
invested time and energy into Wellspring Water,
biding his time, putting in long hours to help move
the company forward. While his financial livelihood
was not tied to his father, his career aspirations and
dreams were tied to Wellspring Water. And as long
as his father was alive and controlled the company,
Brooklyn would worry about Parker. *I should have
just stayed.* Marrying Sterling would have been like
a slow, eventual death. But it would have at least
kept the peace. Now, she wasn't sure when the next
blow was coming.

When Brooklyn was a little girl, she'd announced
to her mother that her sole purpose in life was to
marry Lil Bow Wow. She'd really fooled herself
into believing that she would be Mrs. Lil Bow Wow
before she turned twenty years old. Her mother
had even driven her to Auburn Hills, Michigan, to
see him in concert, even bought backstage passes
so she could meet her true love.

Unfortunately, Brooklyn realized that she was
only one of many little girls who had visions of
marrying the rapper. And he'd barely noticed her.
She'd been a devastated fan that day, and had sunk
into a depression so deep, she wouldn't come out
of her room for days. It was then that her mother

had sat her down and told her *Life isn't fair, but the good stuff will outweigh the bad stuff.*

From the outside looking in, it might seem like Brooklyn lived a charmed life. In many ways she had. Aside from the rough patch she'd had after her mother died, she'd breezed through school, had never struggled to pay bills, never experimented with drugs, and was never physically abused by anyone. Her clients . . . they had serious situations, life-and-death problems. Brooklyn couldn't relate to eating dog food, sleeping with a knife for protection, feigning for a hit of something. But the one thing she could give her clients was her undying devotion to seeing them live better lives. She wondered what advice they'd give her if they saw her.

Living in a luxury condo, food in the fridge, nice clothes on her back . . . she really had nothing to complain about. Nothing at all. So *why do I feel so alone?*

Because now she was by herself, forced to figure things out on her own. It was uncomfortable for her, outside of her plan for her life, to know she had to start over with her savings and postpone getting her house. Thinking about her clients, though, provided the punch to the gut she needed to snap out of the pity party she'd been stuck in for the last few hours. When her problems seemed insurmountable, like they did at that very moment, she'd often take stock in what she did have and pray for those less fortunate, because her life could be so much worse than it was. It gave her a much needed perspective that often served to give her peace about any situation she found herself in. Sucking all her emotion in, she sent up a silent prayer for forgiveness, for forgetting that she really was blessed.

Picking up her phone, she dialed her brother. When he answered, she told him, "I'm all settled. Thanks for everything."

"Any time," his said, his voice raspy.

"Did I wake you?"

"I was almost sleep. Do you need anything?"

Brooklyn nibbled on her thumbnail. "Actually, I do need something."

"What is it?"

"Can you come here and stay with me tonight? I don't want to be alone."

Carter gripped the arms of the wicker chair he sat in. He couldn't sleep, so he'd ventured out onto the balcony. But as much as he'd wanted to chalk up the reason for still being outside on his dark balcony—over an hour later—to the new town and the strange bed, he knew that wasn't the reason. The truth was he'd spent the last twenty-five minutes debating whether he should reveal himself to his new neighbor. Brooklyn.

Instead he'd watched her stare out into night like she had the world on her shoulders, listened to her crying. For some reason he couldn't say anything, but he couldn't tear his eyes away from her petite form either. The light from her condo illuminated her like an angel under a halo.

Now she was on the phone, talking all low and sexy. *Is that her normal phone voice or is she talking like that because of the person on the other end of the line?* He wondered who she was talking to, who she was asking to spend the night with her. Earlier, she hadn't seemed like she was with someone. Carter could have sworn she was eyeing him in the way that someone did when they were interested. After all, she'd invited *him* out for dinner or coffee.

He heard her laugh, saw her dash a tear from her cheek. *Who made her cry?* The thought of some man bringing her to tears made him want to fight. Although he couldn't figure out why. He'd seen her cry twice. And both times, she'd brought out every protective instinct he had.

Maybe it was because she was small? Brooklyn was tiny, couldn't be much more than five feet tall. Carter was a giant compared to her. Honestly, he'd be worried he'd hurt her. *Wait. What the hell is wrong with me?*

"I know it's late," he heard her say. "But it's been a long day and I can't get my internet up and running." She paused. "I know, I know. It's not that, I just . . . I can't be here by myself tonight."

Carter practically ripped the arm of his chair off, he was gripping it so tight. He'd been reduced to eavesdropping. What business was it of his, if she did have a man that she called over to . . . ? *Damn.* And why was she begging that person to come over? Brooklyn was beautiful. If she had to beg a man to come keep her company, that man was a fool.

"Thank you. I appreciate it. See you when you get here."

She hung up the phone and he opened his mouth to finally announce his presence. Nope. He was still a piece of shit, but now he was a Peeping Tom, creepy piece of shit. He watched her step out farther onto the balcony. *What the hell is she wearing?*

Not only was her skin glowing like the sun, she was wearing a short little see-through nightgown that showed off her legs and her flat stomach. In March. In Michigan. And he was rock hard. The feeling surprised him so much that he almost toppled over in the chair. Unfortunately, the beer he'd been sipping on did fall onto the balcony.

"Shit," he hissed.

Her gaze flashed over to his balcony. "Who's there?"

Carter cursed himself to hell and back before he stepped forward, into the light. "Me."

Brooklyn's mouth fell open. With wide eyes, she stuttered, "Wha-whe-why . . ." She swallowed. "You? You're my neighbor?"

Carter approached her hesitantly, trying not to look at her breasts, all perky and firm under her nightgown. He sucked in a deep breath, focusing on her eyes. "I moved in Friday."

"Wow, I moved in today, a few hours ago."

She averted her gaze, and his dropped to her painted toes. "This really is a small town." He stepped closer. "I heard you. I didn't mean to, but I heard you crying." He tilted his head to meet her beautiful eyes. "Are you okay?"

With a tentative smile on her face, she said, "I'm fine." She licked her lips, and he followed the movement like a hawk would its prey. Her voice sounded like a song. It was like balm to dry skin. "I had a rough day."

"I'm sorry to hear that. I've had a few of those myself." That was the understatement of his life.

"Sometimes it helps to go to bed and start fresh in the morning."

"I thought you were going to say that it's good to talk about these things."

"I'm not a big talker."

"I wouldn't have guessed that." She was teasing him. He could tell by the smirk on her face and the gleam in her eyes.

"Nice night."

She looked up at the sky, hugged herself. "Yes. Hard to believe it was snowing a little over a week ago."

Spring was a few weeks away, but snow could be right around the corner. It was best to enjoy the warmth while it lasted. "That's Michigan for you," he murmured.

Brooklyn looked at him then, tilting her head to the side. "Where are you from?"

"Detroit," he admitted.

"Ah." She shot him a playful grin. "Figures."

"What is that supposed to mean?"

"I knew you were from a big city."

Carter laughed. "Is that a bad thing?"

"Not really. I like Detroit. I've been there a few times. There's a lot to do. A friend of mine moved to the Detroit area a few years ago. She stays in . . ." She tapped her chin as if in deep thought. "Westland?"

"Okay, that's not too far from the city." Westland was a city in the metropolitan Detroit area, about sixteen miles from downtown. Carter was familiar with the area because Krys used to drag him to the Westland mall to shop. For some reason, she enjoyed

the smaller mall more than the bigger one near
their home. "I've actually spent a lot of time there."

"Really? She used to stay in Detroit, but her fiancé
works in Ann Arbor and they wanted to move
somewhere in the middle."

Of course Carter knew Ann Arbor. He was a University of Michigan alumnus. "I went to school in
Ann Arbor." He said it before he could stop himself.

"Shut up. You went to U of M? I wanted to go
there, but my father insisted I go to Michigan State."

"You're a Spartan, huh?"

The rivalry between U of M and Michigan State
was strong in the state. Carter had never been a fan
of the "green and white." Kendall had defected and
decided to head to East Lansing for college. It made
game days very spirited in the Marshall household.

"I am. You got a problem with that?"

"I guess you can't win them all."

"Wow." Brooklyn smiled. "Good comeback. Now
if only your team could actually win a game."

"Ooo . . ." He chuckled. "And you would know
how it feels to have a losing team."

"I'm also a BU Terrier," she said.

"Boston U, huh? So you haven't lived in Michigan
all your life?"

"Nope. I've actually spent a lot of time in the
Boston area. I went to a boarding school out there
for three years, and then went back for grad school."

"What made you come back here?"

Brooklyn shrugged. "I wonder the same thing
sometimes. But it always comes back to my childhood. It's the last connection I have to my mother,

there are some fine people here in Wellspring. It's home. My family is here."

Carter understood that. After he'd graduated with his bachelor's degree, he'd stayed at U of M for his graduate degree, while Martin went off to Duke University. At the time, he'd told himself that he stayed for Krys, but it was really because Michigan was home. He never really wanted to live anywhere else.

"Don't get me wrong," Brooklyn continued. "I love Boston and have considered a move more times that I can count. But I enjoy what I do here."

"That's a bonus." Carter wanted to ask more. He'd enjoyed their friendly banter, and couldn't help the smile that seemed to get wider when they'd traded barbs about each other's teams. "The connection," he blurted out when the conversation died down.

Brooklyn blinked. "Excuse me?"

"The internet. I also overheard you saying your internet isn't working. I can help with that." *Yes, I can.* He was a computer engineer after all. He'd made his living off knowing computers and developing software.

"Oh, okay. Sure, I'd love the help."

He pointed toward the patio door. "I'll come over."

"Right. I'll open the door."

A few minutes later, he was standing on the other side of her door. He lifted his hand to knock, but the door swung open. Brooklyn stood before him, a smile on her face and a robe covering her beautiful body.

Carter knew he shouldn't feel disappointed, but that's exactly how he felt. The thought made him feel like a straight-up pervert.

"Come in." She pulled him inside and he followed her to the kitchen table, where her laptop sat.

It didn't take him long to hook up her connection—if anything he went slower than he normally would. Once he was finished, he pointed down at the laptop. "You're all set."

She leaned forward, clicked on the internet browser. Carter closed his eyes as her scent floated to his nose. Vanilla. "Yes!" she shouted, with a fist pump in the air. "You are a genius!"

He was so wrapped up in her energy that he was rendered speechless when her mouth met his. A warmth shot through his body, right before it disappeared. Because she disappeared. And he couldn't say if he was relieved or disappointed.

"Oh my God, I'm so sorry." She backed away. Far away to the other side of the kitchen. A flush spread across her cheeks. The mortified look on her face would have offended him if he could think about anything other than her lips on his. It wasn't a passionate kiss. It was soft, and the first time he'd kissed any woman since Krys died.

The thought sobered him and he bolted out of the chair. "It's fine, no big deal." *Except it is a big deal.*

In the two years since he'd lost his wife, he hadn't even really thought about being with another woman. Yes, he liked sex and had been propositioned many times, but he'd gotten used to not getting any. This was different. *She* was different.

He was sure if Aisha were here, she'd give him the big thumbs-up. Everyone wanted him to move on, to meet someone. How could he do that when he felt guilty for even looking at another woman? He looked at his wrist and cursed inwardly because he didn't have on his watch.

Brooklyn approached him tentatively. "I'm . . . I didn't mean to kiss you like that. I just got caught up in the moment. Please forgive me."

He smiled tightly. "Nothing to forgive." And he wanted her to do it again. He wanted to do more than kiss her. The admission, even to himself, was enough to make his entire body go tense. "I should probably go, though. I have a long day ahead of me tomorrow."

Needing to put as much distance between them as possible, he left without another word.

"Don't go," Brooklyn murmured, clinging to her big brother. Parker had driven her to a fast food joint to pick up breakfast, and he was dropping her back off at her new place. "Can't you spend the day with your little sister? We could watch movies, eat, talk."

Actually they could sit looking at each other in silence and it still would have been better than being alone. Brooklyn used to love the solitude of being by herself, but she missed having someone around to chat with or play games with. Nicole had her own life and Brooklyn hated to intrude.

As much as she pretended to like freedom, she longed for strings. By now, she'd expected to be settled in a committed relationship and on the road to marriage—just not with Sterling. The sad part was she hadn't actually met a man in recent years who would even qualify for husband material. Dating was like walking a mine field. One false move, and *BOOM*!

"Brooklyn, you're going to be fine." Parker pinched her earlobe, like he used to do when they were kids. "It'll be an adjustment, but you're going to end up loving it here. Why don't you head to town and pick up some décor? Spruce up the place. Make it Brooklyn's place."

"Considering I have no money, that would be a negative."

Parker pulled out three crisp hundred-dollar bills from his wallet. "Here, take this." She opened her mouth to protest, but he rushed on. "And don't give me a hard time about this. You're my sister, and I love you. Whatever I can do to help you, I will. So take this money, and go buy a vase or a painting to put on the wall."

Brooklyn closed a fist around the money in her palm. "Thank you," she whispered. "I love you, too. Thanks for coming last night. I'm sure your date wasn't thrilled that you walked out on her like a thief in the night."

When Parker had arrived the night before, he wasn't in the greatest of moods. It wasn't until they'd settled in for a movie that he'd admitted that she'd ruined his little plans. Her brother was the most eligible bachelor in Wellspring, but once again he'd pushed his own personal needs aside for her. She was grateful to him for everything, but she also wanted him to be happy. She felt bad that she'd basically guilted him into dropping whatever he was doing to come and keep her company.

"She'll be alright." He waved a dismissive hand in the air. "Not like she won't answer the phone when I call to make it up to her later."

He wiggled his eyebrows, and Brooklyn turned up her nose in disgust. "Ew, that's too much information."

"Hey, I'm a grown-ass man, and you're an adult now. I refuse to sugarcoat my life anymore."

She laughed. "Like you ever did."

Growing up, Brooklyn was well aware of her brother's reputation with the ladies. No, he wasn't a manwhore or anything, but there weren't many women who wouldn't want what Parker had to offer. He was charming, had an infectious laugh, but more than that, he was a genuinely good man, nothing like Senior.

Parker pulled her into a tight hug. She swallowed rapidly, as emotion bubbled up inside her. "I love you, big brother."

"Love you, too, big head."

Chapter 10

Brooklyn waved as Parker drove off. *This sucks.* Once he was out of sight, she made her way up to her front door. She shifted her bag of greasy food under an arm and fished for her key. Shaking her purse, she cursed as she dug in and pulled out her key, and a receipt for gas, and her earbuds.

"Good morning."

Brooklyn glanced up and found Carter standing outside his door. *Has he been there this entire time?* She scanned the area, before meeting his gaze again. "Hello. I didn't see you come up." She allowed herself a few seconds to take in his outfit. He was wearing sweats that rode low on his lean hips and a T-shirt that showed off his ripped body. *Damn.*

"You were busy trying to find your keys, I'm guessing. I went and joined the gym down the street and decided to stop at the Starbucks." His voice was like warm coffee—hot and addictive. He eyed the fast-food bag under her arm. "That's not breakfast."

For some reason, she felt ashamed under his perusal. It was almost like he could see the contents of her bag and was picking apart her love for greasy hash browns and sausage biscuits. She wanted to defend her choice, but found herself saying, "There's nothing much around here, and I was in a rush."

It wasn't even a convincing lie. Truth was, Parker had offered to take her into town for breakfast at the Bee's Knees—not that her favorite item on the menu was much better—but she'd turned him down, instead opting for quick and greasy.

"Ah." He smirked and she knew he didn't believe her excuse. "Smells good."

Her mouth went dry at the sarcasm in his tone. *Really?* He was judging her when he was sipping on coffee? Coffee was unhealthy, even though she loved it and couldn't operate without it.

"Are you judging me with that cup of coffee in your hand?"

"It's tea." He winked. "Nice try."

Her mouth fell open, before she closed it. He was actually joking with her, teasing her really. "Oh."

He chuckled. "I'm just playing with you. Did you bring me some?"

The better question was *Does he want me to give him some?* Because the way he was looking, she was definitely down. *Bad girl.*

"Um, I actually do have an extra sandwich, if you're interested." His eyes were on her, assessing her. She grew uncomfortable under his stare. "You're staring again."

He blinked. "I'm sorry."

Truth be told, his dark stare made her squirm in her shoes. Not in a bad way, but in a *damn-I-want-you-to-want-me* kind of way. "Well, if you don't have any other plans," she continued, "I don't mind sharing." Herself or her sandwich.

"Do *you* have any plans?" The question seemed like a challenge, like he expected her to tell him she did. Like he knew something.

"I'm actually free all day. I did plan to run to the store to get a few things for the condo. It's a little colorless in there. One big beige explosion."

She knew Parker hadn't picked out each piece of furniture himself, but he'd probably instructed the interior designer to go with neutral tones. Unfortunately, Brooklyn wasn't a beige type of person. Gray, yes. Beige, yuck.

"I don't mind some company, if you want to see more of the town," she added.

Brooklyn waited for a response. Every second that passed without an answer frayed her nerves. It was a simple yes or no. One word and she'd know where she stood. He'd already turned her down for dinner *and* coffee. And now it appeared she was a glutton for punishment. Maybe she'd spooked him last night with the crazy kiss? *Who kisses someone for fixing their internet?* Apparently, she did.

She chalked it up to temporary insanity. Why else would she ask him out again, like a desperate, horny teenager? Or a grown-ass woman who didn't have options? Because damn it, she did. *I'm a catch.*

Carter took a step toward her. He was like a big, hard wall of muscle. He smelled like sweat and woods. He was downright distracting. "I wish I could join you," he said finally. "I have a conference call that I have to hop on in an hour."

Crushed, she nodded. "That's fine," she lied.

"No worries. We are neighbors, after all. I'll see you around." She pushed her key into the lock, biting back a curse.

"Hey," he called to her.

She froze, but refused to look up at him. "Yes?"

"Since you have an extra sandwich, I wouldn't mind sharing it with you."

Sighing, she glanced over at him. Smiling, she told him, "Sure. Come on in."

Carter sat, his back ramrod straight on Brooklyn's couch. *What the hell am I thinking?* He'd had an out, told her he couldn't go out with her to shop. Then he'd turned right around and agreed to eat breakfast with her?

He didn't have an excuse for accepting her offer for a greasy breakfast sandwich. Not a logical one, at least. He didn't even eat sausage, or biscuits. Unless his mother made her famous biscuits and gravy. And that was pretty rare these days, since he'd made it a point to stay away from family functions in recent months. But Brooklyn . . . He'd hurt her when he turned her down, even though she'd tried to play it off. Carter wanted to let her know that it wasn't her. It was him. It was always him.

This isn't a date, though. Wasn't it? Two people, eating with only each other. Regardless of the less than fancy fare, the fact that he was sitting across from Brooklyn, trying like mad to not stare at her mouth as she talked, screamed "date" to him.

He didn't know what to do with his conflicting emotions. He was torn between pushing her away and pulling her closer. One minute, he was resolving with himself to stay away, and the next he was anticipating the next time he'd see her.

"Don't you agree?" she asked.

Caught off guard by her question and the fact that he had no idea what she'd been talking about, he nodded. Carter stared down at his half-eaten sandwich. "What do you do?" he asked.

A wide grin spread over her face. "I'm a social worker. I work at the Wellspring Clinic."

He found it very hard to concentrate when she smiled. It was genuine and warm, showed off the tiny creases around her mouth. "Do you enjoy it?" he managed to ask.

"I love it." She rested her chin on her hand, staring at some point behind him. "Watching my clients find their footing after dealing with addiction or mental illness is so rewarding."

"What made you choose that career?" The more she talked, the more he wanted to hear. Brooklyn wasn't anything he'd expected. Instead of the pampered princess he thought she was when he'd first laid eyes on her, she was a woman who wasn't afraid to lend a helping hand to those less fortunate.

She pushed at her sandwich. "My mother struggled with an addiction to pain meds," she explained, her voice so soft Carter had to strain to hear her. "And I wish I could have helped her. Unfortunately, she died when I was young, so I figured since I couldn't help her, I could help someone else."

Carter knew all too well the damage that a parent with an addiction could inflict. His father was a raging alcoholic who hadn't thought twice about beating his mother in front of them. It wasn't until

Carter was old enough and big enough to stop his father that the abuse ended.

"Did your mother die of an overdose?" he asked.

She shook her head. "No. She died in a car accident. I was in the car with her."

"How old were you?"

"Twelve. We were on our way back from Woodland Mall in Grand Rapids, because I just had to have the new . . . I don't even remember what I wanted. Anyway, she was driving home, and a semi cut us off. Next thing I remember, my father and my brother were standing over me in the hospital. My mother had been killed instantly."

The grief in her tone sparked something within Carter, made him want to comfort her. But he didn't know her, so he wouldn't assume she needed his comfort. Instead, he gripped the edge of the small kitchen table. Hard. "I'm sorry to hear that," he said. "Must have been hard for you."

"Hard is an understatement. But I was lucky to have my brothers. And Nic. They're my family."

"What about your father?"

She rolled her eyes. "Me and my father have a complicated relationship. So, no, I didn't feel lucky to have my father during that time and after."

He wanted to tell her that he knew about that as well. But once again he refrained from sharing too much. A few moments passed with no words spoken. "Well, I better get going." He stood, wrapping up the rest of his sandwich. "I have work to do."

She rose to her feet. "I can toss that." She gestured toward the sandwich. He handed it over to her. "They don't taste too good warmed up."

Carter watched her toss both sandwiches into the wastebasket. "Thanks for breakfast."

She followed him to the door. "No problem. I'll be seeing you around. Good luck with your conference call."

"Thanks."

He walked out but was stopped by his name on her lips. "Yes?" he asked, turning around to face her.

"I saw you at the Bee's Knees. Did you enjoy the food?"

"I did. And you were right. That was the best western omelet I've ever had."

"Good. I'm glad. Wellspring isn't Detroit, but I think you'll come to appreciate the hidden treasures here."

Carter wondered if she realized that the treasure he wanted to unearth was standing right in front of him. "I don't doubt it."

Brooklyn stood out on her balcony later in the day. A storm was coming. She'd been watching the weather reports all day. Severe weather was a source of anxiety for her. When she was a kid, she'd pack a suitcase full of her underwear and her dolls and hide down in the basement during a thunderstorm warning.

Panic rose in her at the thought of being alone during a tornado warning. What would she do? Cower under the kitchen table? There were too many windows, and no storm shelters around. She knew because she'd already called. The units weren't built with basements and the developer hadn't added storm shelters yet.

Thunder sounded to the west, and she took a deep breath. It wasn't a calming breath, because she wasn't calm. She was scared as hell. Hugging herself, she peered out at the dark clouds.

A few years ago, there was a storm so bad, Brooklyn almost had a heart attack. She had hunkered down in the basement, inside a closet. The only problem with that was she hadn't told anyone that she was there. When the storm was over, she'd emerged from her hiding place only to be yelled at for disappearing and driving them all crazy with worry. Parker had been beside himself, scared that she'd got caught in the storm and was lying dead in the woods somewhere.

The fear never abated. In fact, when Nicole went on her honeymoon last year, she and Kyle had caught a weather report about storms in the region, and called to check on her. That was Nicole, though. She'd drop everything for Brooklyn, and Brooklyn would do the same.

Tempted to call Nicole and Kyle, she weighed her options. The storm was due to hit within the next forty minutes to an hour. *Selfish* would be the word to describe her for begging her pregnant friend to come and sleep with her in the middle of the storm. But she could go to them. She might be able to make it before the worst hit.

"Are you okay?"

She let out a surprised yelp and whirled around to find Carter standing on his balcony, staring out at the darkening sky. *When did he show up?*

"I'm fine. I hate severe weather."

"My sister is the same way," he said. "But she can't

stay away from the TV, has to watch the weather channel."

Brooklyn knew the feeling. She'd reasoned that it had more to do with safety than paranoia. "Your sister is a smart woman."

"I prefer to watch the storm coming."

She glanced at him out of the corner of her eye. "I do that sometimes, too. It's almost like I'm a glutton for punishment."

He chuckled. "Maybe you're just trying to be prepared?"

Brooklyn watched the river below, noticing how the current sloshed against the rocks. "I've never lived by myself before."

He didn't respond, so she forced her eyes away from the raging river to him. He was studying her, staring at her in *that* way again.

Rubbing the back of her neck, she cleared her throat. "I don't even know why I said that. How was your conference call?"

He leaned against the railing, looking down at the ground. "It was like all conference calls. Boring and full of people who like to hear themselves talk."

"Gosh, you're so right. I'd rather be out in the field any day than stuck at the office in a meeting."

The thunder was closer now, and Brooklyn tried to remain calm. The hair on her neck rose, but she was rooted to her spot. *I need wine, preferably lots of it.*

"So, you've never lived alone?" he asked. "Where did you live before?"

"With my father." Brooklyn stopped short of revealing who her father was. She hadn't gotten to last names yet, and she was okay with it. Things inevitably changed once people knew she was Parker Wells's daughter. "And a roommate in college."

She heard the crack of lightning and jumped. As if on cue, her phone rang. She picked up. "Hey, Nic."

"Hun, are you good?" Nicole sounded out of breath.

"I'm fine. Are you okay? You sound like you're sick."

"We can come get you." Her friend screamed in her ear for Kyle. "I can come right now."

"Nic, you don't sound too hot. Where are you?" She glanced at Carter, who was watching her intently. Like always.

"Damn it," she heard Nicole say.

Brooklyn didn't like the way her friend sounded and backed up toward the door slowly, ready to spring into action. "Nic, you're scaring me. What's going on?"

"Oh hell. Yep, I'm in labor."

"What?" Brooklyn screeched.

"Brooklyn?" It was Kyle. "Nicole's water broke. I'm taking her to the hospital."

"Oh shit!" Brooklyn looked at the menacing rain coming their way. *Oh no.* She gripped the phone. "I'm coming."

"No, don't drive. You'll have an anxiety attack. We'll swing by and get you on the way to the hospital."

She heard Nicole scream in the background. "You don't have time for that." She took a deep breath. "I'm . . . I'm going to drive there. I'll be fine. Just hang up and get Nicole to the hospital. I'll be there. I promise."

Ending the call, she rushed to the door. "I have to go," she told Carter. "Nicole is having the baby."

"Are you going to be okay to drive?"

"I have to be. Talk to you later."

Brooklyn rushed through the house, packing up a bag of clothes. She unplugged her phone charger and threw it in her bag. She also grabbed her laptop from the kitchen table, shoving it into her tote.

Thunder rolled in the sky, closer than it was even two minutes ago. She looked out the window. It was getting darker by the minute. She gripped her shirt, willing herself to focus. *Nicole needs me and I have no choice but to be there for her.*

Sighing, she locked up the house and ran out to her car. Of course, she would drop her keys. Cursing, she scanned the area for where they fell. The first raindrop landed on her shoulder and she shuddered. *Great.*

The light sprinkling turned into a stinging rain fairly quickly and she still couldn't find those damn keys. Finally spotting them next to the front tire, she went to grab them and tripped over a rock. Losing her balance, she reached for the door handle, anything to keep her upright, but she missed. She toppled over, dropping her bag and her purse into a puddle. Fortunately, she'd managed to turn her body so that she landed on her side and not her face or the car itself. *Ah, that hurts.*

The tears came next. Covering her face, she cried into her hands as the rain fell down on her. Then she felt two arms come up around her and lift her up. It was Carter.

"Are you okay?" he asked.

Unable to hold her tears, she nodded her head.

"I am so clumsy. I fell." It was more a sob than an explanation. Not that she needed one.

His eyes softened and he brushed a hand over her cheek, then her neck. "You're scraped up, but you'll be okay." He picked up her stuff, placed her bags in the back seat, and put her keys in her hand.

Thunder clapped in the sky and she closed her eyes. *I can do this.* "Thank you. I have to go." She slid into the driver's seat, gripping the steering wheel so hard her hands hurt. Only she couldn't bring herself to start the car. The sky opened up even more and the rain battered down on her car. *God, please don't let me blow away in a tornado.*

She jerked back, startled when Carter touched her shoulder. She peered up at him. "Yes? Is something wrong? Did I forget something?"

"Scoot over. I'll drive you to the hospital."

Thank you, God. She climbed over to the passenger side and he climbed in. "I appreciate this, Carter."

"No problem." His gaze dropped to her mouth before he tore it away and focused front. "You just need to tell me where I'm going."

Growing up on the east side of Detroit, Carter thought he'd seen everything. Well, he was wrong, because he saw two things he'd never seen before.

He was born and raised in Michigan, very familiar with the erratic weather, but the storm that was raging outside the hospital was unlike anything he'd ever experienced. The sky turned green, almost black, and the hail was the size of a softball.

When they'd pulled up at the hospital, which was

actually in Grand Rapids, he waited for the valet to come out. He was tempted to pick up a ball of hail and ship it to Aisha, because he didn't think his sister would believe him if she couldn't see it for herself.

Then there was Brooklyn. He'd given up on her giving him directions to the hospital. The woman was terrified. So he'd let Siri lead him. On the drive, she'd pulled her knees up to her chin and buried her face in them. She was so quiet, it made him feel uncomfortable because she'd never struck him as the quiet type. He had to keep looking over at her to see if she was okay.

And even now, almost an hour later, the rain was still battering the building, the wind was pushing the trees like they were pieces of paper. It truly was a sight to see. He glanced out the waiting-room windows.

But even the raging storm had nothing on his other first. Brooklyn. She was like a storm of raging emotions, a contradiction of sorts. To see her so defeated, so scared, had been eye-opening, but the woman in the hospital with him now was a totally different person. Brooklyn was controlled, calm, and collected. She'd held Nicole's hand, calmed down another woman in the hospital who was freaking out because her son had been struck by lightning, and talked to the medical personnel like she'd done it every day of her life.

"Carter?" He turned and found Brooklyn standing there. She'd changed from her wet clothes into blue scrubs. She held him out a pair. "For you. I don't want you to catch cold."

He was soaking wet, and thankful for the change of clothes. "Thank you."

After he'd changed, he walked out into the waiting room. Brooklyn was on a chair, reading a magazine. When she saw him enter, she grinned. "Hi, Carter."

"Hi, Brooklyn."

The room they were in was pretty deserted. An older couple sat on the other side, watching CNN on television. A young mother and her child were over by the fish tank. Music played softly over the speakers.

"Oh God," Brooklyn said.

"What?"

"This song. It reminds me of being a kid." He listened. It was an 80s classic, "Roxanne." "When I was a kid, I was the queen of misinterpreting lyrics."

Curious, he asked, "How so?"

"My mother used to listen to a lot of old-school R & B. And there was a song called 'Juicy Fruit.'"

Carter knew the song very well. His mother used to listen to that song every day. It played on repeat, over and over again. Chuckling, he shifted in his seat to face her.

"So, one day I was singing it at the top of my lungs because I thought it was about gum. Anyway, my mother chastised me for it and banned me from singing the song anymore. It wasn't until I became an adult that I actually sat down and listened to the words."

He smiled. "It wasn't about gum."

"Right?" She laughed to herself, seemingly swept away by the memories. "It's actually pretty erotic."

The lyrics to the song were racy for the era. There was no disguising the meaning, in his mind.

"And this song? 'Roxanne.' I was bowled over when I realized what it was really about. A man who falls in love with a prostitute."

He barked out a laugh. "Yeah. But it's not raunchy or anything. It's still a love song."

She eyed him, a small smile on her lips. "I guess. Anyway, those were good days. When my biggest worry was disappointing my mother for singing a song."

There was a story there that he wanted to know. But he wouldn't push her to talk. He watched her lean her head back against the wall.

"There you go again," she said, her eyes closed.

Frowning, he asked, "What?"

"Staring again." She opened one eye. "But it's okay. I like it."

Then she closed her eyes again.

Chapter 11

Brooklyn walked into her condo early the next morning, ready to climb into bed and not wake up for a day or two. She'd finally met her godson, Kyle Elijah Jr., after eleven hours of hard labor. And he was a doll, with a head full of hair, which explained why her best friend suffered from heartburn during her pregnancy.

The storm had passed sometime around three o'clock in the morning, but when it was over she was still in one piece and Carter was still next to her. He'd stayed the entire time. It could've had something to do with the fact that he'd driven them there in her car, but she appreciated it nonetheless.

Through the night, they'd actually talked. He'd opened up a little about growing up in Detroit and they'd bonded over a love of chewy SweeTarts and crime dramas. His favorite was *Criminal Minds* and hers, *NCIS*.

Brooklyn flicked the light switch. Nothing. The power was out. So much for chilling in front of the TV. She checked in with her job, to let her boss

know she wouldn't be in. She was grateful she
worked for such an understanding company. She
hadn't had any problems so far. During their quick
conversation, she found out half the town was without power. The last time a storm like that swept
through the town, it had shut down businesses for
days due to power outages.

After she checked her emails, she jumped in the
shower and washed her hair. Glancing at one of her
older wigs, perched on the shelf, she crinkled
her nose. Parker was right, the wigs had to go. She
picked it up and tossed it in the small trashcan.
She'd donate her new and barely used ones to charity. She'd only started wearing them because her
father hated that she cut her hair. Getting rid of
them was another step toward independence.

Brooklyn was supposed to drive to the credit
union to speak with the manager in person about
her account, but the storm had prevented that. The
more she thought about her money situation, the
angrier she got. There was no way it was legal for
her father to access that cash, not when it was her
account. She'd decided to fight tooth and nail to
get her money back. She was thankful for her
brother, who'd slipped her a few hundred bucks
when she saw him last. He'd always taken care of
her, even when it caused him personal hardship.

Plopping down on her couch, she texted Parker,
who told her that Wellspring had suffered wide-
spread damage throughout the county. The expressway leading to headquarters was blocked by a fallen
tree, preventing people from traveling to work, so
they'd closed for the day.

Briefly, she wondered what Carter would be doing now that he didn't have to go to work. She considered inviting him over to dinner. But she couldn't be held liable for what she'd do if he turned her down again. *What if he says yes this time?*

A few hours later, Brooklyn awoke to a knock at her door. Stretching, she slid off the couch and padded to the front door. When she opened it, Carter was standing there with a pizza in hand and a few beers.

"I was hungry and had a taste for pizza."

She held the door open for him, and he walked in. "Isabelle's is open?" The pizza place was only about ten minutes from them, and she was surprised they had power.

He set the pizza down on the kitchen table and took a seat. "Not really. I was driving past and saw a line of cars, so I stopped. Strangely enough, they don't have power so they fired up their gas ovens and started making pizzas so that their food wouldn't go to waste."

"Good idea."

"I figured I'd share."

Still pleasantly surprised that he'd taken the initiative to come to her, she walked into the kitchen and pulled out a few plates. When she turned around he was watching her, his intense gaze glued to her like a hawk. Swallowing, she tugged at the hem of her oversized shirt. It was all she was wearing. Well, that and a pair of panties. She hadn't thought to put on clothes because she'd been so surprised to see him.

"I'm going to go and change." She brushed past

him, but his arm on her wrist halted her steps. Looking down at him, she sucked in a deep breath. "Yes?"

Carter stood to his full height. He towered over her, the heat of his body searing her skin. She searched his face. "Carter," she breathed as he stepped into her, "what are you doing?"

With his gaze fixed on hers, he ran a thumb down her face and over her jaw. "I don't know."

Brooklyn arched into him when his breath fanned across her lips. His breath was warm against her skin. It smelled like beer, and something uniquely Carter. She wasn't sure what had changed to bring them to this point, but she wanted it. So much she could taste it. But there was something holding him back, preventing him from stepping completely over the line. *Or is it someone?*

He rested his forehead against hers. Smoothing a hand up his chest, she gripped his shirt in her fist. Caught in his gaze, she managed to formulate a response. "I think you better make a decision. Quick. Because—" Her sentence was cut off by his lips on hers.

Carter couldn't believe he was kissing Brooklyn. More importantly, Carter couldn't believe that he wanted to kiss her. It had been so long since he'd been close to a woman, since he'd felt skin against his skin. He wanted more, so much more.

He cupped her face in his hands, grazing his thumbs over her cheek as he continued to kiss her senseless. It was all tongue and teeth, and nothing else mattered to him in that moment but her mouth against his. For once, Carter couldn't think about what they were doing because he wanted her, and didn't want it to stop.

Carter found himself giving in to the feeling, wrapping his arms around her and pulling her closer to him. He allowed himself to get lost in her scent, the feel of her curves molding to his hands, the sound of her soft moans as he nipped and sucked at her lips as if they alone would save his soul. Every stroke of her tongue against his pulled him deeper into her. It was too much, and not enough at the same time.

Reluctantly, he pulled back, sucking in a deep, steadying breath. Her eyes were closed and her lips were parted, swollen from his kisses. She was absolutely stunning. He'd done that to her. Unable to resist, he bumped his nose against her, sucked her bottom lip one last time.

Brooklyn opened those beautiful brown orbs. "Carter," she whispered. "That was . . . you—"

He smiled. "I know."

She retreated back a step. "No, I mean you *kissed* me."

"I'm aware of that."

"Why? I've asked you to go out with me, invited you for breakfast. I don't understand. You've been turning me down. I kissed you and you bolted out of here so fast . . ."

He understood her questions, and wished he had an answer that sounded halfway decent. "I'm sorry. There is a lot you don't know about me."

She dropped into the seat, picked up a piece of pizza, and bit into it. It would seem that he'd kissed her hungry. "Have a seat," she said. "Because I need to hear something from you. Something more."

He sat down, followed her lead by grabbing a slice of pizza. They ate in silence for a few minutes before he said, "I'm sorry if I made you feel like it was you. It's not you. I wanted to kiss you before, but I couldn't bring myself to do it."

Pausing with pizza slice in hand, she dropped it on her plate and slid her chair closer. "Why? Are you married? Do you have a girlfriend at home?"

Carter swallowed. He hadn't expected the question, but he understood why she'd asked. He still acted like a married man, as though even looking at another woman was a betrayal to Krys. "No. I'm not married." It wasn't the right time to bring his past into the conversation, though. Not yet.

She was still, observing him quietly before she asked, "What is it? Are you a virgin?"

He barked out a laugh. "Hell no."

"Thank God," she mumbled, chewing on the pizza crust.

"I don't want to just jump into bed with you either. It's been a long time since I've met a woman I wanted to get to know."

"And you want to get to know me?"

"I do. I haven't laughed in a long time. And you make me laugh. It kind of caught me off guard at first. I'm not used to giving up control."

"So don't. If you need to be in control, then take control."

Carter narrowed his gaze on Brooklyn, who was

busy picking pepperoni off of her pizza. "It's that easy for you to give up control?"

"I didn't say that. I like to have control, too. During the day."

His brain wrapped around her words. *Does that mean she's willing to give up control at night?* The thought made him want to put her to the test.

"How about we start with a first date?" he asked.

She smiled, wide and sexy. "Are you asking me out?"

"Are you saying yes?"

"I have a couple of conditions. You asked me out on a first date. I feel like we've already kind of had a few dates. So I'm assuming you have something official in mind."

Carter chuckled at the way she held up air quotes and did a quirky shake of her head when she said *official.*

"You can't act all stuffy and intense like you do." She held out her beer, allowing him to open it for her. "I don't like fancy dates with high expectations. I don't set rules like that. I'm not the kind of woman that needs big overtures. I order for myself. I don't make a guy wait thirty days to have sex. If I want someone, I'm not shy about it."

Carter hardened at her admission. Brooklyn was refreshing, honest, and sexy as hell. He loved to hear her talk, loved the way her mind worked. He could see himself falling for her. Which was why he needed to take it slow. Brooklyn was her own woman, and what he felt for her was unique to her, and nothing like what he'd felt for his wife.

She deserved to be first in any man's life because she was good, kind, intelligent, and passionate. She didn't deserve to be left dangling on a string if he wasn't truly ready to move forward.

"Carter?" She waved a hand in front of him, bringing him out of his thoughts. "Are you still here?"

He gripped her wrist, stroking her skin with his thumb. "I'm here."

"Does having a first date mean I have to forget about that kiss?"

He brought the inside of her wrist up to his mouth and nipped at the skin there before soothing it with his tongue. "I don't think I can forget about that kiss."

"Damn," she whispered.

Meeting her gaze, he smirked. If he wanted to throw caution to the wind and take this to the next level, she would say yes. The thought sobered him, made him want to really go about this the right way. "Save Friday night for me, Brooklyn."

"Am I going to see you before Friday, Carter?"

"That would be a definite yes." He liked the idea of making plans with Brooklyn, although he had a feeling that nothing would be cookie-cutter with her. And that made him want her more.

"Any idea what happens now?" he asked. They had just set up a date, but was he supposed to just go home? This was new to him.

She smirked, leaned forward. "I think it's pretty clear what happens next."

Oh shit. Carter drew in a deep breath. He'd already told her that he didn't want to jump into bed with her, but his mind was slowly racing to that end game. She was simply irresistible. "Really?" he asked.

Brooklyn's gaze dropped to his mouth. As if she were a magnet, he leaned forward even closer. Their mouths were almost touching, her breath mingling with his own. "Yes. I think it's time we take this . . ."

He swallowed, bit the inside of his cheek. He wanted to kiss her again. He wanted to kiss her so hard and so long, it made him feel a little unhinged. Crazy. "To your bedroom?"

She giggled, and he felt stupid. He'd told her that he wanted to take her on a date, and yet he'd skipped right ahead to her bedroom. "Is that where you want to go? Because I'm okay with that, too."

This woman was a breath of fresh air. So open and honest. She'd basically just given him permission, but he couldn't do that. Not yet. He owed her the truth before they took it too far. Clearing his throat, he settled on some of it. "I don't think we should do that tonight." He closed his eyes to avoid her penetrating stare. "But I want to."

He felt her hand on his cheek, and leaned into her touch.

"Carter?"

Opening his eyes, he met her gaze. "Yes."

"I was going to suggest we take this party outside . . . to the balcony. To talk some more."

Carter felt the corners of his mouth quirk up in a smile, and nodded. "Sounds good to me."

They spent the next several hours talking out on her balcony, watching the sun set. As darkness settled over the surrounding land, she went into the house and lit a few candles.

Brooklyn stood up and held out her hand. "How about a game?"

Unsure where she was coming from, he asked, "What kind of game?"

"Pool."

There was a hint of mischief in her brown eyes, but he took her hand anyway. "Where is there a pool table?"

"In the clubhouse. We can take a few candles over there and play."

Never before had he shot pool by candlelight, but something told him it would be an unforgettable experience.

The walk to the clubhouse was quiet, the only light was the one from his flashlight. Yet, Brooklyn didn't feel uncomfortable or unsafe. It could have been the fact that they were both armed with their pool cues, but she suspected it was Carter. The entire way there, he held a hand at the small of her back, guiding her through the dark as if he owned the land and knew everything about it. There was so much she didn't know about him, so much she wanted to learn. Had he served in the military? Did he have kids?

She knew he had a sister, because they'd talked about her. But did he have brothers? Was his family close? Perhaps it was the social worker in her that wanted answers to those burning questions, but she was smart enough to know it would take time for Carter to truly open up to her.

In his eyes, she still saw torment. But she also sensed new resolve that hadn't been there prior to their adventure in the storm last night. Had that sparked this change in him? He went from avoiding her, turning her down, to . . . devouring her.

Her mouth still burned from that kiss. Brooklyn wouldn't consider herself an experienced woman, far from it, but she'd had her fair share of kisses. And she could say, beyond a shadow of a doubt, that Carter had put everyone she'd ever kissed to shame. At first, she'd tried to convince herself that it was just a kiss. But hell . . . it was not *just* a kiss. It was more like a revelation, or a confirmation—definitely a precursor. Brooklyn looked forward to feeling his lips against hers again.

They arrived at the dark clubhouse, and she let them in with her key. He shined his light inside and she walked in first, leading them to the game room.

The eight-foot pool table was new, and she couldn't wait to break it in. She set up several candles and lit them.

"Ta-da," she said, her arms outstretched. "You ready?"

"Are you sure you want to do this?"

Brooklyn liked that Carter was confident in his abilities, but she wasn't worried about him beating her. "I'm not scared, if that's what you're wondering."

He racked the balls, motioning to the table. "Ladies first."

She brushed past him and applied chalk to her cue stick. "I'll take it. I've been known to break and run. You may not get a turn."

Chuckling, he leaned forward, rubbing a hand over the back of her head. "I'll believe it when I see it."

Settling into her stance, behind the head string, she aimed. Brooklyn focused, then shot the ball, scattering the balls and knocking two into corner pockets.

"Solid," she said, as she circled the table looking for the next shot. Leaning against the table edge, she tapped the end of her cue stick on the right corner pocket. Brooklyn's pose, and the intense look in her eyes, almost did him in. When she shot the ball, dropping it into the pocket, he realized that he'd underestimated her abilities.

"Good shot," he mumbled.

She sauntered around the table, grinning at him. "I know. So how about a wager?"

Carter took in her confident stride, the focused look in her eyes as she strategized on her next move. "What am I winning?"

She laughed. "I think I should be asking you that question."

He stepped forward, close behind her, dwarfing her. "The fact that you clearly know what you're doing on this pool table is making me want to re-think my earlier assertion."

Carter had never met a woman that made him feel like control was slipping away. Until now. And judging by the way she wiggled her ass against his hardening dick, she knew it too. "I know my way around a lot of things," she told him.

"Let's play for breakfast. If I win, you cook me breakfast. If you win, I'll buy your breakfast."

Her laugh went straight to his groin. "Don't cook, huh?"

"Not breakfast."

"How do you know I cook?"

"I actually don't picture you as a cook, but seeing as how you've consistently surprised me, I figured I'd give it a try."

"You're not wrong. I do know how to cook. I just don't do it much."

Carter had more questions, and he knew he needed to move, to make his way around to the other side of the table, away from her. But he stood rooted to his spot, with her in front of him, dangerously close. "Did your father cook?"

She glanced at him then, lifted a single brow. "My father? Cook? Yeah, right. To answer your question, I learned to cook from the housekeeper, Arlene." Her family was wealthy enough to employ a housekeeper. He made a mental note to do some investigation of his own. "Who taught you how to shoot?"

He took her change in subject as a sign that she didn't want to talk about her father or her housekeeper. Deciding to let it go for now, he answered, "My mother. She's the best player I've ever had the pleasure of beating."

"That's so awesome. A woman after my own heart."

Carter wondered what his mother would think of Brooklyn. The thought almost made him retreat back a step. A date was one thing. Introducing Brooklyn to his mother, his family, was quite another. It was also a step that indicated more about his growing feelings for her than he dared to admit out loud.

She bent low over the table, seemingly not as affected as he was by their position. He took in the arch in her back, the round curve of her ass against him. Then she looked back over her shoulder at him and winked before she took her shot, sinking another ball into the pocket.

Carter didn't get a turn until she'd sunk all but one of her balls. His mother would definitely like this woman. He liked her, too. "The game isn't over yet."

That playful grin on her face would be the death of him. She walked around to the other side of the table and stopped right at the pocket he'd called. He imagined she'd swindled many men out of their money with her smile and the gleam in her eyes.

She leaned forward, bracing herself on the edge of the table and giving him an unobstructed view of the tops of her breasts. Arching a brow, she asked, "Isn't it?"

Carter took his shot, grumbling a curse when he came up short. He laughed when she did a cute little twerk of victory. His mother would definitely love her. It didn't take long before she won the game, but he couldn't care less. For the first time in years, he'd let himself go, let himself feel, and he'd enjoyed every minute of it.

Chapter 12

Five o'clock in the morning. *Wait. Five o'clock?* She peered at the battery-operated alarm clock, rubbed her sleepy eyes, then peered at the offending phone that hadn't stopped ringing. Frowning, she picked up the phone, sent it to voicemail, and pitched it across the room. It was her father. She covered her face with her pillow. *What the hell does he want?*

The phone rang again, and Brooklyn rolled out of bed, landing on her butt. Growling, she crawled over to the still ringing instrument of torture. She hesitated before answering. "Yes, Daddy?"

"Brooklyn, I've had enough of this. Where are you?"

"I'm in my skin. I don't even know why you're acting concerned about my whereabouts, especially since you had me kicked out of the hotel."

"I told you I would do it. You disobeyed me, so I made arrangements. Where. Are. You?"

Brooklyn's pulse raced, her heart pounded in her ears. There was no way in hell she'd tell him where she was. It would only cause problems and increase her anxiety. No, he couldn't kick her out of Parker's place, but she wasn't going to fool herself into believing she was untouchable. "Senior, why did you call me at five o'clock in the morning? I have to go to work soon."

"Really?"

She didn't like the tone in her father's voice. Something was off. "What do you want?"

"This has gone on long enough. I expect you to come home tomorrow. And I expect you to fall in line and do what I told you to do."

"Marry Sterling?"

"Exactly."

"What's riding on this? There has to be something to make you treat me like this. I don't deserve it, and I'm not marrying Sterling."

"Tomorrow, Brooklyn *Wells*." The emphasis on their last name wasn't lost on her. "I want to see you at the house tomorrow."

He hung up before she could tell him off. Not that she would. Despite everything he'd done to undermine her, she still couldn't tell him what she really thought about him.

The power had come on sometime during the night. Unable to sleep, Brooklyn showered and made a cup of coffee. She decided to try and get some work done before she headed into the office. She pulled her patio door open, letting the light breeze in. She heard a creek, and peeked out.

Carter was leaning against the railing and staring out at the river. She smiled, remembering the feel of his lips against hers and the billiards game by candlelight. She'd killed him, all three games, before they'd decided to call it quits.

Taking in the solemn look in his eyes, the way he seemed almost in a trance, made her feel uneasy. *Does he regret last night?* She hoped not. The promise of a date with him, an after-the-date with him, made everything in her spark to life.

Carter had told her that it had been a long time since he'd enjoyed the company of a woman. And she was glad to be the first, but she wondered why. She wanted to ask him, but she supposed the answers would come when he was ready. Just like she'd refused to go into further detail about her father.

For now, she enjoyed getting to know him without adding the complication of her family into the equation. She cleared her throat, and he spun around to face her. His face softened when he realized it was her.

Gazes locked, they stood like that for what felt like forever. "How long have you been up?" she asked finally, stepping toward him.

He walked to the side of the patio closest to hers. She didn't know why the builder had made the decks so close together, but she was glad for the proximity that morning. Being able to reach out and touch him was a gift that she'd accept freely. She brushed her fingers over the top of his hand, and he flipped his over, clasping her hand in his.

"I don't sleep well," he admitted.

"I can't say that. Sleep is one of my favorite things to do."

He chucked, low and soft. "You're so funny."

Her heartbeat quickened, and she grew warm under his steady eye contact. "I try."

"You're beautiful, too."

"Thank you." Her voice cracked with overwhelming emotion.

Brooklyn loved sex, had no problem articulating it to any man that she'd been with. Every lover she'd had—and it hadn't been too many—had relinquished control to her. For some reason, she knew Carter was different. She sensed that giving over control to him would be the best part of making love, if they should ever make it to that point. *Oh God, I hope we make it to that point.*

Just standing there with him, the early morning breeze against her skin and the slow rise of the sun as the backdrop, she wanted nothing more than for him to make a move. She knew he wouldn't, though.

"What are you doing up so early?" he asked, brushing his thumb over hers.

"Trying to get some work done." It wasn't a complete lie. Just a tiny omission of the truth. "Hungry?"

Something like desire flared in his dark eyes. And it made her feel woozy. "I believe I owe *you* breakfast."

Grinning, she thought back to his face when she kicked his butt at the pool table. "If I remember correctly, you owe me three. Is it safe to say I'm collecting on one of those this morning?"

His smile widened. "You know I've never lost to anyone except my mother."

"There's a first time for everything," she teased.

His bark of laughter made her giggle. "I think we need a rematch. This is going to your head."

"How about Thursday at Brook's Pub?"

"You're on. I went easy on you last night."

Getting her butt spanked on the pool table was exactly what she wanted. Literally, and eventually. But as much as she wanted him, she'd still kick *his* ass in the actual game.

"I'm looking forward to it."

His fingers brushed up her arm to her shoulder. "Me too."

"Just kiss me."

His head jerked back and his eyebrows rose.

"I said that out loud, didn't I?"

He laughed. "You did. But I'm not complaining."

Tipping her head up with his index finger, he leaned down and placed a chaste kiss to her lips. She moaned at the light touch, immediately wanting more. But he didn't give her what she wanted. Instead, he kissed her forehead.

She frowned, opening her eyes to find him waiting, a secretive smile on his full lips. Lips that she wanted to kiss. Lips that she wanted to hear talk dirty to her. More than just dirty—filthy. Yeah, she wanted to hear him melt her panties off with his words.

"You know you're wrong for that," she said, finally finding her words. "But it won't last. Before long, you're going to be trying to hop across the balcony to get a taste of me."

"I already want to."

"Tell me how much," she said on a shaky breath.

He blinked then. "Tell you how much?"

"Yes. I didn't stutter. The dirtier the better. Tell me how much you want to taste me."

The challenge was clear. Sometime in the last few minutes, she'd decided that she wanted him to truly let go with her. They didn't really know each other, but when she thought about him, when she was this close to him, she wanted to give herself to him. She wanted him. This would be a start. She wouldn't push him to take it further than he was ready for, but he'd opened the door when he admitted that he wanted to taste her.

His jaw ticked, but she knew it wasn't because he was disgusted with her. It was just the opposite if the grip he still had on her hand was any indication. If he wasn't turned on, or even curious, he would have let her go when she'd thrown down the gauntlet.

"Okay," he said, tracing his finger down her arm. "I can't wait to taste you, to lick you until you scream out my name."

"Carter," she said, shocked by the words that had just come out of his mouth. He'd risen to the occasion—her gaze dropped down to the front of his pants—literally and figuratively. The soft, shy smile that graced his face, heated her as if he'd lit a flame inside of her.

He leaned low, his lips now against her ear. "Is that good for you?"

Brooklyn's head fell back as he kissed her ear. "Yes. That's good."

His phone rang from inside his condo, and he grumbled a curse. "I have to get that. I'm expecting a call from my business partner."

"It's cool. I have to get ready for work. But I'll see you later?"

"Count on it."

* * *

Carter had taken two cold showers after the little liaison on the deck that morning. Neither of them helped because he was still on fire for Brooklyn—three hours later. She'd asked him to put into words how much he wanted to taste her. Before she'd asked him to do that, he hadn't really thought about it. Now, it was all he could think about.

He tried not to think about her, but inevitably his mind would drift back to her smile, her smell, her laugh. He was trying to work, trying to do what he'd came all the way to Wellspring for. But he thought about her on his commute and he was currently thinking about her during his meeting with Parker Wells Sr.

Today was his first meeting with the man, and he wasn't impressed. He wasn't sure why, but it appeared that everyone in the room was scared. Everyone except Parker Jr., who'd sat in the meeting detached and emotionless. He wondered about the dynamic between the two and wondered if the senior Wells was like that with all of his children.

He glanced at the face projected on a television hanging on the wall of the conference room. His partner, Martin, sat relaxed but focused. Which was more than he could say for himself. Martin reiterated their mission and assured the room that Marshall and Sullivan was the right firm for the job and added, "We won't leave until everything is up and running."

Being distracted by his next-door neighbor didn't bode well for him or his business. He'd come there to do a job and to decompress, not become enamored of a woman he didn't really know much about. *Maybe that's the reason why. I don't know her, and she doesn't know me. That could be a good thing.*

He was sure Martin had caught on and he'd be asking questions later during their afternoon conference. Carter wasn't sure he'd actually be able to tell his best friend everything. Once he put words to it, once he admitted out loud that there was a woman, it would make it real.

As Martin yapped on about business, he scanned the room. It was Parker Sr.'s personal conference room, connected to the older man's office. It was painted a taupe color, outfitted with the newest technology, but it was cold. *Just like the man himself.*

When Carter's gaze locked with Parker Sr.'s, he straightened in his seat and focused on the screen. "Martin will be here on Monday," Carter said. "We will present our recommendations next Friday."

Parker Sr. nodded. "I trust you've been getting the cooperation you need from our employees."

"They've been very cooperative, yes. You have a great staff. I've already identified several ways to streamline processes and make their workday more efficient. The system you're currently using is difficult to navigate. It is our hope that the changes we make will decrease the time spent working on a single project."

A loud commotion from outside of the room drew their attention to the door. The woman on the other side of the door wasn't talking loud, but she was insistent. He could tell in her voice. A very familiar voice. *Is that Brooklyn?*

Before Carter could rise to check it out, Parker stood, and excused himself from the room. Parker Sr. didn't even seem phased. He continued talking to the room as if there was nothing going on outside the door. He heard glass break, and then he heard Parker's voice before it went eerily quiet.

Carter glanced at the door, then back at Martin, who shrugged.

Parker Sr. crossed one leg over the other, steepled his hands together. "I like the plans that you've mapped out. I look forward to hearing your recommendations next Friday." He turned to Carter. "I trust you've enjoyed your stay in Wellspring. Parker told me you're residing in temporary housing. I hope the accommodations are sufficient for you and your team."

"I appreciate the hospitality. I've enjoyed seeing the town. It's quite impressive, the history and the people." Carter closed his laptop and packed his bag. "I'm planning on bringing my sister out for a visit as well."

Martin added, "I'm looking forward to visiting Wellspring myself."

"Great. When you arrive, we'll set up a dinner or something." Parker Sr. tapped his pen against the table. "My wife loves to entertain."

Carter opened his mouth to say something, but he was rendered speechless when the door burst open and Brooklyn stormed in with Parker right on her heels. She stopped in her tracks, then faltered back a step when her furious gaze locked on his.

"Brooklyn, you know better than this." Parker Sr. leaned back in his chair, as if he didn't care that the meeting had been interrupted. "I'm in the middle of something. Get out."

Brooklyn's eyes widened and her chin trembled. And Carter wanted to throttle Parker Sr. "Senior, you have taken this too far." Her gaze met Carter's for a second before she turned it back to her . . . *father?*

Parker Sr. eyed Brooklyn, unbothered by her obvious distress. "You did this to yourself. I warned you to fall in line. There are consequences to every action, my dear daughter."

It was a loving term, one he'd used for his own daughter, but there was no love, no warmth in the older man's tone. Carter clenched his fists and drew in a deep breath. His next move could make or break his relationship with Wellspring Water and with Brooklyn.

"You got me fired from my job!" Brooklyn shouted, pounding her fist against the table.

"What?" Parker roared.

Brooklyn looked at Parker, tears in her eyes. "I went in to work this morning and was informed that my services were no longer needed." A sob tore from her throat and Carter stood to his feet. "Parker, he donated thousands of dollars to the clinic for much-needed renovations, on the condition that they let me go."

"This can't be true." Parker turned an angry glare on his father. "Tell me this isn't true, Senior?"

Parker Sr. smiled. "Son, this is no concern of yours. This is between me and Brooklyn."

Brooklyn laughed. The sound was harsh and humorless. It seemed so unlike her it took him by surprise. She was pissed. "You mean, it's between you and the King family. Right? I wouldn't agree to marry a man I don't love, for the benefit of Wellspring Water and your business endeavors. So you decide to not only wipe out my bank accounts, but take away my job."

Parker Sr. shrugged. "It's the economy. The clinic was forced to make a hard decision. You or a new building. They can easily hire another social worker. But when will they ever raise enough money to repair the furnace or the air conditioning system or the bathrooms? It was an easy decision for them, once I assured them that I had another job lined up for you at Wellspring Water."

"Another position? That's rich. The only position you want for me is Stepford Wife so that *you* can have more power. Well, I won't do it. Wellspring is not the only company in town. I can work somewhere else."

"Where? My reach is farther and longer than you think, Brooklyn. Your best bet is to come home from wherever you're staying."

Carter's best bet was to get the hell out of there before he jeopardized his job. But he couldn't. He stepped forward.

Brooklyn pinned him with her gaze and shook her head slightly. All the color seemed to drain from her face. Her arms fell to her sides, like her father had stolen her breath, her life. With a downward gaze, she said, "I won't return to your house. If that means I have to leave Wellspring and everything else behind . . ." She glanced over at Parker, then back to Parker Sr. "I will do that. And I won't look back. So what is it, Senior? Are you so heartless that you'd rather I leave town with nothing, risk never seeing me again, and still not get your precious wedding?"

"Brooklyn, don't," Parker warned. "Can we talk about this? It doesn't have to come to that."

"You're damn right it won't come to that," Parker Sr. said, finally standing to his feet. He stalked toward Brooklyn, but Carter stepped between them.

"I wouldn't do that." Carter glared at Parker Sr.

"Carter," she hissed, from behind him. "Don't."

Parker Sr. took a step back. "When did the two of you meet?" he asked.

Carter glanced over at Parker, because if he had to look at Parker Sr. again, he'd pummel him to the ground. He wasn't going to stand there and let him continue to denigrate Brooklyn. "What I won't do is let any man treat a woman like this in front of me. I'm sure she got the picture. She can't depend on her family to have her back."

Parker stepped closer. "Don't you dare talk about my sister like you know her or anything about our relationship."

"Parker, please," Brooklyn said, her voice weak. "Don't make this worse."

"I only go by what I see and hear," Carter continued, not giving a damn about the job anymore. "And from where I'm standing, you're not doing or saying anything that would lead me to believe that you would protect her."

He felt Brooklyn's hand around his forearm. "Please, just go. This is not your fight. I can handle this."

Carter wouldn't look at her, because he'd be a fool to take his eyes off of Parker Sr. or Parker at that point. "Brooklyn, I don't think you understand. Your father looks like he would have no problem

beating you into submission. And I'll be damned if
I let that happen."

"I'm only going to ask this one time," Senior
growled. "How do you know my daughter?"

"I met him when he moved to town," Brooklyn
answered. "He actually saved my life the night of
the charity gala, pulled me out of the way of an oncoming vehicle. That's how I know him."

Carter ground his teeth together. Brooklyn had
simplified their interactions for a reason, so he
wouldn't say more than she did. "Step back," Carter
ordered. "We're going to leave, and you're going to
let us."

"You're making a huge mistake, Mr. Marshall,"
Parker Sr. sneered. "You don't want an enemy in me."

"Then you don't know me well. I don't need your
money, or this job."

"Well, then this won't hurt you one bit. You're
fired."

Parker spoke up then, directly to his father. "You
won't fire him, Senior. Not because of this. The
contract has already been signed. The work has
started. And *you* put him the position to have to
defend Brooklyn. I can't believe you went this far."
Parker turned to Carter and Brooklyn. "Go home.
I'll come by to see you later."

Chapter 13

Brooklyn paced her living room floor. She still couldn't believe the mess she'd caused. She'd barged into her father's office and dragged Carter into her drama. And now his job was in jeopardy. No matter what Parker had said, she knew it wouldn't stop her father from exacting revenge on Carter for daring to even get involved in the first place. Now, she just had to get Carter to understand what was going on.

She rubbed a hand through her short curls. She hadn't missed her father's unappreciative glance at her short hairstyle. The man was a monster, worse than any boogeyman she'd ever been scared of. She didn't doubt for minute that her father had done worse things than forcing her to marry a man like Sterling. He was a cold, unfeeling bastard.

"Are you going to stop pacing now?" Carter asked from his seat on her couch. He'd been sitting there quietly for the past thirty minutes, just watching her, an unreadable expression in his dark eyes.

"What possessed you to risk your job?" she yelled,

her arms out at her sides in frustration. "He will destroy you."

"I'm not scared of your father." Carter folded his arms over his chest. "I've gone up against worse."

Brooklyn plopped down on the couch and buried her face in her hands. Tired. She was so damn tired of everything. "You don't know my father. You don't know what he's willing to do to get his way."

"I have a pretty good idea," Carter said.

"What is your deal?" she asked. "You're so guarded. You don't know me, not really. You didn't even know I was a Wells before today. By all rights, you should be angry with me for keeping my last name from you. But instead, you're all knight in shining armor, fighting for me. I didn't ask you to put yourself on the line for me. Don't you see that it only makes me feel even more shitty?"

"I'm sorry, Brooklyn. I don't mean to make you feel shitty. I just want you to be okay. Your father basically strong-armed you, like you were a stranger on the street, to do his bidding. And he walked up on you like he was going to hurt you. What kind of man would I be if I let that happen? And I'm sure Martin would agree with me. I'm sure he already does, because he was in the room, and he heard everything."

Brooklyn flinched, shaking her head. She had forgotten about the man on the television. They'd been having a video conference. "I shouldn't have barged in like that. I didn't think. I was just so angry, so damn pissed."

Carter scooted closer to her and pulled her

against his side. "I know. I'm sorry you have to go through this."

Brooklyn relaxed into his arms. "You are wrong about one thing."

"And that is?"

"Parker. He's always protected me. He's the reason I have a place to stay, the reason I have money in my pocket right now."

"You have no money?"

"I do. Well, I thought I did. I had an account in another city. But my father got to it." But seeing how she had no job to go to anymore, she could take the afternoon and head to the credit union and get some answers.

In a way, this may have been a blessing in disguise. At least the clinic would be able to do some good in the community. She didn't blame her boss for taking the offer. The funds her father offered would be used to benefit the many people who needed their services.

"What are you thinking about?" he asked.

She peered up at him. "All the good the money will do for the clinic and the community. There are so many people out there who need access to things we take for granted. I'm glad some of them will get the help they need. I'm glad that the clinic will be able to update their facility."

"Did you mean what you said about leaving Wellspring?"

She shrugged. Up until that point, she'd hadn't seriously considered leaving Wellspring. She really did love their little slice of heaven and the people there. But she couldn't very well expect to live off her brother for the rest of her life.

"I don't want to go," she admitted softly. "What else can I do? My father will threaten everyone in town if they help me. He's right. His reach is too far."

"Have you considered going into business for yourself?"

Brooklyn had always envisioned starting a non-profit organization to assist the homeless with finding housing, employment, and education. She wanted to help them get the necessary medical care they needed, treat the mental illnesses that run rampant among homeless people.

"I've thought about it, starting my own non-profit. But I guess it seemed way off for me. I wanted to work a few years, get some experience in my field. That's why I took the job at the clinic. I loved every minute of it, even the exhausting parts. I should have known it couldn't last long."

After her mother died, Brooklyn quickly learned that life wasn't fair. Instead of allowing her to grieve, her father had brought another woman into the home within weeks of her mother's passing. He even had the nerve to order them to call Darcy "mom." It had infuriated her, and she'd lashed out.

"When I was a kid, after my mom died, I wanted to die with her. I knew my father wasn't right, but I didn't have a way out. So I acted out." She paused when his muscles tensed beneath her. She glanced up at him. "Are you okay?"

He nodded, kissed her forehead. "I'm fine. I just . . . know the feeling."

The look in his eyes touched her, and she reached out to stroke the frown line in his forehead. "Maybe we should talk about something else?"

"No, go ahead. I'm listening."

Brooklyn told him about her time at the clinic. When she was fourteen years old, and a hard-headed brat, she'd had to go to the clinic after a sobering experience. One night, after the home-coming dance, Harper Thomas, the star player on the football team, had approached her, told her that she was who he wanted to be with. Like the naïve teenager she was, she went for it. They went to the back of the bleachers and she let him do things to her that she shouldn't have been doing at that age.

"I didn't know any better," she continued. "I thought he cared about me, so I did what I thought would keep him there. The next day, he acted like he didn't even know me. I'd see him around the hall, walking with other girls and he'd whisper things about me. I was the laughing stock for a few weeks."

The humiliation didn't end there. After weeks of torment, she'd drowned her sorrows in a bottle of gin, and Nicole had found her slumped over the bathtub. Nicole and Kyle had rushed her to the clinic to get her stomach pumped.

"My father eventually found out and immediately sent me to the boarding school in Massachusetts as punishment. Turns out it was the best thing for me. It was there that I volunteered at my first homeless shelter. I got a chance to see how much good people can do in the world. So I changed my life, and real-ized my calling. When it came time to go to college, I attended State and majored in Psychology and Sociology, instead of pre-law like Senior wanted."

"I really want to give you kudos on turning your life around, but I can't approve the Michigan State choice."

She laughed at his joke, and shoved him. "You're crazy."

"Seriously, though. That took a lot of guts to blaze your own trail and not follow the path your father set out for you. You should be proud of yourself."

"I am. I love the work. I took the job at Wellspring Clinic because they'd not only helped my mother and so many others in our community, but they helped me. And I figured I could help them, help fulfill their mission."

Carter pulled back and shifted so they were face-to-face. "You can still do something big, something better. Start your own homeless shelter. Create that nonprofit, and watch it grow."

Her stomach flipped, as a warmth spread through her body. "You make it sound so simple."

"Because it is, if you have the desire and the connections. Lucky for you, I have plenty. And I'll help you."

Brooklyn ducked her head. "I can't ask you to do that. Like I said, you barely know me. My father can—"

He brushed his thumb over her bottom lip. "I know that you think your father will ruin my life, and I'm not even going to say that he won't try. But I don't scare easily, and I'll fight for what's right. And what he's doing to you isn't right."

Brooklyn wanted to ask him why he was so passionate about this. What had made him react so swiftly in the meeting room? They'd just agreed to a first date, had only shared a few kisses and played a few heated games of pool. There had to be a personal reason.

"You were so angry earlier," she said, hoping he wouldn't push her away. "I know it's not just because of me."

"My father used to abuse my mother. It does something to me to see a man berating a woman like that. It made it worse that it was you. I know we don't know each that well, as you've pointed out several times tonight. But I like you, and I feel like we've started a nice friendship." She opened her mouth to speak, but he rushed on. "Maybe more?"

Her shoulders fell on a sigh. "I'm sorry about your mom. That must have been hard to see."

"It was. But me and my siblings had each other. And from what you tell me, you and Parker have had each other's backs. It makes it easier to deal with shitty parents when you're not alone. At the same time, it did shape how I view relationships, how I react when I see violence. And watching your father charge toward you was enough for me to jump into action."

His heartfelt admission made her want to pull him closer. "Thank you." She pulled him into a tight hug, taking in his scent.

"I'll help you any way I can," he said. "Are you hungry?"

She pulled back. "Hungry? Who can eat when their life is in ruins?"

He kissed her nose. "You can."

He was so right. It was kind of jarring that he seemed to get her in a way that no one else had ever been able to. How would he know that she liked to eat when she was stressed? It was a wonder she hadn't gained weight over the last few days.

"Okay, I can." She cupped his face in her hands. "Where did you come from?"

"Detroit."

She laughed again. "I never pegged you as a joker."

"I told you there's a lot you don't know about me."

"I want to find out more. I want to explore this more."

His mouth was on hers within seconds. He pulled her closer, taking her mouth like he was thirsty for her, like his very life depended it. She let him control the kiss, enjoying the low groan in his throat when she opened for him. His tongue stroked hers, teased her.

Before long, they were grasping at each other, pulling at clothes. He pushed her skirt up her thighs inch by excruciating inch. She unbuttoned his shirt, revealing his muscled chest. He kissed down her throat, nipped at her shoulder blade before tracing the line of her bra with his tongue.

Brooklyn couldn't breathe. She wanted this man, needed him to take her right then. *Will he?* She got her answer when he stopped and pulled back.

"Tell me," she whispered. "Tell me what you want."

His eyes flashed to hers. "I want . . . I want you."

"I want you, too. But something is holding you back. Even now, when we're so close, when I can feel you against me, there's a part of you that won't let go."

He rested his forehead on her breasts, and she

kissed the top of his head. "I want to. I just want to make sure the timing is right."

Disappointed that she wouldn't have the orgasm she craved that night, Brooklyn sighed. She understood where he was coming from. It wasn't actually the best time to be intimate. She'd just had a terrible argument with her father in front of him. He probably didn't want to take advantage of her. *I wish he would take advantage, though.*

"I understand."

There was a knock on her door, and Carter sat up. She missed the contact already. Giving him a once-over, she straightened her clothing and hurried to the door.

When she opened the door, Parker pushed in past her. "We need to talk."

"What the hell is going on in Wellspring?"

Carter opened a beer and took a seat on his couch. He'd excused himself from Brooklyn's place when Parker showed up wanting to talk. Martin and Aisha had been calling him back-to-back for the last several hours. Once he'd showered and changed into a pair of sweats and a T-shirt, he'd finally called Martin back.

Martin had immediately conferenced in Aisha.

"Mr. Parker Wells Sr. is an asshole. That's what's going on."

Carter still couldn't believe the turn of events. The day had started out normal enough—an early morning conversation with Brooklyn that left him wanting more, then an early morning argument about Brooklyn that left him wanting . . . something else entirely.

Apparently after he'd left, Parker Sr. had disconnected the video call and Martin was left wondering what was going on. "Listen, Carter. If this is too much for you right now, just say the word. I'm there."

Carter shook his head as if Martin could see him. "I'm fine. He fired me, but then Parker told him he couldn't fire me. So I'm going to go along as if nothing happened. That's all."

"I just don't understand what happened that made you get involved," Aisha said. "You should know better than to jump into someone else's family business. How do you know this woman?"

Carter wanted to tell his sister and his best friend just how well he knew Brooklyn. Well, since he didn't know her *that* well, he wondered if he could tell them how much he *wanted* to know her.

"I heard her explanation to her father," Martin added. "You saved her life? That's crazy."

"She was on the phone," Carter explained. "She was so distracted she didn't see the car coming. I just pulled her out of the way. And since then, we've been cool."

Cool was an understatement. But it was all he was prepared to say at that time.

"Okay, so she's just someone you met in town?" Aisha asked.

"Because that seemed like more than a casual acquaintance," Martin said.

"She's my next-door neighbor, too. We talk, we've eaten together . . ." Carter finished his beer and slammed the empty bottle on the table. "I took her to the hospital the other day during a storm because her best friend was having a baby. We're kind of friends."

There was silence on the other end. After a few seconds, he peered at the screen to see if the call had dropped. It had not.

"What?" Carter asked. "Say something."

"I didn't know you were done talking," Martin said.

"Aisha, I know you want to say something." Carter knew his sister had something on her mind. It wasn't like her to be so damn quiet. Especially with him talking about being friends with another woman. "What is it?"

"Is Brooklyn a friend, or is Brooklyn a *friend*?" The change in tone in that last *friend* made him burst out in laughter. Martin joined him. "What? It's a simple question, brother."

"I like her," Carter admitted. "A lot. But we're just taking things slow."

"So this *is* a thing?" Aisha asked, her voice soft.

"Yes, it's a thing." Carter closed his eyes. He'd said it out loud, and the world didn't open up and suck him in.

"I think that's great," Aisha said. "But I want you to be sure that this is good for you. She's the daughter of the man that hired you to come to Wellspring in the first place. Are you sure you want to start something with a woman that could potentially cost you money?"

He'd expected that. Although his sister had been clamoring for him to meet someone and have a life, she was still a numbers person. She was a bottom-line person, and that's why they'd hired her to be the chief financial officer of Marshall and Sullivan.

"Aisha is right," Martin said with a sigh. "At the end of the day, we are running a business. You have to make a decision. Is this account something that you're prepared to lose?"

Carter was normally the stickler for professionalism in the workplace. Along with Martin and Aisha, he'd worked long and hard to make the company what it was. He'd foregone time with his family for Marshall and Sullivan. He didn't want to do it anymore. He didn't want to work so much that he couldn't live.

After so much pain and grief, Brooklyn, had slowly breathed new life into his lungs. He hadn't looked forward to anything for so long, and he looked forward to seeing her, to being with her.

If Parker hadn't arrived at her condo when he did, Carter wasn't sure what would have happened. She wanted him to let go with her. *Can I do that*? The first answer that popped into his head was yes. But then there was that part of him, the part that felt guilty for moving on, for having a life when Krys's life was cut short.

Krys was more than his wife, she was his best friend, and she was snatched from his life so fast. His baby girl had never even experienced her first steps or her first orange. And he was deprived of seeing her off to prom, of giving her away at her wedding, of meeting his first grandchild.

Carter knew that it was time to stop wallowing in his grief, and let himself give in to the feelings for Brooklyn that seemed to be building by the hour?

"I haven't been fired yet," Carter said finally. "We'll see what tomorrow brings. Okay?"

There was a soft knock on his door.

"Alright, man," Martin said. "I want an update tomorrow. I'll drive in on Friday morning. I may bring Ryleigh. Aisha booked a room for me at the hotel."

Carter opened the door, surprised to find Brooklyn on the other side. She had changed into a pair of shorts and a tank top.

"I don't feel like being alone." She held up a bottle of wine. "Mind having some company?"

Chapter 14

Brooklyn needed a break. And her first impulse was to come to Carter, because he had been her safe place. He'd proven that he was solid, that he would protect her. And she needed that.

With his phone against his ear, he held the door open for her to enter. "I have to go," he said to whoever he was talking to. "I'll talk to you tomorrow." He hung up, tossed his phone onto the couch, and turned to her. "Have a seat."

"Do you have a corkscrew?" she asked.

He took the wine bottle from her and walked into the kitchen. Brooklyn followed him, watched as he opened the bottle and pulled a wineglass from the cabinet.

"You're not pouring yourself a glass?" she asked, walking up behind him.

He handed her the full glass, never taking his gaze off of her. "I'll just finish my beer."

She sipped on her wine, and gestured to the

open beer bottle on the table. "You already started without me, I see?"

"Long day," he said simply. Once he picked up his beer, he led her back to the couch.

Brooklyn sat down gingerly right next to him, so as not to spill any of her red on him. "Tell me about it."

He sipped his beer, pinned her with a concerned gaze. "How did your talk with Parker go?"

Shrugging, she pulled her legs under her. "He's upset. With my father. They had an awful argument after we left, and Senior basically told Parker to mind his own damn business."

Parker had been so pissed, he'd almost quit on the spot. Brooklyn was glad he didn't, though. Her brother had a vision for Wellspring that their father didn't seem to understand or want. But she knew that once Parker was able to make more decisions, once their father was gone, Parker would be able to make lasting changes.

"What's with your father wanting you to marry Sterling?" Carter asked.

"His father is a state representative. Having an in with the Michigan legislature would be no small feat for my father, and would no doubt help him with Wellspring Water business. Apparently, he's trying to buy up land in the state and Senator King is working with him to do so in exchange for a merger between the families. Mr. King is looking to build Sterling's political career and he needs a wife. So they both have something invested in this."

She didn't like being nothing more than a bargaining tool for her father. Love never factored in, and it hurt. It sucked to not have the love or respect of her only living parent. It was bad enough that her mother died, but today her father died, too. At least, he was dead to her.

"You made it sound so easy to start over, to start a business." She took another sip of her wine. "I almost believed you."

Her eyes welled with unexpected tears. She didn't want to cry. She was tired of crying over her father and his actions.

Carter brushed away the tear that fell. "It won't be easy, but it's definitely worth it if it's what you want."

She bit down on her bottom lip. "You know what I want? I want to do something that has no connection to my father or his company. Because once he's involved, he won't let go. I want to be my own person. I want to be with a man because *I* chose him." She sucked in a shaky breath, closed her eyes when she felt his lips press against her temple.

Brooklyn hadn't meant to break down. Tonight wasn't about her dad. It wasn't about her brother, or Wellspring Water, or even her dream job. She'd come over to Carter's because she wanted to be near him.

"How did you leave it with your brother?"

"He told me he's mad that I didn't tell him about us."

Carter nodded. "I get that. Why didn't you?"

I wanted to keep you to myself for a little while longer. She wouldn't say that out loud, of course. "I don't know. I'm sorry, though. I knew who you were. I should have told you who I was. That was unfair of me."

He swept a hand over her leg. "You don't have to apologize. I should have asked what your last name was. But I didn't care who you were."

Ouch.

"I didn't mean that the way it came out." He squeezed her leg. "I meant that your last name didn't matter to me. I'm sure it matters to most people, but not to me."

"It's when you say things like that . . . I want to jump on your lap or something." Her eyes widened and she slapped her hand over her mouth.

Carter laughed, pulling her hand from her face. "It's okay."

"Oh my God, did I just put it out there like that?"

Yes, she was attracted to him. That much was obvious. She liked being with him, hanging out talking about nothing in particular. She liked the way he stared at her, the way his eyes followed her every movement. It could have been a side effect of being so close to him. They lived next door, seemed to always run into each other. But she didn't think so.

Plain and simple, she wanted to be with him. But more importantly, she wanted *him* to do her. Hard. All night.

He scratched the back of his neck. "I'm not complaining."

His gaze dropped to her mouth, sending a thrill through her body. She wondered what she could say, what it would take to propel him forward the last few inches.

"What's your magic word?" she asked.

He raised a brow. "My magic word?" he repeated.

She finished her wine in one gulp and set the glass down on the table. "You like control. We've already established that. But what is that one word that will get you to lose it with me? What do I have to say to get you to do what you described to me this morning?"

The smirk that played across his face was downright adorable. And she melted. He reached out and traced her lips with his thumb. She licked the tip of his thumb, enjoying the way his eyes narrowed on her.

He feathered his fingers down her cheek. His touch was warm, warmer than the wine that slid down her throat. *Will I ever grow tired of his hand on my skin?* She loved the way it felt when he touched her. Her body loved it, too, because every inch of her responded to him like she was metal to his magnet.

Deciding to take the initiative, Brooklyn climbed on his lap. Hell, she didn't have to work in the morning. All she had was time to explore Mr. Carter Marshall. And she would.

His grip was tight on her hips, holding her in place, keeping her from making intimate contact. But she still felt him, though—his hard length pressed against her inner thigh. "Brooklyn, I—"

Bending down, she licked his neck, bit down hard on his shoulder. "Tell me to stop."

With one move, Carter tossed Brooklyn on her back and settled between her legs. They fit. He had tried hard not to react, because he knew that if he let go even a little bit, he would be lost. But she was determined to make this hard for him.

Wrapping her legs around his waist, she rolled her hips.

He groaned, pushing forward. "Brooklyn," he murmured against her mouth.

She slipped her hands under his shirt, dragged her nails across his back, digging in. It was her fault he'd lost every shred of control he had. She moved her hips, sliding herself against his hardness.

"The magic word"—he nuzzled her nose with his, before he brushed his lips against hers—"is *please.* Say please."

"Please," she whispered, her breath catching in her throat when he pushed against her.

"You're so damn beautiful." He reached between them, palming her in his hand. "And you're so damn wet." He rubbed her clit through her thin panties. "You want me to taste you."

Brooklyn nodded.

"I can't hear you." He slipped her shirt up and off. "Say it."

Carter grinned when she growled out a tense yes. He nipped at her chin and made his way lower, kissing her as he descended. He took his time, sucking each of her nipples until she cried out his name. He dipped his tongue into her belly button, then pulled her shorts off.

Tracing the line of her panties with his tongue, he pushed down on her clit through the thin cotton. She arched off the couch. "Carter, please."

Carter slid onto his knees and peered up at her. "Say it again."

"Please," she whimpered, biting down on her lip.

He gripped her panties and ripped them off of her, flinging them across the room. His heart pounded in his ears as he buried his face in her core, licking and sucking until she begged for mercy. But he couldn't stop. He wouldn't stop. He continued, taking pleasure from her moans, from the way she held him to her, from the way she rolled her hips against his tongue. She came on a hoarse scream, her body shaking wildly as her orgasm rolled through her.

The silence of the room was drowned out by the turmoil in his head. He pulled back, took in the way her body looked after receiving pleasure. It was lithe, ready to be taken fully. But he was hesitant about taking it too far.

Carter recognized the need in her eyes when she'd asked him what his magic word was. And he wanted to give her what she wanted. Damn, he wanted it more than he'd ever wanted anything.

"Carter?"

He met her curious stare. "Yes?" He kissed his way back up her body to her lips. Settling between her thighs, he deepened the kiss and let her taste herself on his tongue.

Reaching between them, she stroked him through his sweats. "Take these off," she ordered. "You have on too many clothes."

She pushed his pants down, and he kicked them off the rest of the way. He reached back and pulled his T-shirt off. "Better?" he asked.

Smiling up at him, she bit down on his chin. She was spicy, unafraid to show him just how much she wanted him. "Much."

"I can't get enough of you, spicy." He kissed her. "I want this. Do you believe me?"

She searched his face. "I do."

He rested his forehead against hers. Carter knew himself. Being with Brooklyn like this meant something to him. And he needed her to know that. "But I need you to be sure."

"I'm sure. Carter, stop thinking so hard. You can be free with me, I won't break. What do you want?"

To bend you over this couch and take you hard and fast. "You," he answered.

She studied him, almost as if she could see right through him, to his soul. "Then take me to bed."

It was a silent dare. Rocking her hips, she snapped the waist band of his boxer briefs. "I think you still have on too many clothes."

He stood then, pushing his underwear down to the ground. He gripped her wrist and yanked her to her feet, her body crashing into his. Skin to skin, he took her mouth in a kiss, lifted her in his arms and walked her back to his bedroom.

Take me to bed is a figure of speech. Brooklyn didn't mean it literally, because she would have given it to him right there on his couch. The short walk to his room was too long. She was on fire for this man, wanted to do everything with him.

He stopped in the hallway, pressed her back against the wall. *Yes, right here.* He buried his face in her neck. "Brooklyn, you're driving me crazy." He gently bit down on her neck, before soothing the area with his tongue.

"It's okay," she whispered. "I'm already crazy, so . . ."

He chuckled. "Damn, you make me want to do things to you."

She sucked his earlobe into her mouth and scraped her teeth against it. "Freaky things? Tell me."

There was nothing sexier to Brooklyn than a man that knew how to articulate exactly how he wanted her. She loved dirty talk, and it drove her wild to know how she affected a man.

They moved again, finally stepping into his room. He tossed her on the bed, and she burst out laughing. *He's playful. I love it.* Scrambling to her knees, she scooted toward him. Brooklyn trailed her fingers over his sculpted chest, tracing his hard muscles.

Gripping him in her hand, she squeezed, smiling when his eyes rolled into the back of his head. She kissed his neck as she stroked him. His hand on her wrist stopped her. "Problem?" she asked.

"I want inside you. Now."

She fell back against the mattress. "Come here, then." He climbed over her, taking her nipple in his mouth, sucking it and pinching the other. He brushed his fingers over her clit, circling it until she let out a frustrated groan. "Carter, please."

"You're not ready yet." He pushed one finger inside her, then two, pumping slowly. She rode his fingers hard, chasing the release that had been building since they'd started the trip to his bedroom.

His thumb was replaced by his tongue, lapping at her like she was his favorite meal. And when he sucked her clit into his mouth, she came. Loudly.

He kissed her down to earth again, resting his body against hers. "Tell me to stop," he said. He'd used her own words on her.

Shaking her head, she said, "No, because I don't want you to stop."

Then he pushed inside her. Her mouth fell open on a wordless sigh. *This is really happening.* Brooklyn was making love to Carter. Just the feel of him against her, of him inside her, was enough to trip her right over the edge. They stayed like that for a minute as she adjusted to his size.

When she was ready, she rocked her hips, taking him deeper. Carter pulled out almost completely before pushing back in, slowly. She threw her head back as his hard length impaled her, branded her as his.

Soon, they settled into a rhythm. Brooklyn locked her ankles together around his back, holding him to her. He sucked her lip into his mouth, groaning when she dug her nails into his scalp.

"Carter, please."

The bed creaked as his pace quickened. With each thrust, Brooklyn gave herself over to him, urged him to go faster, go harder, go longer. He buried his face in her neck, lightly scraping her skin with his teeth.

"Beautiful, come for me. I need you."

Those were her magic words. *He needs me.* Her orgasm ripped through her like an explosion, stealing her breath away with its intensity. Carter stiffened, and then followed her over the edge, her name tumbling out of his lips over and over again.

Carter fell against her, breathing hard against her sweaty skin. She rubbed his head, whispering nonsensical words to him. When his breathing evened out, he rolled over, taking her with him.

"Damn," he breathed.

She tilted her head up and kissed his chin, sucking the skin there for a few seconds. "I know," she agreed.

He shot her a lazy grin, kissed her nose and then her lips. "You're beautiful."

Brooklyn didn't think she'd ever grow tired of hearing him call her beautiful. It made her feel treasured, safe. She dropped her head to his chest, giggling. "You make me feel that way."

When he said it, she actually believed it. She had never been told she was beautiful, not by any man. The one person that was supposed to make her feel that way, her father, had been more than eager to point out her shortcomings, often.

"I haven't been able to stop staring at you since I met you," Carter said softly.

She laughed. "I like that about you."

He ran a lazy finger over her back. "Not at first you didn't."

"No, I actually did. I just didn't know why you were staring. It was giving me a bit of a complex."

"You have nothing to be insecure about, beautiful." He kissed her brow. "If you haven't guessed, you had me once you landed on me out in that snow."

Brooklyn felt a blush creep up her neck and

bloom on her cheeks. "Stop. You tried like hell to get away from me."

"I already told you it wasn't you."

They'd never actually discussed *why* it was him, though. What was he running from? She hoped it wouldn't come back to bite her in the ass later. They'd already slept together, and she was falling fast.

"What do we do now?" she asked. "I mean, I did put out before our first real date."

He stared off behind her, as if he was thinking of the right answer. "I still have Friday reserved with you, beautiful. That hasn't changed."

"What about Brook's Pub tomorrow?"

"I'm still planning to spank that ass on the pool table tomorrow night."

She snorted. "In your dreams."

Her stomach growled, and he lifted a brow. "Hungry, huh?"

"Famished."

A few hours later, Brooklyn slipped out of the bed. Carter was asleep after they'd finally christened his couch. There was so much going on with Brooklyn, and despite her earlier bravado about her father and not talking about it, she needed to talk to one person in particular.

She pulled on the discarded T-shirt and tiptoed out of the room. Once in the living room, she grabbed her cell phone and walked out on the deck to make her call.

Nicole's groggy voice came over the receiver. "Are you okay, hun? It's late," her best friend asked.

"I'm fine," Brooklyn whispered. "Were you asleep?"

"Not really. Why are you whispering?"

"I'm sorry if I woke you."

"It's hard to sleep in here."

Kyle had called Brooklyn earlier to let her know that Nicole had to stay in the hospital another day. The doctors wanted to be sure her blood pressure dropped down to a normal range before they released her.

"We still haven't established why you're whispering," Nicole continued. "What's up?"

"I slept with Carter," Brooklyn blurted out.

"That fast?" Nicole was the only one that could say that to her and get away with it. And only because she'd said something similar to Nicole when her best friend gave it up to Kyle on their first date.

"I feel like we haven't talked. Today was the day from hell. But it ended on a high note."

"What happened?"

Brooklyn explained the situation with her father to her bestie. "And so I knocked on Carter's door to chill and now . . . I'm in his T-shirt on *his* balcony talking to you."

"Your father is a dirty bastard. I can't believe . . . well, I can believe it. But damn. This is ridiculous."

"I know. I still haven't been able to go to the credit union to get my money."

"I'm sorry, hun."

"When are you coming home?" Brooklyn asked, perching her feet up on the railing. "I miss you."

"Hopefully, tomorrow. I've had twelve straight hours of normal BPs. I just want to be at home, in my own bed, with my baby."

"I know you do."

"So, since I'm all stretched out and laid up, tell me about this night of hot sex. Was it good?"

Brooklyn didn't want to gush, but she couldn't help thinking about it. "No details, Nic."

"Take pity on me since I'm laid up in the hospital."

"The only thing I will say is Carter is an amazing man."

"Seriously? That's it?"

"Well, I told you. There was something about him. He's mysterious, but he's compassionate. He stood in front of my father and my brother and dared them to disrespect me one more time. It was a sight to see."

Nicole grumbled, "It should have never happened in the first place. What are you going to do without a job?"

Brooklyn wondered the same thing. "Nicole, I'm thinking about finally starting my nonprofit. I know I didn't get all of the experience I wanted to have before I got fired, but I know people in the industry that would be interested in helping me. Once I get this off the ground, I'll be working for myself."

"I always told you it was a good idea."

Nicole had always been her number one cheerleader. Brooklyn appreciated that in her friend. "You did. But I wanted to work for a while, network, so it wasn't a priority—until now. I think I can do this. It will take some time, but I'm willing to put in the work."

"Well, you know I'm here to help you in any way I can."

Carter had said the same thing. And judging by the way he barely flinched when her father fired him, she trusted that he really wasn't worried about the job. "Thank you, Nic. I love you. Call when they release you. I'll come and spend the day with you, cook dinner and help with my godson."

The two talked for a few more minutes, before Brooklyn hung up.

"Everything okay?"

Brooklyn turned to find Carter standing in the doorway. Smiling, she answered, "Yes. I was just talking to Nicole."

"You sure?"

"Very sure."

He pulled her to her feet, kissed her thoroughly.

When he pulled back, Brooklyn swayed on her feet. "Is that your way of asking me to come back to bed?"

Chuckling, he leaned forward, brushing his lips over hers again. "Or we could just stay out here."

Chapter 15

"How can we move forward from yesterday's unpleasant conversation?"

Carter shrugged, looking at Parker. "I don't know. I *do* know that your sister is not going to be disrespected in front of me. I don't care who is doing the disrespecting."

"I feel you on that," Parker conceded. "I am the same way."

Carter narrowed his eyes on Brooklyn's brother. The man in front of him obviously loved his sister, but Carter wasn't sure Parker had done everything in his power to protect her. "Listen, I'm prepared to walk away from this job if I have to. I'm not going to beg anyone to do business with us. And it seems like your father is used to getting his way, so it will be doubly offensive to him if I stay after he fired me."

"I know who my father is. I've never had any illusions."

Carter scratched his head, looked at his watch. Brooklyn should be on her way to the credit union

at that moment. They'd awakened that morning,
tangled in each other's arms. Spending the night,
making love to a woman, had been the last thing on
his agenda when he'd arrived in Wellspring. But
Brooklyn Wells was not just any woman.

"Good," Carter said. "Then me and you won't
have any problems."

Parker sighed. "How is she?"

"She's good, on her way to the credit union."

Waking up with Brooklyn's naked body pressed
against his body was surreal. He'd immediately
hardened at the feel of her. And it didn't take long
for him to wake her and show her just how she
affected him.

He thought he'd feel guilty about being with
Brooklyn, but the guilt didn't come. Instead, he
had peace about his decision to let go with
Brooklyn, to move forward. He wasn't sure the
peace would last, but it felt good to have it in that
moment.

It was sometime during the night, after they
made love on a chair on the balcony, that he'd figured out what had scared him about Brooklyn all
along. She was a free spirit, and she'd made him
feel free. It made him almost feel invincible, like he
could do anything, be anything. For once, it felt
like he had life ahead of him.

He didn't know what his revelation would
mean for their relationship, or if she even wanted
a relationship with him. All morning, long after
Brooklyn had left, he'd been thinking about how
he was going to tell her about Krys and Chloe.
Because he needed to tell her, if only because he
wanted to be transparent with her.

"Carter, what are your intentions with my sister?" Parker asked, pulling him from his thoughts.

"What do you mean?"

"It's a question. Is this just a fling, or it is more serious?"

"There hasn't been a conversation between us about it yet. Right now, we're just getting to know each other." And he'd explored every inch of her body, gotten to know her intimately.

"Well, just so you know, you hurt her and you'll deal with me."

Carter nodded. "As long as you know that I don't plan on hurting her, but I will protect her as long as I'm here to do it."

"You do realize that you aren't a resident of Wellspring."

Frowning, Carter sat back in the chair. "What are you getting at?"

"Brooklyn lives in Wellspring. Whatever you're doing, be careful. You two live on different sides of the state. Unless you have plans to move to Wellspring or move her to Detroit, you need to tread lightly. Don't make any promises you can't keep."

Parker hadn't said anything wrong. Essentially, he'd only pointed out a truth that Carter hadn't even considered. He'd been so wrapped up in the haze of their night together, so intent on being with her, that he hadn't paid a single thought to what would happen when his project was over. Would he stay? Would she go?

Carter knew he was jumping ahead, but it was a necessary evil. "I know you're concerned, but Brooklyn and I are grown people, capable of making our own decisions. We'll handle things as they come."

"Okay." Parker leaned forward, tapping a pen on his desk. "So, let's get to work."

At the Bee's Knees, Brooklyn started her business plan. She'd driven to the credit union and had no luck gaining access to her money. Then she'd hightailed it back to Wellspring, just in time to beat the lunchtime rush.

Will Clark slid into the booth, across from her. "Hey there, Brooklyn! Aren't you supposed to be at work?"

Brooklyn glanced up at Will and smiled. "I am currently unemployed."

The older man frowned, confusion written on his face. "What? You loved that clinic. What happened?"

"My father happened, Will. He's upset because I won't bow down and marry Sterling King. So he's basically declared war on me."

Will shook his head, a disgusted look on his face. "That's cold. I'm sorry, darling."

"There's really nothing I can do. I just have to deal with it, and move on."

"I wish you didn't have to go through this." Will patted her hand tenderly. "You deserve better than that. You've made good on your life. Your mother would have been proud. Never forget that."

Will and Dee had been good friends with Brooklyn's mother, despite their age differences. Brooklyn had spent many an evening with her mother at the Clarks' home and even more time at the Bee's Knees in her younger years. "I know. I'm so glad I've been able to come here and hear stories about her."

After her mom died, her father had wiped

everything of her from the house. It was almost as if he wanted to wipe her existence from the earth, make it like she'd never existed. Her mother was a brilliant and wise woman. Brooklyn often thought about how her life would have turned out had her mother still been alive. Would her father still be the overbearing man that he was now?

Brooklyn had naïvely hoped that her father would actually listen to her. She'd wished that he'd tell the King family, her mean and hateful step-mothers, and everyone else that meant her harm, to fuck off.

Unfortunately, her father always fell short. He'd never had her back. Ever. And that hurt Brooklyn to her core.

Will sighed heavily. "What do you need?"

"A job?"

Brooklyn had to do something for money, especially since she would need it to aid in her new business endeavor. It made sense to get a job, from someone who would not be bullied into firing her because her father requested it.

There was no love lost between the Clarks and the Wellses, and it had all stemmed from a time before Brooklyn was even a thought. She'd heard bits and pieces of it over the years, but everyone was still pretty hushed on that part of Wellspring history.

"You got it, darling." Will stood. "Start Saturday morning, and we'll see how you do."

Brooklyn slid out of the booth and hugged the old man. "Thank you so much. I appreciate you."

"Your father is a ruthless bastard. He doesn't

deserve you." Will pinched her chin like he'd done so many times in her life. "Now, you finish eating. It's on the house."

Before she could argue, Will had walked away and started yapping with another couple on the far side of the restaurant.

Carter left WWCH a few hours later. On his way to his car, he dialed Aisha. "Hey, can you set up a phone conference later today with Martin? So far, we're still on the job, but I want to have a contingency plan in case something goes down."

"I'll let Martin know about the conference call later. His travel arrangements have already been made, and he'll be there Monday morning."

"Thanks, Aisha."

"Is everything okay?"

Telling Aisha about his night with Brooklyn would probably mean another two hours on the phone, and he just didn't have any time to answer a trillion questions about his feelings. "I'm fine. Just leaving work for the day. I have plans tonight."

"With Brooklyn?"

"Actually, yes. It's a Wellspring thing, to party on Thursday night, so we're going over to a local pub to shoot pool."

"She shoots pool? Mom would love to hear that."

Carter smiled. "Mom would love her."

"Well, I may have to come with Martin so I can meet this woman. She sounds amazing. I haven't heard you talk about any other woman since you met Krys over a decade ago."

"Aisha, please stay home. You can come when things die down."

"Okay, punk. But I'm coming soon."

Carter laughed, told Aisha to give their mother a hug from him, and disconnected the call. He had just made it to his car, when Sterling pulled up beside him in his Mercedes-Benz.

"Well, if it isn't Mr. Marshall, the hero."

Carter glared at the other man. "What do you want?"

"I heard about your little show in the office. I hope you know this is the beginning of the end for you. Mr. Wells doesn't take kindly to being told what to do, especially about his kids."

"Well, that's where your problem is. Mr. Wells treats Brooklyn like she's a child when she is a grown woman."

"You don't know them. And here you are, inserting yourself into business that doesn't concern you."

Carter wanted to wipe the smug look off of Sterling's face. "Why don't you get out of the car and tell me that to my face?"

Sterling shut his car off and climbed out. "I don't have to explain anything to you. But I think you owe Brooklyn an explanation for not telling her that you have a wife and a daughter."

Carter's body tensed, and his vision grew cloudy. "What did you just say to me?"

"I said Brooklyn will be so upset to find out that you have a wife and daughter."

Carter gripped Sterling by the collar of his suit and jacked him up. "I would suggest you shut the hell up. I don't care who your father is, I will beat the shit out of you."

Sterling found his footing and pulled away from Carter's grasp, nearly falling to the ground in his haste to get away. "I got you. You're going down." Sterling jabbed a finger in Carter's direction. "You're no good for Brooklyn. You've been snowing her this entire time. And I can't wait to tell her all about your deception."

Rage filled Carter, swift and hot. Before he could even reason with himself, or even count to ten, he swung on Sterling. His fist connected with the jerk's jaw, and he felt the bones crack under the force of the blow. A writhing and screaming Sterling on the ground in front of him drew the attention of onlookers. He registered mortified gasps behind him as people gathered.

Several employees, curious about the crowd in the front of the building, walked out. Some of them he recognized from his interviews. A security guard also rushed over to them, and ordered Carter to have a seat. It was going to be a long evening.

Chapter 16

Brook's Pub was live, people crammed into the space, drinking and laughing and shooting pool. Brooklyn sat at the bar, nursing a drink, Carter was late. Not just late, he was three hours late.

Brooklyn tried to call him numerous times but had gone directly to voicemail. *Did he stand me up?* If so, she'd scratch his eyeballs out later, right after she had her pity party of one.

"You okay, Brooklyn?" Juke said, from his spot behind the bar. "You look like your dog died. Or something."

Brooklyn snickered, touched by what constituted Juke being concerned. "I'll be fine. Just disappointed is all."

She wasn't a great judge of character. In fact, she'd been wrong about people on numerous occasions. But Carter . . . She thought she had a good read on him. He struck her as the honest type, a man who would tell her the truth, no matter how much it would hurt her. He'd never given her any indication that he wasn't going to meet her for a game of pool. It was just the opposite, actually. After she'd left him that morning, he'd kissed her and promised to see her soon. Then he'd texted her during his lunch break with a "See you soon."

Where is he? She glanced at her phone, willing it to ring. No such luck. Frowning, she turned the phone off. At this point, even if he was coming, she was leaving. She'd be damned if she sat there much longer, waiting on someone who wasn't coming.

Motioning for Juke, she told him that she was out of there, paid him, and walked out into the cool night. As she strolled through town, she thought about the last time she'd walked the strip. With Carter. She passed the ice cream shop, waved at a few of the customers, before veering east down Baker Avenue. Earlier in the day, she'd looked forward to having a cone with Carter after they left the pub, but she didn't even want her favorite cool treat now.

Her mind rolled over every detail, every word. Nothing. There was really no excuse, and no good explanation, aside from death or jail. And both of those explanations were horrifying in their own way.

Grinning down at Mr. Paul, a homeless veteran she'd often helped at the clinic, she pulled a twenty-dollar bill from her pocket and placed it in his hand, closing his fingers around it. Mr. Paul had served two tours in Afghanistan and settled in Wellspring. The war had done unimaginable things to his mind, and he'd been unable to keep a job. When his mother died, he was left with no family, no one who cared. But he was a proud man, stood tall no matter who was in the room. It was unfortunate that he didn't have a place he could call home.

A homeless shelter would be perfect for Wellspring and its surrounding communities. The growing homeless population needed help. Maybe she could build her own clinic, attached to the Loving Brooklyn Homeless Shelter. Smiling, she made a mental note to jot that name down when she returned back to her house.

"Marie?"

Brooklyn froze. It wasn't a coincidence. It couldn't have been. Her mother's name was Marie, so what were the odds someone would call her by her mother's name by accident?

Turning around slowly, she laid eyes on a petite woman, unkempt, with dirty hair and dirty clothes. She was sitting on a cardboard box, rocking back and forth. Brooklyn walked up to her and asked, "Did you call me Marie?"

"Marie, it's been so long since I've seen you," the woman said. "I missed you."

Brooklyn swallowed past a lump in her throat. "I'm not Marie, ma'am. She was my mother."

The woman turned startling blue eyes on Brooklyn. "Your mother is Marie." The pale woman smiled. "You look just like her. Where is she?"

It was obvious the woman had been through a lot. Her eyes were bloodshot, her pupils were dilated and she was shaking uncontrollably. She was an addict. There was no way to tell what she was on, but Brooklyn suspected heroin or opioid addiction. "How do you know my mother?"

"Sweet Marie went to my school. She always smiled. That's what I remember."

Brooklyn knelt down in front of the woman. Her face looked familiar, but she couldn't place her. It was too late to take her to the clinic, but Brooklyn didn't want to leave her by herself, out in the open. The crime rate in Wellspring was pretty low, but there were several people in town that wouldn't think twice before they took advantage of the woman's mental state. "What's your name?"

The woman chuckled. "Marie called me Lisa Lisa."

Brooklyn smiled. Her mother's favorite '80s group was Lisa Lisa and Cult Jam. She remembered hearing "All Cried Out" nonstop one summer. The song was so sad she'd grown to hate it over the years. But she was grateful she could actually recall her mother's angelic singing voice.

"Lisa Lisa, how can I help you?"

Lisa Lisa looked at Brooklyn. "Your mother loved you."

Brooklyn's breath caught in her throat, and she fought back tears. "I know. But you need help. Let me get you to someplace warm. Would you like to sleep in a bed tonight?"

"I haven't slept in a bed in months."

Brooklyn's heart broke for the woman. She wanted to help her get back on track. But not all people wanted help, and she wasn't sure where Lisa Lisa fit on the spectrum. She reached out and wrapped an arm around the woman, pulling her in close. "I can get you a bed."

She led Lisa Lisa down the street and back over to Brook's Pub. Juke had a few rooms over the bar that he'd often rent to patrons who were too drunk to drive. If she asked, he would give up a room in a minute. Then she could call her good friend Dr. Warsaw, to come and check her out.

As they walked back over to the pub, she wondered about the history between Lisa Lisa and her mother. Had they known each other long? Or were they passing acquaintances?

"Parker Wells is a bad man," Lisa Lisa mumbled, taking Brooklyn by surprise.

"You know my father?"

The lady nodded. "He's bad. He treated Marie bad, and took her money. He deserves to rot for what he did to Marie."

Brooklyn continued forward, ignoring the talk because she was focused on caring for the older woman. She lead the woman through the crowd gathered in front of the pub.

One look at her and Lisa Lisa, and Juke immediately shook his head. "No."

Brooklyn pleaded with her friend. "Please. She has to go somewhere tonight. I need your help."

Juke sighed. "Why do you always do this? She's a pill popper. I've seen her around here on many occasions, trying to steal food."

Brooklyn glanced over at Lisa Lisa, who was sitting on a nearby stool, biting her fist and mumbling something to herself. With a heavy sigh, she turned back to Juke. "I promise I'll stay with her."

"No. You don't know what she's capable of. I would burn this place down if something happened to you under my roof."

Juke didn't issue idle threats. She knew he'd move heaven and hell to avenge her if she found herself in dire straits. He really was a big, soft teddy bear—with scary tattoos. "Okay, how about we—"

"Call the police. That's what they're for. She can stay the night in a holding cell. It's clean and she can have a shower and a meal."

"But she knows my mother. I can't take her to jail, Juke."

"Seriously, I know you have a big heart. But she needs help you can't give her here. If you want, I'll walk with you to the jail, to drop her off."

Biting down on her lip, she nodded. "You're right."

Juke ordered one of his employees to take over at the bar and he walked around, helping Lisa Lisa to her feet. They left, and walked over to the police station.

When they arrived at the jailhouse, Sheriff Walker took pity on her and allowed her to help clean the woman up. He even gave her clean scrubs to put on her. Once Lisa Lisa was settled in a cell, with a Subway sandwich, Brooklyn joined Juke and Sheriff Walker in the front room.

"Thanks, Sheriff," she said, taking a seat next to Juke. "I just didn't want to leave her out in the streets. It's cold at night."

Sheriff Walker smiled kindly. "You've always had a big heart. She'll be safe here."

"Do you know her?" she asked.

With a far-off look in his eyes, Sheriff Walker nodded. He was born and raised in Wellspring, just like her parents. He'd actually graduated in her mother's high school class. "Her name is Lisa Castle. Both of her parents worked for Wellspring Water."

Lisa Castle. She remembered that name, and recalled her mother mentioning her friend Lisa who lived out of town. "She called me Marie."

"Makes sense. She hasn't been in her right mind. I don't even think she remembers your mother died. They were very close. They spent a lot of time together. I'm surprised she's back in town."

Brooklyn wondered why the woman had returned and how she ended up an addict. Juke wrapped an arm around her and squeezed. "I wonder if she has any family."

"Her parents died years ago." He stared off at a point beyond her, seemingly in deep thought. "I think her brother is still living, though. I'll see if I can reach him. He lives in Grand Rapids. Well, he did the last time I checked."

Relief flooded Brooklyn. At least there was hope. "She said something to me tonight."

Sheriff Walker looked at her. "What?"

"She said that my father deserves to rot for what he did to Marie."

"Whoa." Sheriff Walker shot her a strange look, which did nothing to ease the feeling of dread that had seeped into her soul.

"I'm going to find out what she meant."

The sheriff, another man who had been like a surrogate uncle to her, squeezed her shoulder. "Some things are best left in the past."

Brooklyn flinched as if he'd slapped her. "Really? I'm not sure what's worse, Sheriff—the thought that my mother died because of something my father did, or the knowledge that the people who claimed to love her knew about it and did nothing." She turned to Juke. "Let's go. I'll be by to check on her in the morning."

* * *

Carter could have sworn he heard Brooklyn a little while earlier, but he figured it must have been a dream. *Why would she be here?*

It had been hours since he'd cracked Sterling's jaw. The melee at WWCH had drawn the attention of everyone, from senior management down to the mail room clerk, who'd given him a high five.

He knew he'd messed up. Big-time. And he had no one to blame but himself. Well, he blamed Sterling for being such an ass. The man had goaded him about cheating on his wife with Brooklyn, and accused him of leaving his family behind to dally with another woman. The thought made him want to slam the man's face into hard cement.

Carter had wanted to call Brooklyn, to let her know that he didn't stand her up. But then he'd have to ask her to come help him, and he didn't want her to see him in his current state. So he'd called Aisha.

He heard a heavy door slam, and the taps of shoes against the linoleum. Then silence.

"What the hell were you thinking?"

Carter sighed, peered up at his sister through the metal bars. "I wasn't."

Aisha gripped the bars and leaned forward. "You're in jail, Carter."

"I know that. Get me out of here."

His sister looked tired. Her normally bouncy hair was pulled back in a haphazard ponytail and sat on the top of her head. She had bags under her eyes, and they were puffy, as if she'd been crying.

Leaning her head against the bars, she grumbled a curse. "I've posted bail. But I need an explanation.

What possessed you to break Sherman King's son's jaw?"

She's said it like that name was supposed to mean something to him. It didn't. Not that he didn't know who Sherman King was. He definitely knew who he was. He just didn't care. Wrong was wrong. And Sterling King was dead wrong if he thought he'd just sit by and let that shit slide.

"Carter, I'm worried about you." Aisha's chin trembled, and he stood, crossing the small cell to her. "You're being reckless. It's not like you to not care about your job or your reputation. One wrong move can do detrimental damage to Marshall and Sullivan. It's not just you that would be affected. Martin has a lot riding on this deal. I have a lot riding on this deal."

Now he felt bad. He hadn't thought about the ramifications. He'd just wanted the guy to pay—for disrespecting Brooklyn, for disrespecting him and the memory of his wife and daughter. Leaning his forehead against hers, he sighed. "I'm sorry."

She retreated back a step, searched his face. "Are you? Because it seems like you're on this mission to push everyone away, to prove that you don't need anyone."

That wasn't true. Carter knew that he needed his family. He needed his sister. "I do need you," Carter told her. "You know that."

"Then act like it. Act like you care."

"I care, Aisha. Damn. I care." *Too much.* "I hit Sterling because he disrespected my relationship with Krys."

Aisha blinked, then a frown settled on her face. "What? How does he even know about Krys?"

Carter bowed his head. "He must have done a Google search, I don't know. But he brought up Krys and Chloe like he had any right to speak their names. I don't know what happened, I just snapped. I couldn't hold it in, so I clocked him."

Aisha sighed, her eyes softening. "You did more than clock him, Carter. You put him in the hospital. He has to have surgery, for Christ's sake. This is bad."

"I know I messed up, Aisha. I'm willing to do what I have to do, even if that means admitting my guilt and serving time."

She shot him a wary glance, scratching the back of her neck. "We secured representation. According to the sheriff, you'll have to appear for an arraignment on Monday, first thing in the morning."

"Okay. Whatever I have to do."

"Martin wants you to leave Wellspring. And I agree."

Carter knew it was coming, and he tended to agree with his partner and his sister. He'd messed up bad, terminating their contract seemed like a foregone conclusion. But Martin would have to be the one to fight on behalf of the company. There were too many hard feelings, too much water under the bridge for Carter to remain on the project.

There was just one problem—Brooklyn. If he left Wellspring, he'd be leaving her behind, and he didn't want to do that. He would have to come up with a solution, one that would solve all of their problems. That is, if she'd even want to see him again after she found out what he'd done.

He wondered what she was doing. Was she pissed that he didn't show up? Did Parker tell her what happened? There were so many wild cards at play. He hadn't even shared with her that he'd been married. When she'd asked if he was married, he'd told her no, without elaborating.

It wasn't a lie, but it wasn't the truth either. No, he wasn't married now. Their love story didn't end with divorce and hard feelings, it ended in two tragic deaths. How would Brooklyn feel about that? He imagined she'd have misgivings about being with him after the lie, and knowing that he'd loved another woman so deeply it had nearly killed him when she died. And he didn't want her to feel like she was second choice. But there was a good chance she would, and then they'd be over before they even started.

The realization that he didn't want it to end was like a swift kick to the gut. Making love to her, letting himself be with her on that level, was huge. Especially since he'd felt he didn't deserve to be happy after he'd failed Krys and Chloe. And even more so because they barely knew each other. She didn't know important things about him, things that would make or break their bond. But the thought of losing her, of missing the instant connection they had with each other, was enough to drive him insane.

Carter didn't know what he was going to do, but he'd figure that things out. "Okay," Carter said. "I'll leave Wellspring."

"The attorney suggested you come home with me tonight, and drive back Monday for the court date. This way, you'll be able to speak with him and iron out your defense."

Not that I have a viable defense. "Fine. But I don't want to drive back tonight. I need time to take care of some business."

Aisha seemed like she was going to argue with him, but she shocked him when she told him, "I'm okay with that. You take care of what you need to take care of. Martin is still planning to come today."

Carter nodded. "Sounds like a plan."

Chapter 17

On Friday morning, Brooklyn showed up at the jail bright and early. Sheriff Walker let her into the cell. Lisa Lisa was sitting up, hugging her knees. She couldn't wait to talk to her mother's friend. The woman had constantly muttered something about money and her father, and Brooklyn was curious about it.

"Lisa," Brooklyn called softly.

Lisa jerked back. There was a marked difference between the Lisa of today and the Lisa of yesterday. Her eyes were clear and her face wasn't as pale.

"Do you remember me?" Brooklyn asked, sitting next to the woman. "I found you on the street last night."

"You're Marie's daughter." Lisa rested her cheek on her knees. "I remember."

"How are you this morning?"

Lisa shrugged. "I'm tired."

Sheriff Walker had given Brooklyn the good news that he was able to locate Lisa's brother and he would be arriving soon to pick her up. She only prayed that Lisa would be able to get the help she deserved. "I know. But I hope this is the start of you getting back on your feet. I hear your brother is coming to get you."

She nodded, tears filling her blue eyes. "I haven't seen my brother in five years. I'm surprised he's coming."

Brooklyn swept a comforting hand over the woman's back. "He loves you. And he wants to help."

They sat in silence for a few minutes, before Lisa said, "Your father hurt Marie. He took her money, and then tried to drive her crazy."

Brooklyn frowned. *He took her money?* As far as she knew, her father was the one with the inheritance. Wellspring Water was his family's business, passed down through the generations. She was sure the woman was mistaken.

"Your mother, she supported me when I didn't have anything. Your mother was a godsend to me. When she died, I was devastated."

Brooklyn had been devastated, too. She'd blamed herself for years. If only she had seen the car approaching instead of being engrossed in some computer game.

Lisa turned to her. "Her grandmother made it possible."

Brooklyn frowned. "Made what possible?"

"Wellspring Water. Marie saved it, and your father hurt her."

Brooklyn turned over all the information Lisa Lisa had shared in her head. "What did you mean by my father hurting my mother?"

The woman swallowed roughly. "I visited Marie

at the mental hospital in Kalamazoo because I lived there at the time. She was so medicated, so out of it, she couldn't even articulate."

Brooklyn recalled her mother being gone for an extended period of time, but she had no idea she'd been in a mental hospital. She remembered because she'd had a piano recital and she'd cried the entire ride there because she was told her mother wouldn't be attending. Her father didn't even come. He'd sent their housekeeper, Arlene, with her.

Lisa Lisa had been talking nonstop, mostly incoherently, so it was hard to follow. But Brooklyn instinctively knew there was truth in the older woman's words.

"What happened?" Brooklyn croaked, as bile lodged in her throat. Had she been right about her father and his role in her mother's death?

"She eventually was released, but he'd successfully taken control of her shares.

"Shares? What do you mean shares?"

"Your mother was smart, though," Lisa Lisa continued as if Brooklyn hadn't even spoken. "Check her will. Her shares of Wellspring are in your and your brother's names."

Brooklyn was shocked, angry, devastated. Lisa's story contradicted everything she thought she knew about her family's money. And this all had something to do with Wellspring Water. "How did you know all of this?"

"We couldn't see each other. My husband was abusive and forbade me to see Marie. We wrote letters, though. She told me that she felt her life was in danger. But she wanted someone to know what was going on."

Unable to hold it in, Brooklyn rushed over to the toilet and threw up. She hadn't eaten anything and barely had drunk any water, so it hurt. Tears pricked her eyes as she gagged over the small, cold toilet.

After a few minutes, she sagged down against the wall. It had always seemed very plausible that her father had done some shady business and made her mother's death look like an accident. She honestly didn't know what her father was capable of.

"Are you okay?" Lisa asked, concern in her eyes.

Brooklyn nodded and drew in a shaky breath. "Do you think my father killed my mother?" Her voice sounded foreign to her own ears. She was scared of the answer.

Lisa dropped her gaze to the ground. "She wasn't happy and wanted to leave him. Divorce is messy."

And Senior wouldn't have wanted her to leave, especially if she had the money. He would have fought tooth and nail to keep her there because a divorce would have cost him a fortune. Unless . . .

She died. The person who benefited most from her mother's death was her father. It definitely wasn't her or Parker. And since Bryson had a different mother, it didn't affect him.

In hindsight, there was a lot she didn't know. For instance, she didn't know why her mother had chosen her father in the first place. They seemingly had nothing in common. But if her father knew that her mother had money, she could see why the union happened. He was just that cold, just that calculating.

"Thank you, Lisa." Brooklyn finally stood and walked over to the older woman. She reached out and grabbed her hand, giving it a good squeeze. "Please, never hesitate to call me." She handed Lisa her business card.

The other woman scanned the information on the card. "You work for the clinic?"

"Not anymore, but my personal cell phone number is on the back. Please call me, and let me know how you're doing." Brooklyn handed her a piece of paper. "These are the names of some contacts that I have in Grand Rapids. I've already told them you're moving there, and they are available if you need the support."

Lisa nodded, folded the piece of paper, and closed her hands around the small card. "I will. And let me know if you need any help."

Brooklyn pulled Lisa into a tight embrace. "Thank you again. Take care of yourself."

On her way out of the jailhouse, she dialed Parker. When he answered, she told him, "Meet me at the Bee's Knees. I have something important to tell you."

"Is this about Carter?"

Brooklyn blinked. "No. What about Carter?"

She'd been so busy, so distracted by her family secrets, that she'd forgotten about Carter. When she'd gone home, he wasn't there. His place was dark, untouched.

"Have you seen him?" Parker asked incredulously.

"No. I ended up spending the night at Nicole's house. She and the baby were released late yesterday. He wasn't home when I went back there to pack a bag, so no . . . I haven't seen him. He stood me up last night. We were supposed to meet at Brook's Pub and he didn't show up."

"Probably because he was in jail."

Brooklyn froze. "What?"

"Carter broke Sterling's jaw yesterday after work. The sheriff had to arrest him for assault."

Unbelievable. "Did they say why he did that?"

"Senior told me why."

Brooklyn shook her head rapidly, as if Parker could see her. They couldn't afford to believe anything her father said. "Really? What does Senior know about it?"

Parker explained that her father and Sterling had joined forces to split her and Carter up. Sterling had told Senior about Brooklyn asking Carter out and her father ran with it, assuming they were an item. It hadn't helped that Carter had been so protective of her in the office that day. "And I guess Sterling confronted Carter with something they found out."

Brooklyn sighed, placing a hand over her queasy stomach. "What is it? Just say it." It was better to rip the Band-Aid off fast.

"Carter has a wife and a daughter, according to Sterling."

It took a few seconds for his words to sink in, and when they did, Brooklyn was livid. Carter was *married*. Just to be sure she heard her brother right . . . "Did you just say Carter is married with a child?"

"That's what Sterling told Senior. And he also told him that he was going to confront Carter with what he found. Unfortunately, Sterling can't talk, so we can't get the details."

Irritated, Brooklyn paced the sidewalk in front of

the jail. She needed to get the hell out of there before she lost her composure. She stomped to her car, phone gripped to her ear. "Is Sterling okay?"

"He has to have surgery."

Brooklyn closed her eyes tight. "You mean to tell me Carter hit Sterling so hard, he broke his jaw? All because Sterling confronted him about being married?"

"It appears that way. It just doesn't ring true, though."

"Why else would he react that way then? Why would he assault him for something that wasn't true?"

She jumped in her car and sped off. Parker's voice came through her Bluetooth. "Are you there?"

"Yes, I'm in the car."

"If you weren't going to tell me about Carter, what were you calling me for?"

There was too damn much going on. She couldn't think, she wasn't sure she could even feel anymore at that point. Her father lied to her, Carter lied to her. How could she have been so wrong about him? So blind?

Brooklyn knew he had secrets. She'd suspected it from day one, with one look into his intense eyes. But he'd treated her with respect. He didn't force her or push her. And to find out he was lying the entire time?

Brooklyn sped through town, intent on confronting him. He deserved her wrath and he was going to get it. He'd made her look like a fool. He pretended to be so torn about making a move with her, invited her out on a freakin' date like he was such a gentleman.

"Brooklyn, I'm going to need you to calm down."

"I'm not upset," she lied.

"And I'm Barack Obama."

"Shut the hell up, Parker." She stopped at a traffic light, cursing the car in front of her for driving five miles under the speed limit.

"Look, I expect Carter to have an explanation. He doesn't strike me as the cheating type."

"How would you know?" Brooklyn shouted. "He's a stranger. We don't know him."

"So why are you so upset?"

"Because . . ." *I liked him.* Not just "little like," but "big like." For the first time in her adult life, she was ready to embrace the connection, to allow herself to feel it with someone. That was the one thing she missed about being in a relationship. She missed being in sync with someone, in tune to their habits, to their moods. Carter made her feel things she hadn't ever felt with another man. Hell, he'd made her come so hard and so much, she couldn't see straight.

"Wellspring Water is going to have to terminate his contract," Parker explained. "Senior is chomping at the bit, too. He's already rallied the board, he's even talked to his attorney about suing Marshall and Sullivan for breach of contract. He's out for blood. He wants to destroy Carter."

Brooklyn knew her father wouldn't take Carter's defiance lying down. And the assault charge would only be the beginning. Call her soft, or even crazy, but she didn't want her father to ruin Carter's life.

"Okay. I don't want to hear about Senior. And I don't want to hear any excuses from Carter either. *If* he's married, no matter what his explanation is, he's a damn liar. I asked him flat out if he was married, and he told me no."

Parker muttered a colorful curse. "I'm sorry, Brooklyn. I know you liked him."

Was it that obvious? Of course, it was. She'd been downright giddy when he was in the room, or near her. She couldn't help but smile at the mere thought of him. She had thought she'd felt a connection to him, something deep and strong. And to think he had been yanking her chain since the day they met . . .

"It's okay, Parker. I'm not blameless. I went after him. He kept turning me down, but I kept asking." *That'll teach me.* She wasn't meant to be the aggressor. She pulled into her subdivision and parked right next to Carter's car. He was home. Finally.

She hung up on Parker without saying goodbye and stomped up to Carter's door. She pounded on it frantically, almost daring him not to answer it.

But when the door swung open, all her bravado faded into oblivion and she was left speechless. The woman standing in front of her, looking ever so comfortable in Carter's home, was wearing nothing but a robe.

"Who is it?" Carter walked out into the living room and stopped in his tracks at the sight of Brooklyn standing in the doorway. "Brooklyn?"

He'd waited up for her the night before, but she never showed up. He'd called her countless times, but it went straight to voicemail. Where the hell had she been?

"Carter," she said, her voice cold and almost robotic. There was no feeling, no warmth. Not like the other times she'd called his name.

He closed the distance between them, pushing past Aisha. "Where have you been? I've been calling you. I have something to tell you. I didn't want to leave Wellspring without being honest."

Brooklyn pushed past him into the condo. Her gaze dropped to the suitcases in the middle of the floor. She spun around. "You're leaving?"

"How much do you know?"

Brooklyn jabbed a finger in his face. "I know you're married, with a child, Carter. How could you do this to me?" With her hands on her hips, she gestured toward Aisha, who was watching the situation with wide eyes. "Is this your wife?"

Frowning, he started to explain, but she cut him off.

"Shut up." She sliced a hand through the air. "I don't want to hear any excuses. I guess I shouldn't be surprised. Men lie. Period. I don't care if your wife is standing in this room, practically naked. You're a married cheater. And I'm going to need you to stay the hell away from me." Brooklyn turned to Aisha. "Good luck with him. I hope you can find someone that will treat you right."

"I hope so, too," Aisha said, covering her mouth to hide her grin. Carter shook his head, knowing his sister was enjoying the scene in front of her. Soon, everyone would know that he'd just got his ass handed to him by the little, spicy, beautiful Brooklyn Wells.

Brooklyn jerked her head back. "Excuse me?" She turned to Carter.

Her assumptions, the story concocted based on that asshole Sterling's word, was downright laughable. Married cheater? That couldn't be further from the truth. Carter pointed at Aisha. "That is not my wife. Aisha is my sister."

Brooklyn's mouth fell open and her fingers flew up to touch her parted lips. "Oh."

Carter stalked toward her, and she took a small step back, retreating from him.

"I'm not married. I told you I wasn't married."

Brooklyn tugged on her ear. "But Sterling . . . I heard about the fight. You broke his jaw because he accused you of being married with a child. Why would you do that if it wasn't true? Why would you risk your livelihood for a rumor?"

"I asked the same question," Aisha said. Carter glared at his cosigning sister.

"Well?" Brooklyn asked incredulously. "What is it?"

"I'm not married, but I was." The words tumbled from his mouth in a rush.

"You're divorced?"

"My wife and my daughter died a couple of years ago. In a fire."

Brooklyn gasped. "I'm so sorry, Carter. I . . . I don't know what to say."

He moved forward, closing in on her. "There's nothing you can say. I should have told you from the beginning, before we . . ." He couldn't finish the sentence. What they'd shared the other night was perfect, from beginning to end. He didn't want to sully it with this conversation. The two didn't go hand in hand.

"No. I shouldn't have . . ." She let out a tortured laugh. "I barged into your house all crazy and deranged." Brooklyn turned to Aisha and held out a hand. "I'm Brooklyn, by the way."

Instead of shaking her hand, his sister pulled Brooklyn into a hug and told her, "We don't shake hands, we hug."

Brooklyn met his gaze over Aisha's shoulder, and mouthed, "I'm sorry."

When his sister finally stopped hugging his woman . . . *Wait, my woman?* Carter had just referred to another woman as *his woman* and it felt right, natural. New. He took Brooklyn's hand and pulled her toward him. "Can we talk? Alone."

A few minutes later, they were in Brooklyn's house, sitting on the couch. He leaned forward, resting his elbows on his knees. He was really about to have a conversation about Krys with another woman, the only woman.

Brooklyn sat down next to him. "Tell me about your wife and your daughter."

Carter's head snapped up, and he met her concerned gaze. Swallowing, he nodded, knowing she deserved the truth.

"Krys was my college sweetheart, my first love. I proposed right after college graduation," he explained. "But we didn't get married until I finished grad school. A few years later, we found out she was pregnant. My daughter, Chloe, was born during a heatwave on July fourteenth."

"Do you have a picture of them?" Brooklyn asked.

"I pretty much lost everything that day." The only thing he had left was Krys's wedding ring, the heart ornament, the files in his file cabinet, his tools, and his cookware. Aside from her wedding ring, nothing else that was salvaged had any emotional value to him. Everything else, all his pictures, his other keepsakes . . . gone. "There was nothing much left of them. Everything that mattered to me was destroyed in the fire. Everything." His voice broke and he paused to take in a deep breath.

His mother had gathered a few pictures of their family that she'd had around the house. She'd also kept a few of their wedding pictures in a small photo album. And he'd been able to snag pictures from Krys's Facebook page. But that was it. The fire took the wedding garter, her favorite pillow, Chloe's little stuffed bunny, his daughter's first pair of shoes.

He felt Brooklyn's soft hand on his back. "I'm so sorry, Carter. I can't even imagine the pain you've gone through. Or how it must have felt to lose your family in such a horrific way." She leaned against his shoulder.

He rested his head on top of hers, taking comfort in her. "So when you told me you'd wanted to die with your mom, I knew how you felt. I almost died with them," he admitted softly. "I wanted to die with them. But I didn't."

Carter finished the story, telling Brooklyn about the trial and the subsequent lawsuit and civil trial. When he was done, he bowed his head, the weight of the conversation taking its toll on him. A tear fell and he felt exposed. Weak, even.

Brooklyn massaged his neck, whispering in his

ear that he was okay, that she was there, that she understood and wanted to be there for him.

"Carter, I hope you know that I appreciate that you opened up to me. I know it was hard."

"Thanks for hearing me out."

She bit down on her lip. "I have to ask, though. Are you sure you're ready to move on? I know loss. For the longest time, I couldn't even talk about my mother without feeling overwhelmed by my sometimes debilitating grief."

"That's just it. I've spent the past two years seeking justice for them. I won the lawsuit, but it didn't make me feel better. I went to my condo and still felt alone. That's when I realized I needed to get away, to focus on me. That's why I came here. I needed time in a place where people didn't know me or my story. I wasn't here to move on, I was here to heal. Then . . . I met you."

Carter wasn't sure it was even possible to have such encompassing feelings for someone he'd just met. But he did. He wanted Brooklyn. He wanted her to want him. Which he knew she did.

He was suddenly hit with the urge to kiss her, to taste her. So he did, meeting her lips in a tentative kiss, nothing hot and heavy, just soft and warm.

"I'm sorry you had to hear about it this way," he said once he was able to pull away from her. "I wanted to tell you myself."

"I'm just glad I caught you before you left."

"I wouldn't have left without seeing you. You're the reason I'm still here. My attorney got special permission from the court for me to go home. Aisha tried to get me to leave with her last night. But I couldn't leave without seeing you."

"That's good to hear."

"I hope you know how much this means to me, to be able to be honest with you about my past. Makes it easier to be with you now."

Brooklyn nibbled on her bottom lip, but he reached out and ran his thumb over it until she released it. "Does it?"

Carter tilted his head, assessing her. "Are you concerned?"

"I just . . . I'm not sure how we're supposed to move forward. Is there a speed that you prefer? Slow, fast?"

"I still owe you a date. But I think we passed slow the other night."

She laughed, and he let it soak into his soul. It would only be a few days away from her, but it already felt like a few weeks. "Well, I'm ready when you are."

"It's still Friday." Carter watched as the wheels turned in her head. "Come out with me."

"What happened with Sterling?" Brooklyn bit down on her thumbnail. "Why did you hurt him?"

"He's an ass." Carter didn't like the change in subject. In fact, he'd be perfectly fine if he'd never have to hear the name Sterling again. "He disrespected my relationship with Krys. He disrespected my relationship with you. And before I knew it, I swung on him."

Brooklyn let out a deep breath. "Carter, you know this is going to make this so much worse for you. My father plans to destroy your company. They were working together."

He'd already figured that. Sterling seemed too comfortable at WWCH. Carter could concede that the other guy may have played it the way he had in order to provoke him. And he'd fallen right into the trap. Martin and Aisha were right. His head wasn't in the game.

"Your father has already terminated our contract," Carter told her. "By all rights, we can sue him for terminating without just cause. We wouldn't win, but we could do that."

"You don't understand. If it wasn't for me, you wouldn't be in this position. Sterling would have left you alone if he didn't feel threatened by you. My father would have happily let Parker manage the ERP project with little interference. I'm the reason you're in this situation."

Carter gripped her chin, turning her to face him. "Brooklyn, this isn't your fault. I chose to allow that man to push my buttons. I could have walked away, but I didn't."

"We have to do something, Carter. We can't let them win. And I can't let you leave."

Then she kissed him.

Chapter 18

Brooklyn couldn't breathe, but she couldn't stop either. Kissing Carter. She'd heard his explanation and it felt like the truth. She would give him another chance, and clearly she was already ready to move the party to the bedroom, or the floor, or against the wall.

"Make love to me," she whispered against his mouth.

Carter pulled back, sucking on her bottom lip before letting go. "I want you. So damn much. But we need to talk about this, before we get so lost in each other we can't think straight."

Brooklyn grumbled in frustration. "Can we talk later?" she pleaded, cupping his erection in her hand and squeezing.

He let out a low, filthy curse before he took her mouth in his again. She pulled him down on top of her, moaning as his weight rested on her.

Carter quickly descended, tugging at her shirt until the fabric ripped and flew across the room. His hands were rough on her skin as he pushed her skirt up, inch by inch, and ripped her panties off. He kissed her hard, with tongue and teeth.

Desperation speared through her, and a need she'd never felt before filled her to the brim. She wanted Carter, more than anything else in that moment. Everything else could wait, especially right now, while he was strumming her body like she was his own personal instrument.

His fingers dallied over her slick folds as he brushed her clit with his thumb. Arching her hips off the bed, she urged him forward, wanted to order him to take her that instant. But he specialized in driving her crazy.

When she was so close she would cry if she didn't finish, his fingers tightened on her wrists and he pulled her up and over him. She straddled his thighs, peered down at him watching her, touching her.

"Scared?" he teased.

He was right at her entrance, but his grip on her hips prevented her from descending. Meeting his gaze, she replied, "Never."

He slammed her down hard on his dick, and she gasped as she adjusted to his size. Carter was a very well-endowed man. Part of her was a little nervous when she'd first seen him. But they seemed to fit like the pieces of a puzzle.

Bending down, she licked his cheek before she kissed him. Moaning, she rolled her hips, taking him deeper inside her.

"I'm going to make you forget for a minute," he murmured against her mouth. "I only want you thinking of me while I'm inside you."

That's a safe bet. There definitely was no one else

on her mind. She leaned forward, resting her
hands on his chest as she moved over him. His
fingers tightened on her hips and he guided her
into a rhythm all their own.

Soon, they were slick with sweat as she rode him
hard, and he was pushing into her with wild aban-
don. His thrusts were hard, punishing even. She was
sure she'd end up with a few bruises from the tight
hold he had on her hips. But she liked it. She wanted
more. The thought that she was the one that he'd
chosen, that she was the one that unraveled his
control, made her dizzy. He'd let go with her. No
one else.

Brooklyn arched her head back as a wave of pleasure spread through her. One of his hands cupped
her breast, while the other one slid over her stomach, down to her core. He pushed down on her clit,
and she tensed right before her release took her
over.

Sitting up, Carter pulled her closer, wrapping his
arms around her back as she rode him through her
orgasm. Then she heard him let out a low curse, as
he followed her over the cliff.

Brooklyn collapsed against him, grinning when
his arms engulfed her in a hug. "You're so hot."
She laughed when she felt him chuckle beneath her.

"Feeling's mutual."

She lifted herself up, kissed him, and snuggled
back into him. He was still inside her, and hardening fast. He wanted her again, and she wouldn't
deny him.

It had been a crazy day, but she was glad they
ended up back on the same page, in each other's
arms. Hearing his story, seeing the grief he still had

on his face, was heartbreaking. But she was glad that he didn't shy away from telling his truth. It made her want him more.

Carter squeezed. "I'm sure I'll never get enough of you, beautiful."

"Really?" Wiggling her ass, she grinned to herself when she heard him mutter a curse.

"You're killing me," he said with a soft chuckle.

She rested against him, satiated and sleepy. "I don't want you to go home. I want to laze around with you this weekend."

"There's a pretty simple solution to that problem, you know?"

She lifted her head, meeting his gaze. "And what's that?"

He shrugged, ran his forefinger down her nose before he kissed it. "You could always come with me."

"Beautiful, it's okay," Carter told her after several seconds of silence. "You don't have to come home with me."

"No, I want to come with you. But would I meet your whole family, or something?"

He shrugged. "Maybe. We don't all hang out with each other every day. For all I know, they could be out of town."

Every single one of his siblings led busy lives and had challenging careers. They were a family of dedicated hard-workers. That work ethic had paid off, because each of them had made a small fortune in their current businesses.

"I can't imagine not knowing where Parker was."

"I'm sure Aisha can't imagine not knowing where

we are. It's a sister thing. I promise Parker isn't losing sleep over where your other brother is."

Brooklyn giggled. "You're probably right. And Bryson barely calls. I doubt he concerns himself with our whereabouts."

"You don't talk about Bryson. Where is he?"

She shrugged. "I have no idea. I haven't seen him in months. We get along, but Bryson cannot stand Senior."

"I guess that runs in your family."

Chuckling, she said, "I guess so. Well, Bryson has a valid reason to dislike Senior. His mother is my father's long-term mistress. When my mother died, my father moved him into the house. He rarely got to spend time with his mother, because my father is so overbearing. So he's a little resentful, that's all."

"Your father is . . . I'm not even sure I have a word that encapsulates everything that he is." He felt her tense and peered down at her. "Are you okay?"

She shook her head. "I don't want to ruin our snuggle moment with my troubles."

"Hey." He brushed his thumb over her jawline. "Don't be quiet now. Tell me."

Tears welled in her eyes and he frowned. She spoke so soft, so low that he wasn't sure he heard her right. "Promise me something."

"Anything."

"Promise me that when you come back on Monday, you're prepared to fight. My father has done duplicitous things under the guise of Wellspring Water business. He deserves a good dose of his own medicine. And I'm going to help."

Carter narrowed his gaze on her. "How would you help me?"

Brooklyn sucked in a deep breath before blurting out, "My father may have had something to do with my mother's death."

His eyes widened. "What?"

Brooklyn sat up and slipped on his shirt. "I met this woman last night. She was homeless, doped up. She knew my mother."

Carter hadn't asked about her mother much, but he knew she was an addict. "How did they know each other?"

"They grew up together in Wellspring, but the woman had moved away for some time. Sheriff Walker knew who she was right away."

Carter listened intently as Brooklyn explained her theory about how and why her mother died. He couldn't believe a man would be so evil to his own family, his children. If he'd had the chance to be a father to Chloe, he would treat her like the precious child she was.

"And I also believe that my father stole our birthright," Brooklyn continued. "If I'm right, it would mean that Parker and I have controlling interest in Wellspring Water Corp. If that's the case, then we can vote him out."

"So what's your plan?" he asked.

"I plan to break into his office and look for my mother's will."

It wasn't a good idea. Carter knew Brooklyn was determined to make things right, but he didn't trust Parker Sr. And he didn't want to end up in jail for another assault. Shaking his head, he said, "I don't think that's a realistic option. Knowing your father, he'd have you arrested for breaking and entering. You don't want to lose your license. You need it for your nonprofit."

She gave him a wobbly smile. "Thanks for being concerned, but I've got this. And it works out great. You'll be back on Monday. I'm sure my father and all his goons will want to see you being arraigned, so they'll go to court. While they're in court, I'll break into his home office. See. Easy peasy."

Easy peasy, my ass. "Beautiful, you're taking a big chance. Who's going to watch your back?"

"I can get Juke to come with me. He hates my father."

Carter took the opportunity to ask, "Who is Juke to you?"

She smirked. "Are you jealous?"

Pulling her onto his lap, he admitted, "Maybe."

Brooklyn wrapped her arms around his shoulders. "You have nothing to be jealous of. Juke is a good friend. And that's all he is."

"Good."

From her deck, Brooklyn stared out at brilliant blue sky. Carter was still sleeping peacefully, but sleep eluded her. Instead, she'd spent the morning trying to handle her business. She'd agreed to accompany Carter to Detroit, but there was business she needed to take care of in Wellspring.

Last night, Carter had talked her into thinking through an alternate plan that didn't involve her breaking and entering. But in the light of day, Brooklyn wasn't so sure she had time to wait and do things the right way. She'd reluctantly agreed to consult with the family attorney first. And if that didn't work, they'd try the courts.

In Michigan, the Last Will and Testament of any person must be delivered to the county's probate court. If her father had done everything above-board, they could petition the court for a copy. All she needed was a copy of the death certificate, and that was easy enough to get. That also meant that it might take longer to get the information she needed. And Brooklyn wasn't intent upon waiting.

Brooklyn leaned back in her chair and sipped her fresh cup of coffee, moaning low once it hit her lips. A lot had happened in the last few days, and none of it was expected. It was hard not to worry about the future, since it was so uncertain. The only things she was certain of were that she was falling for Carter and her father was full of shit.

She found herself praying that her father wasn't involved in her mother's death, but even as she prayed, she knew she couldn't put anything past him. One way or the other, she would find out the truth. She only hoped she would be able to do something about it before Carter's career was seriously derailed.

Brooklyn picked up her phone and dialed. Mr. Richardson, her mother's old attorney, answered after the first ring. "Hello, Brooklyn," the older man said. "What a nice surprise to hear from you."

"Hello, Mr. Richardson. I'm so glad you took my call. I have a request for you."

"What is it?"

Mr. Richardson had always been kind to her. She'd used him herself for several legal matters, but hadn't seen him since she'd moved back to town. "I need a copy of my mother's Last Will and Testament. Can you help me with that?"

There was silence on the other end of the line.

"Hello?" she called out. "Mr. Richardson, are you still there?"

"I'm here," he answered finally. "Why do you need a copy of your mother's will? Why don't you ask your father?"

"Because I'm asking you. You know as well as I do that I can't ask my father. I don't live in the house anymore. I suspect you already know that. He's taken all my money, had me fired from my job. He's a monster. So, no, I can't ask him for a copy of my mother's will. If you have any compassion, any sense of right versus wrong, you will help me."

"Brooklyn, I don't believe you know what you're doing. Your father will be very upset to find out that you're asking questions about your mother's will."

"Well, then, I hope you don't tell him. And forget it. I will let this go," she lied. "I'll find a way to mend fences with my father. Thank you."

Brooklyn ended the call and dialed another number. If Mr. Richardson wouldn't help her, she'd go to the one place that held the answers. Her father's home. "Parker, I need to see you. Meet me at Senior's house in twenty minutes."

She poked her head into her bedroom. Carter was still sleep. She pulled on a pair of sweatpants and a T-shirt. Before she could leave the house, though, her phone rang. It was her father. *Damn Mr. Richardson.*

"Daddy," Brooklyn answered. "What can I do for you?"

"Brooklyn," her father answered, his voice flat. "Are you ready to come home?"

"No. But I am ready for you to admit that you've taken this too far. I'm not your enemy, I'm your daughter. I haven't done anything to deserve this treatment from you."

"I told you I will do what I have to do. You do realize that your friend could have killed Sterling. His jaw is now wired shut. His father is understandably upset. How do you think that made me feel?"

"I don't really care how that made *you* feel. Imagine how Carter felt when Sterling approached him regarding his personal business. He didn't deserve that. He didn't deserve you and Sterling joining forces to ruin his career, his life. All he did was defend me, and you're gunning for him like he hurt me. The only person who's hurting me now is you."

She wasn't sure why she was appealing to her father. He wasn't going to budge. That much she was sure of. But if there was some off chance that he would let up, even for a little while, it would help Carter in the long run.

Brooklyn hadn't told Carter earlier, but her father had many judges under his thumb. And so did Sherman King. If they wanted him to serve time, he'd have to serve time. That's why it was so important she got the information she needed. It would mean leverage against her father.

"Carter Marshall brought this on himself. I hope you told him that jail is inevitable, because that's exactly where he's going, *if* you don't do what you're told."

She knew it was coming. She'd called it the moment she found out Carter had been arrested

for assaulting Sterling. Her father was going to use
her feelings for him against her. He was dangling
Carter's freedom in front of her. His freedom, for
her cooperation. And she'd choose Carter's freedom, because the thought of him doing hard time
for the assault was too much for her to bear. Her
father knew that, and he'd counted on it. Carter
just fell right into his hands.

"All my life, I've only wanted you to accept me
for who I am. But you never could do that. I always
come up short. I've met someone who makes me
feel beautiful. As my father, you should want that
for me. Except you don't. You don't want that, and
it hurts."

"I'm having a small dinner party at the house
this weekend," her father said, as if she hadn't just
spoken. "I expect to see you there."

"I won't be there. I'll be in Detroit. With Carter."

"You're making a grave mistake, Brooklyn. If you
want what's best for him, you'll leave him alone."

Brooklyn hung up on her father, without another word. It was useless to keep trying to reason
with him. She needed more than reason. She
needed to see her mother's will.

Carter had mentioned that his business partner,
Martin, had been a hacker at one point. And she
wondered if he could help them dig up dirt on her
father. Maybe he could find something on the dark
web that would tie him to criminal activity?

Brooklyn left Carter and her place and rushed to
her family home. When she pulled in the circular
driveway, she was met by Parker. She hopped out of
the car and hugged him. "Thanks for meeting me.

Sorry I'm late, but Senior called to threaten me yet again." She sighed. "When is this going to end?"

"Soon. I'm working on it."

Brooklyn and Parker walked the grounds, took the paved route to the lake. As they walked, Brooklyn updated him about Carter. Then she braced herself and told her brother what she'd found out from Lisa, and her own theories related to her mother's death.

When she finished her story, he clenched his fists. "If he had something to do with Mom's death . . ."

He left the thought open on purpose, she guessed. Because he really didn't know what he would do if they found out their father was responsible for their mother's death.

"I asked Mr. Richardson for a copy of the will, and he refused. So I figured I could try to find it myself. Here."

Guilt crept up in her. She'd told Carter that she wouldn't break in and steal, or do anything that could land her in a cell. But she couldn't just stand by and let her father get away with his lies. Again. He'd been getting away with everything as long as she'd been alive. And she was sick of it.

"No," Parker said with a firm shake of his head. "You're not doing anything. I need you to get out of town for today, enjoy the road trip with Carter, and let me handle this."

"We can work together, Parker. I am sick of him controlling my life. Our lives. I want to help. I didn't bring this to you so that you can fix it while I sit on my hands."

"Brooklyn, if Senior catches you in that house,

it's going to be war. I don't particularly want to have to kill my own father, no matter how evil he is."

She sighed. "Okay. But if you find out anything, please let me know."

Brooklyn opened her front door to find an envelope from Mr. Richardson. She'd mistakenly assumed that her father had called her earlier because Mr. Richardson had told her father that she'd called.

Her father had never mentioned Mr. Richardson, and now she had a manila envelope stuck in her door frame. How did he even know her new address? She unlocked the door and walked in, dropping her keys on the small table near the door.

Opening the envelope, she scanned the documents. *Jackpot.* Mr. Richardson must have taken pity on her because everything was in there in black and white. And there was a note.

Brooklyn,
 You won't hear from me again after today. I did, however, want you to have this. Please read it carefully. You'll have everything you need.

Shocked, Brooklyn leaned her hip against the wall to keep from toppling over. Marie had inherited a fortune from her grandmother, and had invested the money wisely. Her mother had even helped Senior, around the time he took over as CEO of the company, by investing her fortune in the company. Basically, her mother had owned the majority of shares in the company at the time of her death. And she'd left everything to Brooklyn and Parker.

Brooklyn had a feeling Lisa was telling some version of the truth in her fractured state. But she was still shocked to see it all on paper, on the notes written by her mother to Mr. Richardson, in the original copy of her Last Will and Testament.

Staring at the pages, she wondered what to do next. It has seemed almost too outrageous to be true, but it was. Her father was definitely a monster. He'd stolen their inheritance, passed her mother's money off as his own.

"Beautiful, what's going on?"

Brooklyn turned to Carter and handed him the documents. Then, she sent Parker a quick text to hold tight. "My mother's attorney . . . he gave us what we need to get out of this."

Chapter 19

Later on, Carter, Aisha, and Brooklyn headed to Detroit. Aisha left her car parked in front of the condo and hopped in the back seat of Carter's Jeep Grand Cherokee.

It almost seemed surreal, to be with him, on her way to meet his family. They'd only met each other a couple weeks ago. They were moving at light speed, and she realized someone probably needed to put the brakes on everything, but she couldn't bring herself to do it.

She wanted Carter. And she hoped nothing got in the way of the promise they had with each other.

Before they left, Parker had arrived and read over the will. Her brother was a talented lawyer, so she was certain he'd find something in it that they could use to their advantage. In her own review of the document, she'd already seen a few things that had given her pause.

On the way, she'd gotten a chance to pump Aisha with questions about Carter, and found that she loved his sister's dry sense of humor. The two had a lot in common, and Brooklyn couldn't wait to get to know her better.

The Detroit skyline came into view and she couldn't help but smile. It had always been one of her favorite cityscapes. Brooklyn was a proud Michigander, and had made it her mission to visit every county in the state. There was so much to do in her home state, and she made sure that everyone in her circle realized the hidden treasure that she had in Michigan. Her time in Boston had only cemented her love for the "Mitten," as they called it. She couldn't imagine living anywhere else.

Aisha was asleep in the back seat, and Carter and Brooklyn had spent the last hour talking about her plans for her new company.

"What are you going to do, Carter?" she asked. "About the contract?"

Carter shrugged, his gaze focused on the road. "Can't do anything about that right now. We have other projects, so I'm not worried too much about losing the Wellspring Water account. Although, I would prefer we didn't."

"I hate that you lost the account, too. Parker didn't want to terminate it." Her brother had tried everything in his power to prevent it, but the incident with Sterling had been the ultimate deciding factor. Nobody on the board wanted to be on Sherman King's bad side. The man was as ruthless as her father. He was almost worse, because people actually thought he cared, all while he stabbed them in the back.

She reached over and squeezed Carter's hand. "Thanks for inviting me home with you."

He kissed her hand. "I'm glad you took pity on me and agreed."

After she'd read over the will, she'd wanted to stay back in Wellspring and strategize with Parker. But her brother and Carter had double-teamed her. Parker assured her that he wouldn't make a move until she returned, which made her feel somewhat better. She definitely didn't want her brother once again taking all the risks with their father.

Scooting forward, she whispered in his ear. "If only your sister wasn't in the car, I'd show you just how much I want you right now."

"Well, you'll love the surprise I have for you then." He winked at her, and she settled back into the seat.

They arrived at Aisha's house about fifteen minutes later. Aisha hopped out of the car. "Call me later. Mom wants to see you."

"I still don't know why you told her what happened," Carter fussed. "She didn't need to know."

"Bye, Carter." Aisha waved over her shoulder as she walked toward her front door.

A little after three o'clock in the afternoon, they pulled up in front of Carter's condo. He carried her bags inside the house, and before she could even look around, he had her pinned against the wall.

His hands skimmed up her sides, and around her back to finally rest on her ass. "How much do you want me again?" he asked, trailing a line of wet kisses down her neck.

Her head fell back against the wall, as his finger traced her slit through her panties. "I want you more than you know," she murmured.

Then he pulled away and pointed directly at the pool table standing in the middle of his living room. "Want to break this in?"

It was glorious, Brooklyn thought as she brushed her hands over the dark wood. One of the best she'd seen, for sure. It smelled new and she wished she would have brought her stick. "You tricked me. I didn't bring my cue stick. I don't shoot with anyone else's."

"It's a good thing you don't use anyone else's stick." He circled her like a lion would its prey. "I had something else entirely in mind."

Carter had been fantasizing about having Brooklyn on a pool table since their candlelight game. His mind raced with the many ways he could take her, but he settled on one in particular.

"What are you thinking?" she asked, a sexy gleam in her brown eyes.

"I'm thinking I want to bend you over and take you against the corner pocket." He pointed to the spot. "Right there."

Something flashed in her eyes. The challenge was written across her face. She wasn't going to back down, and he wouldn't either. She rounded the table, moving away from him. She wasn't making this easy. He stalked closer to her, gripped the hem of her shirt, and tugged her to him. Her eyes went wide when he placed her hand over his rock-hard erection.

"Carter," she breathed. "You're really glad to see me."

He laughed. "I'd be even more glad if you took your clothes off."

Without warning, or any hint of shyness, she pulled her shirt off and dropped it on the floor. "I like your place," she said, pushing her pants down to the floor.

"Thank you," he croaked, unable to take his eyes off of her. She was lovely, with her black lace boy-shorts and matching bra. Everything about her seemed tailor-made for him, from her narrow waist to her curvy hips to her tight ass. He could barely think when she was close to him, so tempting, so damn beautiful.

Brooklyn turned around and removed her panties. Glancing at him over her shoulder, she winked. "You want to bend me over the table, huh?"

"Hell yeah," he answered truthfully.

"After you bend me over the table, what happens next?" She turned to face him again and unhooked the front latch of her bra. It fell open, giving him a glimpse of her perfect breasts and pebbled nipples.

Brooklyn got off on word play, and he found that he liked turning her on with his words. "First things first, I'm going to kiss every inch of your body, taste you until you come screaming my name, over and over again."

She braced a hand on the ledge of the pool table, swallowing visibly. "Damn, you're getting good at this. And then what?"

He stepped forward, and she took a careful step back. "Then I'll do it again, until your legs are weak and your body is on fire for me."

"Yes," she whispered, her hooded gaze on him. "I want that."

And Carter wanted it, too. More than he wanted his next breath or water or even food.

He stopped directly in front of her. "Once I've had my fill of you, tasted every inch of you, I'll turn you around and sink myself deep inside you."

Brooklyn's eyes darkened. "Carter?" She unbuckled his belt, and slid it off.

"Brooklyn."

She unzipped his pants and pushed them over his hips. "Are you ready?"

"Always."

The slow smile that spread across her face told him that she was definitely in the moment with him. She tugged his shirt over his head, kissed his chest with soft, wet kisses. Then she dropped to her knees and yanked his boxers down.

She sucked him into her mouth, circling the head before taking him in deeper. Carter's head fell back, reveling in the feel of her lips around his length. Teasing, she traced his length with her tongue, cupping his balls in her hands and squeezing.

Unable to control his actions, his hips pushed forward, settling into a slow rhythm as she pleasured him. It was an experience he'd never had before. Brooklyn was a like a force of nature, like an act of God that he couldn't control or predict. The way she trusted him with her body, the way she never shied away from his touch, made him yearn to do anything he could to prove himself worthy of her.

Groaning, he held the back of her head, brushed his fingers through her short curls. He watched her as she blew him, marveling at the pleasure on her face. Almost like she enjoyed it as much, if not more, than he did. "Beautiful, you have to stop."

Gripping her shoulders, he pulled her up and captured her lips with his. Turning her around, he bent her over the table and pushed into her. Emotion filled Carter as she pulsed around him. Leaning his forehead against the back of her neck, he nipped at the skin there.

"So good." Carter felt strung out, like an addict. Only there was no rehab in his future because his life, his existence, depended on her. In the short time he'd known her, she'd seeped into his soul, took up residence in his thoughts. He was lost in her, so addicted to her light and her love. *Love?*

Carter was closer to paradise than he ever thought he would be. From the moment he'd pulled her out of the path of that car, he'd been helpless to stop the rush of feelings that only grew stronger each day he saw her or talked to her. The feeling that he could actually breathe again wasn't lost on him. He'd promised himself that he'd never fall in love again, but then she was there and she made it okay to be himself, to let go. She'd made him feel something that he thought was lost to him. When she wasn't with him, he thought about her. When they were together, he felt a high he hadn't felt in years. *Ever?* No one else mattered but her, but the fire they created together.

Brooklyn pushed back against him, drawing him from his thoughts. "Baby, where did you go?"

Gripping her hips, he pulled out almost completely before pounding into her again. "I'm right here, beautiful."

She glanced back at him, pulled him into a wet kiss. "Don't stop. Please."

That one word was all he needed. Carter swept a hand over her back, tracing her spine with his thumb as he thrust in and out, in and out. Smoothing a hand around her ass, he smacked it lightly.

"Shit," she muttered. "That's it."

"You like that?" he asked, reaching around her and cupping her in his hand. She was wet with desire for him.

"Yes."

With his other hand he gripped her shoulder, picking up his pace, pushing her to the edge that he knew she was close to falling over. Bending down, he whispered against her ear, "You love this, don't you? You love when I brand you, make you mine with every stroke. I won't be satisfied until I've had you in every way possible, until you realize that I'm the only man that will ever make you feel this way. I want you, Brooklyn. So bad I can taste it whenever you're in the room, so bad that I can feel the emptiness in my gut when you're not around. Lose control in me, the same way I've lost it in you."

Brooklyn came then, long and hard, with his name on her lips. He found his release next, digging his fingers into her hips as she milked him, pulling him over the edge with her.

* * *

A little while later, Brooklyn relaxed against Carter's chest. The warm water felt like heaven to her aching muscles. After they'd made love, it was a few minutes before she could even think, let alone move. He'd carried her through the house to the master bathroom and proceeded to run a bath for them both.

He brushed a sponge over her quivering stomach, and she moaned. "I could get used to this, Carter."

"Me, too."

A comfortable silence settled between them for a few moments as he lathered her body and washed her. *How is it even possible to want him again?* Pool-table sex was definitely an experience that would be ingrained in her heart forever.

"I never thought I could do this again," Carter said, his voice soft . . . unsure.

"What do you mean?" He linked his hand with hers, kissed the inside of her wrist. It was a small gesture, but one she felt to her core.

"I almost don't want to say, because I'm hesitant to bring Krys in this bathroom with us."

Krys. His wife. When Carter had explained to her that he'd been married and lost his wife and child to a fire, she was sad for him. The pain still seemed to be just underneath the surface, and it had explained his behavior toward her.

At the same time, she wasn't stupid. Carter had loved his wife. And there was a strong part of her that wondered if he'd ever be able to love her the way he loved his wife. The "fixer" in her wanted to give him space, let him work his way through the emotions involved in finally moving forward with his life after such a devastating loss. But there was another part—the part of her that didn't want to open herself up for future heartbreak, pining after a man that was incapable of loving her the way she deserved.

Brooklyn knew Carter wanted her. That was a no-brainer. But did he care for her? *Can he love me?* She was pretty sure she already loved him. It wasn't even logical to love someone so much, so fast. *Right?* But she knew that she did, just as sure as she knew the sky was blue, the sun was hot, and chocolate and coffee were two of God's greatest creations. Brooklyn wasn't a *love at first sight* believer, but that's what she'd gone and done. She'd fallen in love pretty much the moment he pulled her to safety that cold March night. And every day since then, she'd fallen deeper; harder.

"I think you know you can talk to me about anything, even the uncomfortable things." She pressed his hand against her beating heart. "As long as I'm alive, as long as you can feel my heartbeat in your palm, I'll be here for you."

Carter brushed his lips over her temple, lingering there for a few seconds before he continued. "After Krys died, I wasn't sure I could ever love someone again, not the way I loved her. It was easier to not engage, to not bring another woman into my box of pain. I don't want to hurt you."

Brooklyn braced herself—for what, she wasn't sure.

"For the first time in forever, though, I feel hope," Carter continued. "When I'm around you, when you're telling me crazy things about Juicy Fruit or talking about your dreams, I'm always hit with this urge to keep you. It sounds weird, and even impossible, to want you the way I do, even though we've only known each other for a short time. But I want to wake up in the morning and live every moment of every day because you're here. You're with me, and you actually like me."

"I love you." Her eyes widened and she bit down on her lip. Hard. Her admission shocked even herself. She hadn't planned to say those words to him. And now that it was out there, in the atmosphere, she felt like she'd stripped herself bare, down the bone.

Brooklyn's first impulse was to apologize and tell him she didn't mean to put him on the spot. But she wouldn't apologize because she wasn't actually sorry. And saying the words would be a protection mechanism, a way to even the playing field a little in case he didn't feel the way she did.

When he didn't say anything, she forged ahead. "I've always been the type of person that has no qualms about speaking her mind. So I won't start censoring my thoughts now. I'm already in love with you. And, call me crazy, but I trust you with my heart, even though you don't completely trust yourself yet."

"How?" he asked.

"What makes you feel unworthy to love and be loved again?"

Carter blew out a shaky breath. "I wasn't there, Brooklyn. I wasn't there for Krys when she needed me. I was too busy working, too busy being Carter Marshall to even pick up the phone when she called me the night she died."

Carter explained the circumstances surrounding

the fire, the phone call that his wife had made, the final text that she'd sent. Brooklyn knew that guilt could suffocate even the strongest person. And she didn't want Carter to give in to that feeling.

She wanted to hold him, to wrap him in her arms. Her heart broke at the turmoil she heard in his voice. She turned, the water sloshing around her. Wrapping her legs around his waist, she met his gaze. "Carter, did Krys know your name?"

Frowning, he nodded. "Of course she did."

"Did she know you were Carter Marshall when you married her?"

"Yes, but—"

"But she still married you. She still loved you, Carter. You were the last person she wanted to speak to before she died. And when she didn't get you, she sent you exactly what she thought about you in that text. I suspect she did it because she didn't want you to punish yourself forever."

Brooklyn would have done the same thing, had she been in that position. She wouldn't have wanted the man she loved to succumb to grief, not when each second they had on earth, each minute, was a chance to make it right.

She gripped his chin, forcing him to meet her gaze. "So forgive yourself. You didn't cause the fire and you didn't ignite the flames. You were a victim just like Krys and Chloe were. The only difference is you were the one that was left to pick up the pieces. Just like we have the right to choose our path, you have to choose to move forward. It's not easy. But I have to believe it's worth it, that life is worth the pain. Because on the other side of pain, is joy—even in the midst of sorrow."

Chapter 20

Carter stared at Brooklyn in awe as she mingled with his family. From the moment they'd arrived at his mother's house, Brooklyn had taken to her family like bees to honey. And they seemed to enjoy her, too.

She was amazing. That evening, while he was bathing with her, she'd given him a gift. The gift of understanding. She hadn't tried to belittle his feelings, or make him feel worse. She simply loved him for it, she accepted him for the man he was. Flaws and all.

He watched as Martin and Ryleigh chatted with Brooklyn on the other side of the room. When his best friend had arrived earlier, Martin immediately wanted to meet the woman who had made him lose all of his common sense. And when he introduced them, Brooklyn had managed to charm Martin as well. She and Ryleigh had hit it off immediately, bonding over the joys of small-town living and cooking. They'd already planned a visit to Ryleigh's hometown of Rosewood Heights, South Carolina.

"Son?"

Carter turned to face his mother. Pulling her into a tight hug, he kissed her forehead. "Mama, thank you for cooking for us."

"Aw, you're welcome."

He let his attention drift back to Brooklyn, who was now surrounded by his brothers. Both men were flirting blatantly with her, but he wasn't worried. Because every time their eyes locked from across the room, he was assured that he was the one she wanted. *How did I get so lucky?*

"She's a beautiful woman, son. I like her. And I can't wait to beat her at pool. She told me about your losing streak."

Carter glanced at his mother and chuckled. "She is a beautiful woman, and she did crack my head on the pool table."

He'd seen his mother chatting with Brooklyn a little earlier. The two women had been huddled in the corner, discussing something in a low tone. Carter had been tempted to interrupt, but thought better of it. His mother was a trip on a normal day, and so was Brooklyn. Putting those two together had to mean trouble.

"I'd say it's pretty obvious," his mother added.

A smile tugged at his mouth. "Obvious?"

His mother rocked back on her heels, clapped her hands hard, as if she'd had a revelation. "You're falling in love. And speaking as the mother who watched you drown in sorrow for the past few years, I'd have to say it makes me happy to be able to witness it."

Carter dropped his eyes to the hardwood floor. He felt his mother cup the back of his neck, a gesture she'd done since he was a child, one that let him know that she had his back, that she supported him and wouldn't let him fall.

She tilted her head and peered into his eyes. "It's a good thing, son. Embrace it. Embrace her. It's okay. You definitely have your mother's approval. Not that you need it."

Carter had spent several hours making love to Brooklyn that day. After their bath, after she'd reduced him to tears . . . well, *a* tear, she'd loved him leisurely and thoroughly right in the tub. Then he'd taken her to his bed and worshipped her body for another hour, until his mother had called and broke them out of the haze of desire.

"And you know your mama is right," she continued. "If I tell you a duck could pull a truck, don't ask me no questions, just hook the damn duck up."

Carter barked out a laugh. The duck pulling the truck was one of his mother's favorite sayings. It meant that he'd do well to listen to her, no matter how far-fetched it seemed, just because she'd been the one to say it. He could trust her judgment. Iris Johnston was a wise woman, and she'd been spot-on in her observations 90 percent of the time.

"Alright, Ma."

Brooklyn finally made her way over to the two of them. Her grin was a mile wide and there was a blush creeping up her neck. "Your brothers are crazy."

Carter glanced over her shoulder at his younger brothers. They each tipped their beer bottle to him, and he wondered what they'd said to cause his girl to blush. "What did they say?"

Brooklyn glanced at his mother at his side, then

back at him. She averted her gaze. "They just gave me a few pointers, that's all."

"Oh Lord," his mother said, waving a dismissive hand in the air. "Don't listen to those nasty boys. Probably said something about sex."

Brooklyn's blush deepened, and she let out a nervous laugh. "I can't have this conversation with you, Mama Johnston. But you do know your sons."

His mother laughed. Loud. Clapping her hands with glee, she said, "I really like you, Brooklyn. I'm looking forward to spending more time with you."

"I can't wait to visit again soon. And next time, I'll bring my cue stick."

"Be prepared to lose. Just sayin'."

Brooklyn giggled. "We'll see. It'll be a pleasure to bust that winning streak you have."

In a move that shocked Carter and Brooklyn, his mother pulled his girl into a tight hug. "I would give you my spiel about taking care of my son. But something tells me you already have that covered."

A look passed between the two women, before Brooklyn nodded. "I definitely do."

"What's going on?" he asked.

"I was just telling your mother not to worry about the arraignment. I have it under control."

Carter folded his arms over his chest. "You do, huh?"

Before they'd left his house to come to his mom's house, Brooklyn had taken a call in the second bedroom. When he'd asked her who she was talking to, she told him it was her brother, but hadn't elaborated. Parker had called her several times since she'd been in Detroit, but each time she'd taken it in another room or told Parker she'd call him back.

He knew her brother was just concerned about his sister. He was the same way about Aisha, but something was off.

They chatted with his mother for a few more minutes, until his mother excused herself to take care of something in the kitchen.

Carter reached out and trailed his fingers down Brooklyn's cheek. Being so close to her, and not being able to touch her the way he wanted, was torture. He wanted to yank her to him, kiss her until her legs buckled and she pleaded with him to take her.

Martin walked up to them. "We're going to head home, Carter. I have some work to get done."

Carter nodded. "Thanks for coming by."

Earlier, he'd had a chance to talk to Martin about the Wellspring Water account. "I'll see you Monday morning at the courthouse."

Carter was glad to know that he'd have support in the courtroom. Martin, Ryleigh, and Aisha all planned to be there, which helped. He wasn't nervous about the outcome, but he was concerned. He'd just started living again, and he didn't want to have to spend any time in jail.

Brooklyn had asked if he'd mind going back to Wellspring late Sunday evening, and he'd agreed. He was still curious to know what she was up to, but he wouldn't push her. The dynamics in her family were complicated at best.

On their way out, his mother brought out a bag full of food and shoved it into his hands. "Take this food. You can eat it for lunch tomorrow, or take it on the road. Okay?"

"Thanks, Ma." He gave his mother a hug, then

stepped aside so that Brooklyn could do the same. They said their goodbyes to the rest of his family.

Monday morning came fast. Brooklyn and Carter had driven back to Wellspring late Sunday night. They'd decided to stay at her place for the night. Carter had ordered a pizza and they watched a horror movie before falling asleep in each other's arms.

When she'd awakened that morning, she'd told Carter that she had to make a run to meet Parker, and that she'd meet him at the courthouse. And now she was waiting for one final chat before all hell broke loose.

Martin used his special skills and retrieved a copy of the will that was filed with the court. They didn't want to take a chance of going to the court and asking to see the document, and risk her father finding out that they were looking. Carter then forwarded her the email. When she'd reviewed the document, she went cold. Her father's deception had run much deeper than wills and small secrets. Parker Sr. had committed a crime. He'd changed her mother's Last Will and Testament. He'd successfully taken control of the company, despite her mother's stipulation that all her shares be transferred to her children.

Carter had asked her what was going on, but she'd evaded the question. While they were away, Parker had located several documents that were relevant to their mother's committal. Her father did commit her mother and had attempted to take control of her finances through a conservatorship.

It wasn't long after that that Brooklyn's mother died. The more she found out about her father, the more convinced she was that he did something to her mother. The thought made her sick to her stomach.

"Brooklyn,"

She glanced up at her father. "What?" After what she'd read, she refused to call him *Daddy* ever again, because she didn't feel like he'd been a daddy to her. Yes, he'd supported her financially for years, but he didn't love her like a father should love his child. That much was obvious by his complete and utter lack of respect for her right to choose her own husband.

"You will respect me, Brooklyn Wells."

"You can't demand respect. You have to earn it. And from where I'm sitting, you don't deserve my respect."

"I will not argue with you about this." Her father gestured to the immediate area. "Why did you ask me to come here, of all places?"

Brooklyn snickered. Her father always looked down on everything that wasn't gold plated. He'd refused to help any local charities, preferring to support charities that gave him and Wellspring Water greater visibility and helped his image.

They were in Red Rock Park, which had been owned and operated by Wellspring Water, until her father had tried to sell it a few years back. The community had been so outraged they'd collected the money necessary to buy the park. After the sale, her father had refused to ever visit the place again because the residents of Wellspring had the nerve to undermine his business decision. Which was a shame, because Red Rock Park was a beautiful and popular park.

"I wanted to meet you in a neutral place."

He looked at her with disgust. "I hate that short hair on you."

"It's okay, because Carter loves it."

"Carter will love the jailhouse when he's thrown back in after today's arraignment."

Brooklyn took a steadying breath. "Carter isn't going to jail."

Her father stood over her, dwarfing her and blocking her sunlight. "Either you break things off with him and agree to marry Sterling, or your friend Carter is headed to jail. There will be no more second chances."

"See, that's where you're wrong. I'm not going to stop seeing Carter and you're not going to make me."

"I'm not sure who you've been talking to, or even who you think you're talking to, but you're not going to defy me without huge consequences. And I'm sure your friend likes his business."

Parker joined them, stepping up beside Brooklyn, his hands in his pockets and a scowl on his face.

Her father eyed them both. "Is this supposed to be some kind of double-team?"

"No, nothing like that," Parker said. "We're just done living by your rules."

"What are you going to do about it?" Parker Sr. challenged. "You have no power over me."

"It's simple. If Carter goes to jail, you will go to jail," Brooklyn said.

Her father bit out a humorless laugh. "We'll see about that."

"Yeah, we will. I have Mom's will in my possession. The original one." Her father's face fell. It was the first time she'd ever seen him lose his game face, and she felt the swoosh of victory wash over her. "You used that fake will to gain control of a company that does not belong to you."

"Senior, did you even think about your actions?" Parker asked. "Mom used her money to help you, and how did you repay her? You abused her, and then committed her against her will. All so you could run this company."

"Did you have mom killed?" Brooklyn asked.

Her father's gaze locked on her. "What?" Senior frowned. "Why would you ask me that?"

Brooklyn didn't think her father was that good of an actor. He genuinely seemed shocked at her accusation. "It just didn't feel like it was an accident."

"That was your grief talking. I didn't hurt your mother."

"Why should I believe you?"

"Brooklyn, me and your mother had problems, but I didn't kill her."

There was something about the tone in her father's voice that sounded like regret. And Lord help her, she believed him. It still didn't excuse all the other things he'd done. "I suggest you lay low, call the DA's office, make up any excuse, I don't care. Do whatever you have to do to convince Sterling and his family to drop the charges."

"You're making a huge mistake. I won't take this lying down. You don't want me as your enemy, so think long and hard about this."

"No, you think long and hard about this. I'm not afraid to use this." She held up a manila envelope and handed it to him. "Since you seem to think I'm playing with you."

Brooklyn glanced up at Parker as her father skimmed through the contents of the envelope. Even though she'd waited for that moment for years, satisfaction eluded her. There was nothing to be satisfied about. Her father had manipulated them all for years, lied to them about their mother and everything that happened between them. He'd basically spit on her mother's memory and her last wishes, in order to retain control of Wellspring Water.

And now she was going to make sure he couldn't do that to them or Carter.

Carter sat in the courtroom, his back to everyone. He'd been ordered to take a seat with his attorney. For a few tense moments, he wasn't sure if Brooklyn would make it. She'd rushed into the courtroom right before they'd called his case on the docket.

He glanced over at the King family, seated on the left of the massive space. They'd actively avoided him the entire time he sat in the room—until Brooklyn had arrived. From that moment on, Mr. King had done everything in his power to distract Carter from the matter at hand. He'd taken time to walk over to them and introduce himself.

Carter asked how Sterling was doing. The surgery was a success, and now Sterling had to take some time to heal. His jaw was still wired shut and would be for the next several days. But he'd be okay, no lasting effects, which made Carter breathe easier.

Judge Arnold entered the courtroom and they all

stood. "In the matter of the State of Michigan versus Mr. Carter Marshall, the court finds that there is insufficient evidence to proceed. This case is dismissed."

Carter turned back to his family and friends and then to Brooklyn, who'd stood, her eyes filled to the brim with tears. He shook his attorney's hand and walked around the barrier to his family. His sister pulled him into a tight hug and Martin patted his back.

Turning to Brooklyn, he pulled her into his arms. She held on to him. "Don't let me go," she murmured into his chest. He ran a soothing hand over her back, resting his chin against the top of her head, and she cried.

"I won't," he told her. "I'll never let you go."

Carter meant it. Although he hadn't said the words, he knew that he'd fallen headfirst in love with Brooklyn. And he had no intention of letting her go. The thought of her being with another man, made him want to fight. He was tired of fighting, tired of being angry. He'd let his grief consume him to the point where he'd shut down and shut out the people who cared the most about him. Sure, he'd talked to his sister and Martin, but he'd always held a piece of himself back. He didn't want to do that anymore.

The world was full of disappointment, but he'd been blessed to not only love one person beyond measure, but to feel the warmth of unconditional love with another woman. He'd been given a second chance to do things right, to work smarter, to take time off to be with his family, to laugh more. Those were things he wanted to do with Brooklyn.

Tilting his head to the ceiling, he silently thanked God, and Krys, for sending Brooklyn to him. "I love you," he said.

She pulled back, met his gaze. "Carter, you don't—"

"I do." He caressed her cheek, traced a finger over her ear lobe. "I do. You bared your heart to me the other day and I didn't say anything. But I felt it. I feel it now. You didn't have to be here for me. You didn't have to believe in me. Because of you, I want to be better, I want to do better. So, yes, I love you. And I want to make this work."

He captured her bottom lip in his lips, drawing her closer and deeper into the kiss. She gripped his collar and gave herself over to him. "I'm so happy the charges were dismissed. Now you can focus on Marshall and Sullivan, and getting your life back." She cupped his cheek in her hand. "Let's celebrate."

Later on, at Brook's Pub, Brooklyn and Carter sat at the bar. They'd treated Martin, Ryleigh, and Aisha to dinner at the Bee's Knees, because Aisha insisted on trying the western omelet Carter had told her about. All three were back in their rooms at the hotel, changing clothes.

Brooklyn had planned a walking tour of Wellspring for their out-of-town guests. She wanted them to see everything that made her part of the state unique and fresh.

Juke leaned in. "I'm glad you beat those charges, man," he told Carter. "It's high time someone else won in this town. Senior is a dirty old bastard."

That seemed to be the consensus amongst the townsfolk. Carter had wound up being a sort of hero. Kids had been approaching him all day, asking if he could teach them how to fight. Brooklyn thought it was cute, but Carter, ever the humble person, would brush them off and tell them to concentrate on school instead.

Carter nodded. "I understand that. Maybe this is the start of a new era for Wellspring?"

Brooklyn raised her shot glass. "Let's toast to that." They all raised their filled shot glasses. "To a new era of badass people who aren't content to live in their parents' shadows."

They clinked their glasses together and took their shots. "Brooklyn."

Carter twisted in his seat and nodded at Parker. "Hey, Parker."

"Hey, brother," Brooklyn called over her shoulder. "Have a seat, take a shot."

"I've been trying to call you."

The brisk tone in Parker's voice wasn't lost on Brooklyn, and she turned around. "My phone is dead. What's up?"

Parker bowed his head, grumbling a curse. "It's Senior."

Brooklyn stood to her feet. "What is it? Did he do something? Is he trying to sue Carter? What is it?"

"He's had a heart attack. He's in the hospital. The doctors don't think he'll make it through the night."

Chapter 21

Brooklyn stood at the foot of her father's hospital bed. What a difference a few hours made! That morning, her father had been tall and strong, almost horrific in the way he'd treated them. After they'd shown him the documents, he'd been uncharacteristically quiet.

Now, he was lying in the hospital, wires coming out of everywhere and a tube in his throat. He was so still. Her father had only used stillness as a skill to intimidate or manipulate other's into doing what he wanted. It had worked for years.

Parker stood behind her, his hand on the small of her back. "It's not your fault."

"I pushed this thing with Mom's will. He probably had a heart attack because he thought there was a good chance I'd make good on the threat to expose him."

"Brooklyn, he had a heart attack because that's what people do when they are older and under stress."

But the stress had been caused by her, and her

decisions. Swallowing hard, she approached her father's still form. When they'd arrived, the doctors had ushered them into the room, warning them along the way to expect a change in his appearance. His face was sunken in and pale. Unable to breath on his own, her father was hooked up to a ventilator. Her gaze dropped to his chest, noted the way he seemed to struggle to breathe.

The nurse had informed them that her father hadn't signed an advance healthcare directive, which was a shock to her. She's always assumed he wouldn't want any extraordinary measures taken. It didn't make sense to Brooklyn, knowing how independent her father was. Parker Wells Sr. wouldn't want to depend on anyone. He'd make sure the plug was pulled before he'd have to.

"Get. Out."

Brooklyn spun around and was met with a furious Patricia. Her blond wig forgotten, her dear stepmother was dressed in a pair of trousers and a silk top. Brooklyn tried to put herself in Patricia's shoes. If something were wrong with Carter, she'd make sure that anyone that would do him harm was far away from the hospital. Except, she and Parker were Senior's children.

She didn't agree with her father's actions, but still wished that one day he'd apologize and actually tell her the truth about her mother's life and her mother's death.

Patricia stalked toward them, her arms clenched at her sides. "This is a private hospital room, and neither of you are welcome here."

Parker stepped forward, a deep frown on his face. "Patricia, back the hell up. This is our father. We're going to be his children long after he divorces your ass. So if anyone is going to get out, it's going to be you."

Angry, Patricia yelled, "If it wasn't for you, we wouldn't be here. He told me, you know?"

"What exactly did he tell you?" Brooklyn asked.

"All about you and your new boyfriend, how you disrespected him by snubbing Sterling." She tossed an angry glare at Parker. "And you. He told me about how you overrode him on the decision to fire her boyfriend."

Brooklyn released a breath she hadn't realized she was holding. Her father hadn't told Patricia everything. Which meant one of two things—either he didn't care enough to tell her, or he didn't trust her enough to tell her. Judging by her stepmother's track record, the rumors of affairs that had dogged her around town, she assumed it was the latter. Her father didn't trust his wife. That was saying a lot in itself, and made her wonder why he'd stayed with her. The marriage had lasted a lot longer than the others.

"You don't know what you're talking about, Patricia," Brooklyn said simply. "And I suggest you back the hell off."

The monitors went off, and a slew of medical personnel barreled into the room. Brooklyn's heart sank as they worked on him. A kind nurse asked them to wait outside in the hallway, but she was rooted to her spot and didn't want to take her eyes off of him.

Patricia cried and screamed and acted a fool, and was subsequently escorted out of the room. *Ever the drama queen.* And Parker stood next to her,

his head down. It took several minutes, but the
doctors stabilized her father. Brooklyn slumped
against the wall, relief coursing through her.

She didn't particularly like her father at that
moment, but she didn't want him to die. She
thought about all the times she'd said she hated
him behind his back. Did he ever hear her? Did he
even care if she hated him or not? She wasn't sure
of the answers to those questions, but she prayed
that one day she'd be able to ask him all the questions that haunted her about his actions. And she
hoped to receive an honest answer because it felt
important to her to know his motivation for the
things he'd done.

Several hours later, Brooklyn and Parker were
still at the hospital, waiting. Many of the townspeople had called to see how they were doing. It
really was a testament to the wonderful people of
Wellspring. Most of them couldn't stand her father,
but they cared about her and Parker. So they showed
support. Will and Dee Clark had brought them
food, Sheriff Walker had come to sit with them for
an hour. Juke offered to sneak them in a shot of
something to take the edge off. Of course, she'd
turned him down, but it was nice to feel loved.

Brooklyn had been texting Carter all day. He was
with his family, trying to entertain them. He'd tried
to come up to the hospital, but she'd told him that
she was alright and that he should stay with his
family. But she missed him, and damn it . . . she
needed him.

It had been a long, draining day. Brooklyn felt
icky, like she needed a shower. But the hospital was
so far from town, she didn't want to take the chance

and go home. What if something changed? What if he died?

"Brooklyn?"

Her head snapped up, and she looked straight into the waiting eyes of Carter. She stood up and rushed into his arms.

Carter had been unable to stay away, even though Brooklyn had told him to stay with his family. They'd tried to distract him, asking him a ton of questions about the town. But he couldn't concentrate on them when he was worried about her.

Aisha must have sensed his mood, because she was the first one who said she wanted to head back to Detroit. Martin and Ryleigh had followed suit and soon they were headed back to the "D."

Carter had wasted no time. He stopped by Brooklyn's condo and grabbed her a set of clothes and made his way to the hospital. "I should have come sooner," he said against her neck, taking in her soft scent.

Brooklyn wrapped her arms around his neck. "You're here now. That's all that matters."

He stood like that for a moment, holding her close to his heart. When they pulled apart, he brushed a tear from her cheek. "I brought you a change of clothes."

She smiled. "Thank you."

Brooklyn was still wearing her clothes from that morning, a pair of charcoal-gray slacks and a silk blouse. He'd grabbed her a pair of sweats and a T-shirt.

They walked to a family lounge where there was

a shower and changing room. Carter stood guard while Brooklyn showered and changed. When she was done, they made their way back over to the waiting area where Parker was waiting.

Brooklyn looked down at her brother, who was busy checking his email on his phone. "If you want to go change, I'll stay here with Senior."

Parker sighed. "I guess I could use a break. So can you."

"I'm fine, Parker. Carter is here, so I won't be alone. I need you to take some time, to take care of yourself."

Standing to his feet, Parker hugged Brooklyn and kissed her forehead. "Thanks, sis. I'll be back within the hour."

He shook Carter's hand and disappeared through the automatic doors.

"Did you eat?" Carter asked, pulling her onto his lap. "I can bring you something to eat."

Leaning her head against his, she shook her head. "I'm actually pretty full. Will and Dee brought food up here. I believe there is some left. The nurse put it in the fridge in the back, if you want some."

"I'm not hungry."

"Where did your family go?"

Carter explained that they left so he could be here for her. She tucked herself in the nook of his arm and he hugged her.

"I love your family, ya know? They are so genuine, warm. I can't wait to get to know them better."

Carter smiled. He loved his family, too. One thing was sure, they weren't conventional. They had no filter and didn't hesitate to tell anyone how they felt on any given day. But they were his. He was glad Brooklyn had been received so well. Because he already knew that she was going to be a permanent part of his life. He just didn't know when he would make his move.

Since things had moved with warp speed, he felt that they needed more time to settle in with each other. At the same time, though, he felt like he knew everything he needed to know about her to feel comfortable taking the next step. *Time will tell.*

"I don't really have much family," Brooklyn said. "My father had one brother; he died when he was in his teens. That's it. My mother was an only child. I don't have any cousins, any uncles. The only people I have are my Wellspring family. Until I met you, that is."

Carter couldn't imagine not having family. He'd pushed them all away, but there was something about knowing that they would never truly let him drift too far off course. They'd always be there no matter what, no matter what he'd said in anger to push them away.

He squeezed her. "Well, you can borrow mine. You'll want to give them back eventually, but they're yours."

She laughed, and it was the sweetest sound he'd ever heard. It made him look forward to spending time in Wellspring. He knew it had more to do with Brooklyn than anything, but the desire was still there nonetheless.

"I'd never give them back. They are too much fun."

"Wait until you really see them in action. That little get-together on Saturday was tame compared to the other ones. Barbecues in the summer, the

Christmas Eve party my mom throws every single year. It's almost too much." *But somehow not enough.*

She drew her feet up under her. "My father was always a loner—is a loner. He never liked to have company, and I didn't understand why. I still don't. I like to have people around. I always wanted a big, fun family."

"I'm going to have to take you to the family reunion picnic that my mother's seven siblings have every summer."

"That sounds awesome."

A doctor called from the entrance to the floor. "Ms. Wells?"

Brooklyn stood up and walked toward the doctor. "Hi. Any word?"

"I'm sorry," the doctor said. "We've done all that we can. Your father has slipped into a coma."

"Daddy, they say you can hear me." Brooklyn sat next to her father's bed. "I just want to tell you that I don't hate you. These past few weeks, years, have been rough. I had hoped that we'd be able to talk about things. I have so many questions but they aren't relevant right now. I just wish we could have found common ground."

Brooklyn's conflicted emotions where her father was concerned had colored how she viewed him. A part of her knew that her father wasn't the best husband to her mother, just like he wasn't the best father to her or Parker or Bryson. Had his father treated him the same way, and Senior didn't know how else to be?

They'd never discussed Grandpa much. And she didn't remember him, not like Parker did. Her brother had memories of fishing at the river with him, of spending nights building fires and making s'mores. Brooklyn had always wondered where the disconnect was. But she'd never had a chance to ask her father why it was easier for him to ignore them than love them.

"I want to forgive you. I want to forget the nasty things you've said to me, the way you treated me in front of people. I want to know why I was never good enough for you. I can't understand why."

She picked up her father's hand. "But I'm going to pray for you anyway, like I always do. And I'm going hope that one day, we can actually have the conversation. We can actually move past the disappointment and the mistakes and have a real father-daughter relationship."

She rested her head against the edge of the bed. The doctor had told her that her father could be in a coma for days, for months. She hoped her father wouldn't have to spend the rest of his life laid up in the bed. For a man who'd never really sat still for long, it seemed like being trapped in a body that wasn't working was against God's plan. She wondered if this was his punishment. Was he battling something inside that kept him there?

The door creaked open and Brooklyn turned, smiling when she saw Parker. "You're back."

"Carter called me."

I love that man. "Good. Were you able to reach Bryson?"

Parker shook his head. "The phone number I have

is disconnected. I'm thinking of hiring a private investigator to find him."

Their youngest brother was convinced that Wellspring was the devil, and had promised to never return when he'd left a few years earlier. Brooklyn doubted they'd find him. "I hope he at least calls. It would be good to know he's okay."

"Wellspring Water Corp is in an uproar. The board has called an emergency meeting to discuss how the business will run in Senior's absence."

She shrugged. "That's easy. You'll run it, like you've been training to do all along." Taking his hand in hers, she squeezed. "You got this, brother. You've been working toward this for years."

Parker nodded. "I didn't want it like this. With so much unsaid between us. The last conversation we had with him, we basically accused him of killing Mom. While I'm sad that he's here, I still want answers. And it's just like him to fall into a coma so that he won't have to give them to us."

Brooklyn chuckled. "Wow, Parker." She knew her brother was joking, but it was a joke that had more than a hint of truth to it.

"I can't help it, sis. What the hell are we supposed to do now?"

Brooklyn wished she had an answer for her brother. But she knew there was no answer good enough. "I don't know, Parker. I don't know."

Chapter 22

Carter hauled a box into the house, and set it down onto the dark hardwood floors. It had been several months since Parker Wells Sr. had fallen into a coma. With a little encouragement from him, he'd convinced Brooklyn to focus on the positive changes in her life. She still visited her father every week, but had chosen to focus on healing.

"Baby, did you bring in my box with all of my shoes?"

He grinned at his girlfriend. She stood before him, hands on her hips, dressed in a pair of shorts and a tank top. His favorite outfit on her. "No, it's still in the truck."

Moving in together had been a foregone conclusion. It hadn't taken them long to realize that neither of them wanted to sleep without the other. He'd half expected his family to have a fit, but when he'd announced to them that he was buying a house with Brooklyn—in Wellspring—they all had pretty much acted like it was no big deal. Almost like they already thought they lived together. Even

Aisha was on board with the idea. And he thought she would be the hardest sell.

With Senior still in a coma, Parker was named interim CEO by the board of directors. The first order of business had been reinstating Marshall and Sullivan's contract and releasing Brooklyn's money to her. The King family was livid and threatened to sue. But then Parker had presented emails, sent from Senior to Sterling, concocting the plan to provoke Carter into hurting him. And the threat miraculously evaporated into thin air.

"Carter, baby, we have to get it."

"Beautiful, you don't need your shoes at this moment. I'll get the box later. Right now, we need to concentrate on moving the big stuff."

"That's why I told you that we should hire movers. Period. Who wants to spend all day sweating and moving boxes? We could be chilling on our wraparound porch watching well-paid movers bring in our stuff."

It had been his bright idea to move them into their new house, as a bonding experience. He'd regretted that decision from the moment he'd said it, because everything that could have gone wrong, did. First, the truck he'd reserved got a flat tire on the way to the new house. As if that wasn't bad enough, when they finally arrived at the new house, the key didn't work. And for some reason, there was an open water bottle in the same box as his speakers. And she'd never let him forget it was his idea to bond. Combining homes was no joke. Between that and the new furniture delivery, it had been torture. He couldn't wait until they were settled.

"You didn't have a problem with sweating and

moving last night." He winked when she glared at him. Last night had been a particularly hot night, and they'd taken advantage of the nice weather by getting it in on her balcony. Brooklyn was sexy any day, but Brooklyn bathed in moonlight did him in every time.

"Ha ha. This still could have been done more efficiently if we'd hired movers to do the heavy lifting."

But his girlfriend was stunning, beautiful even, when she was pissed at him. "We don't need movers. Martin and Ryleigh are on their way."

"From Detroit," she retorted, sticking her tongue out at him when he smirked.

She grumbled a curse and stomped outside. He peeked out the door just in time to see her kick a box on the ground. He bit back a laugh when he watched her curse and then hop around, grasping at her toe.

Brooklyn then whirled around and narrowed her eyes in his direction. After she limped across the lawn toward the house, he dropped the blinds he'd been holding open. When she walked through the door, he gripped her around the waist and lifted her off the ground, spinning her around.

She let out a surprised yelp and then smacked him. "Put me down."

Instead of obliging, he held her tighter. "Not until you calm down and savor the experience."

Leaning down, he kissed her nose, then captured her mouth with his. The kiss quickly turned into more, as it had done so many times in the past few months, and they were soon off and running. But with the door wide-open, and boxes scattered around, he reluctantly pulled back. Taking in a few deep breaths, he looked down at her.

"We can't," he said simply. "Not here. There's too much shit around. I don't want you to get hurt."

She pouted. "Wow! Are you serious? Our bed is set up."

"In the bedroom. Our door is wide open and so is the moving truck."

With outstretched arms, she shouted, "We're in the middle of nowhere. Our closest neighbor is a mile away."

"Someone's cranky."

"Someone's hot for her boyfriend."

He stepped closer to her, bringing their bodies into contact. He'd learned over the last few months that he and Brooklyn were truly two sides of the same coin. Where he lacked, she excelled. Where she fell short, he soared. It was the reason he'd invested in the homeless shelter she was opening next year. He knew she would get the job done. And he'd essentially invested in her. He believed in her dreams.

"You know what? I think you're tense." He circled behind her, massaged her shoulders.

She leaned back into him. "I'm tired, Carter. I've been working so many hours, then making sure that Parker has the help he needs . . . it's a lot."

Parker and Brooklyn were in the process of going through the courts to get the fraudulent will overturned. The town was rocked by the scandal, and it even hit the news in Detroit and outside of the state of Michigan. There were reporters, depositions, interviews . . . In short, it was a hot-ass mess.

"I get it. You want me to make it all better." He kissed her neck, sucking it gently before he bit down.

"Oh yes. Make it better." She rolled her hips into his hardening erection. "Make it better all night."

It was moments like these that made him sure he wanted to spend the rest of his life with Brooklyn. It wasn't the sex, it was the true friendship, the real fondness they had for each other that kept him wanting more. He was ready to say *I do.* No big wedding, no big flowers. He didn't need anyone there. He just wanted her and the preacher. That's it. Just the two of them.

Bending down, he picked her up and slung her over his shoulder. She burst into a fit of giggles. "Put me down, Carter."

"I think you're right." He smacked her butt. "It's time we break in that new mattress."

Brooklyn and Carter plopped down on their new sofa. With Martin and Ryleigh's help they had finished moving in. She'd bought her dream house with her dream guy. What else could a girl want?

Leaning back against him, she grabbed his hand and entwined their fingers. She kissed his knuckles. "Your hands are so ashy."

She giggled when she felt the rumble of his laughter beneath her. "Hey, I've done a lot today. I didn't have time to put lotion on."

Turning around, she straddled his lap. "You know what I want?" she asked, running her finger over his brow.

"Anything you want, I got you."

She stared at him. She was so in love with this

man. Everything about him. Brooklyn had never
been in love before. She'd thought she was, but
nothing had ever compared to the level of emotion
she felt well up inside her when he looked at her, or
when he called her *beautiful*. He was the beautiful
one, in her opinion. He'd overcome so much and
still remained one of the humblest people she'd
ever met.

It was a no-brainer to move in with him. As far as
she was concerned, she'd go anywhere with him.
Except to hell—and even then, it would be a hard
decision. Because she wanted to be where he was.

Since they'd made the decision to move in together, she felt that he was going to propose soon.
And she knew Nicole was in on it. But she'd only
had one request. That Nicole at least let her know
if she needed to get a manicure. She couldn't post
pics of her ring with busted nails on social media.
And her best friend had told her yesterday that she
needed to get her "mani" on.

Carter thought he was being slick, too. He'd invited Martin and Ryleigh up to "help them move."
And her brother was uncharacteristically not answering his phone. Even Will and Dee were wink-
ing at each other when they thought she wasn't
looking.

She knew it was coming, she just didn't know
when. "Carter?"

"Hm?"

"I want to break our new pool table in. How about
you bend me over that corner pocket?"

She glanced back at the beautiful nine-foot pool
table in the middle of their den. When he'd suggested it, she'd balked because she'd had plans for

dinner parties and such. But when she thought about it a little more, she'd realized that it was perfect for them. He still hadn't beat her, and she was starting to wonder if he was letting her win because he loved her that much.

Carter ran the back of his hand over her cheek. "I love you, beautiful."

She smiled. "I love you."

"I want you."

She nuzzled his nose with hers. "I know."

He tickled her sides, and she broke into a fit of laughter. "I'm being serious."

Staring into those intense eyes, she nodded. "I know. I want you, too."

"Forever."

Brooklyn froze when he pulled out a small box from the couch cushion. "Oh my God. Carter?"

Even though she'd expected it, she still wasn't prepared for the gamut of emotions she felt when he opened the ring box, revealing the clearest princess-cut solitaire she'd ever seen. She met his gaze, her eyes welling with tears. "Carter," she breathed.

"Marry me," he said simply.

Her heart opened up as his words sank in. It was an ordinary proposal. No grand gestures, no audience. It was them. Simple, but extraordinary.

"Yes," she whispered against his lips, before kissing him. "I'll marry you. Just tell me when and where."

The *where* was at the little glass chapel at the edge of town. The *when* was two weeks from the proposal. They'd decided there was no need to wait. They hadn't done a "long" anything, so it didn't make sense for them to prolong the wedding.

There were less than twenty people in attendance. Brooklyn stood in the small foyer of the chapel, Nicole behind her . . . crying like a damn baby. She shot her friend a look. "You can get it together now, Nic. You're my maid of freakin' honor. No crying."

Nicole laughed through her tears. "I can't help it. You look so beautiful."

"You do," Aisha said from her stance on her left side. Her future sister-in-law looked like she was on the verge of tears, too.

"Come on," Brooklyn said, her chin trembling. "You can't do this to me. If you two insist on crying, I'm going to have to fire you as my bridesmaids."

The three ladies laughed.

"I'm so proud of you," Nic said. "You didn't let your father or anyone else tell you how to live your life. That's something, knowing your family."

Brooklyn thought about her father. She'd visited him after Carter proposed, and told him the news. Even though he didn't respond, she knew that he'd heard her. It had taken a lot for her to forgive her father, but she had. How could she not? It made no sense to hold a grudge against someone who could very well never wake up again. It was healthier for her to let it go. And that she had. She had too much going for her to let it ruin her life.

They'd dressed at her home because there was no bathroom in the small chapel. The glass chapel had been a tourist spot in Wellspring, but it wasn't meant for weddings. Brooklyn had always loved it, so Carter made it happen.

Aisha had brought a tall mirror to lean against the wall so she could see herself before she walked down the aisle. Glancing at her reflection in the mirror, she smiled. It wasn't a big ballroom gown like her mother had worn, and it wasn't a mermaid dress like everyone had expected her to wear. It was a simple, flowing, A-line gown with a sweetheart neckline, designed by up-and-coming designer Allina Smith, out of Belleville, Michigan. And it was perfect.

The music started, and the doors opened. Aisha walked down the aisle first, dabbing at her eyes the whole way. Nicole followed. And then it was her turn. She stepped into the aisle and smiled when she met Carter's gaze.

Unable to stop herself, she broke into a run down the aisle. He scooped her up in his arms and swung her around, kissing her tenderly. The entire church applauded. But all Brooklyn could hear was their hearts beating, in sync with each other, as they'd always done.

Carter buried his face in her neck, kissing her pulse point before setting her down gently. "You're so beautiful," he whispered against her ear. "You're so mine."

Brooklyn laughed, not even mortified that tears had drifted down her cheeks. Nicole could always fix her makeup later.

The ceremony was quick and straight to the point. The minister, Pastor Locke, pronounced them man and wife before he instructed Carter to "salute his bride."

Carter pulled her close to him and dipped his head down, brushing his lips over hers in the faintest of caresses. It left her aching for more, which was exactly why he'd done it that way.

"I love you," he said.

"I love you more." She beamed up at him.

They hurried out of the chapel and into the waiting car.

After the small dinner reception at the Bee's Knees, they returned to their home. She gasped when she opened the door to the flicker of candlelight all over the house.

"Carter, you sneak. Who'd you get to do this?"

"Martin. You didn't notice him and Ryleigh sneaking out of the diner?"

She shook her head and walked over to the pool table where there was a bottle of wine and two beers sitting on top. She pulled the wine bottle out, eyeing the label. "Nice. But I think I'll have a beer."

He opened two beers, and they toasted one another. They'd decided against a honeymoon. There was too much going on with both of their businesses and other things. But they'd agreed to take a trip during the holidays, when things hopefully died down.

Brooklyn noticed her cue stick was sitting on the pool table, next to his. "You definitely know how to make me swoon."

She picked up her stick. "A game?"

He grinned, leaned down and kissed her. "Forever."

Acknowledgments

Writing *Touched by You* was quite the journey. It took me from Southeast Michigan, where I was born and raised, to the western side of my beautiful state. The fictional town of Wellspring came to life through the eyes of Brooklyn, a longtime resident, and Carter, a newcomer. While writing, I envisioned the historic buildings, the ice-cream store, Brook's Pub, and the Bee's Knees, as if I were actually walking into the town. I hope you enjoyed meeting the good townspeople of Wellspring as much as I enjoyed bringing them to life. I appreciate your love and support.

First and foremost, all thanks and praise to God. He has never failed me yet, and it is because of His Grace and Mercy that all of this is possible.

To my husband, Jason, you are the love of my life. I am forever touched by you. I love you.

To my children, Asante, Kaia, and Masai: you inspire me to dream big, to hope for more. You're brilliant, amazing, and beautiful. Never let anyone tell you otherwise.

To my father, Leon, thank you for being someone that I can turn to. Thanks for never turning your back on me. I'm so blessed to have you.

To my brother, Lee, it is because of our close relationship that I can write these awesome brother-and-sister relationships. You mean so much to me. I don't know what I'd do without you.

To my Nanay and Tatay, thank you for loving me and accepting me without question. I love you both very much.

To my sister LaDonna, I can't thank you enough for being that sounding board, that person that I can talk to about anything. You love me without condition. And that means the world to me. Love you BIG!

To my sister Kim, thanks for loving me. Thanks for making me laugh and telling me to take care of myself. I love you!

To my lit sisters, and Once Upon a Bridesmaid crew, Sheryl Lister, Sherelle Green, and Angela Seals: This year has been hard for me, but I'm thankful that we've forged a bond that I only see growing stronger as we continue this journey. Love y'all! You rock!

To my Book Euphoria ladies, you are #BlackGirl Passion. And we are #JustThatDope. Thanks for bringing me into the fold. I can't wait to see what's next on the horizon.

To my #ElleWright Betas (Kimberley, Danielle, Shizzle, Nicole, Keshia, Andrea, Erica, Dwana, Stacey, Latrease, Kim, LaDonna, and Crystal), thanks for reading, thanks for listening, thanks for talking to me about these books. Love you all!

I can't forget about several people who are so special to me. These people have supported #TeamElle from day one. To my writerly boo, Christine Hughes, you're so awesome! You are my family and I'm so glad to have you in my life. A big thank-you to Sheree for being my sounding board when I was creating Wellspring and Brooklyn. It is because of that long, recorded conversation that this book is being published. A special thank-you to Crystal for being my friend, my family. I never have to guess where you stand, and that means more to me than you'll ever know. Love ya! To Tanishia Pearson-Jones, when I think of faith, I see my mother and you. You've shown me what it means to truly trust God. Thanks, friend. To Anita Davis, it has been a pleasure getting to know you. I'm blessed to call you my friend. To all of my friends and family, I love you all. I can't name everyone, but I would be remiss if I didn't thank you all for encouraging me. The year 2017 was rough. So rough. But I'm grateful for you all.

To my agent, Sara Camilli, thank you for talking me off the ledge so many times. LOL. I appreciate you.

To my editor, Selena James, thank you for challenging me, for pushing me to be better, to look deeper. I've already learned so much from you. Thanks for taking a chance on me.

I want to give a shout-out to the City Chicks and Southern Belles, Brenda Jackson, Beverly Jenkins, Lutishia Lovely, Renee Daniel Flagler, Iris Bolling, Tiffany L. Warren, Sherelle Greene, Sheryl Lister, Yahrah St. John. Our #RT17 event rocked the house! Thank you for everything!

I also want to thank to Priscilla C. Johnson and Cilla's Maniacs, A. C. Arthur, Brenda Kidd-Woodbury (BJBC), MidnightAce Scotty, King Brooklyns (Black Page Turners), Sharon Blount and BRAB (Building Relationships Around Books), LaShaunda Hoffman (SORMAG), Orsayor Simmons (Book Referees), Tiffany Tyler (Reading in Black and White), Naleighna Kai (Naleighna Kai's Literary Café and Cavalcade of Authors), Delaney Diamond (RNIC), Wayne Jordan (RIC), Radiah Hubert (Urban Book Reviews), and the EyeCU Reading and Social Network for supporting me. I truly appreciate you all.

I also want to thank my readers. Thanks for your feedback, thanks for your encouragement, thanks for reading. Without you all, this wouldn't be possible.

I hope you enjoyed Brooklyn and Carter!

Thank you!

Love,
Elle

Parker Wells, Jr., meets his match in

ENTICED BY YOU

Enjoy the following excerpt . . .

Chapter 1

For the last several hours, Parker Wells Jr. had been asking himself the same question over and over again. *What the hell was his father smoking when he met, then married Patricia Lewis Wells?*

Sighing heavily, he watched the movers cart box after box from his father's mansion. It seemed Patricia had made out quite well for herself considering she'd been a "reformed" stripper when she became wife number five to Parker Wells Sr. With her bright blond weave, long fake nails and lashes, and her enhanced face and breasts, he often wondered how she really looked under all of that . . . fakeness.

Gesturing to one of the movers, he grabbed the huge painting his father had commissioned of his latest wife. At least, she got to keep it. The other four wives, including his own mother, hadn't faired so well. The paintings ended up in the incinerator the moment the divorce was final. Or in his mother's case, the death certificate was signed.

Parker wondered if that was the moment he realized he didn't care for his father. Hell, he borderline hated him for most of his thirty-one years on this Earth. For the life of him, he couldn't remember any redeeming qualities.

Senior, as they were instructed to call their father, had made it a point to not engage with his sons. His younger sister Brooklyn had a different experience as a little girl, when their mother was alive. She remembered their dad as kind and protective back then. Things didn't change for Brooklyn and Senior until Mama died.

Parker, on the other hand, never remembered feeling secure in his home, or even in his own skin. Everything about him had been picked apart since he could form a coherent sentence. His first memories of his father were painful ones, discipline for even the smallest infraction. His pants weren't ironed right, his hair was too long, he didn't enunciate his words properly, he wasn't smart enough, he wasn't fast enough on the football field. Never mind, he'd never received less than an "A" on anything, had made the All-State team and won MVP for every year he played football. After a while, he'd stopped even bringing home trophies or awards because they just didn't matter. And things had steadily gotten worse as he grew into adulthood.

After his mother died, he'd become a shield to his younger siblings, taken their punishments so they wouldn't have to be subjected to their father's wrath. Although, neither one of them had escaped unscathed. Most recently, his father had waged a war against Brooklyn for daring to say no to the arranged marriage Senior had set up.

The last time his father had hit him was the one time he'd ended up in jail. Parker could still remember the fury that tightened his bones, turned his blood hot, yet cold, at the same time. He'd defended himself that day, and his father had never stepped to him again.

Of course, the punishment for that transgression had been banishment from the house and the family company, Wellspring Water Corporation. At the time, Parker didn't care. He'd considered it a blessing that he wouldn't have to be around Senior and his cronies.

Everything changed once he'd graduated from law school. He'd made it his mission to work his way back into his father's good graces, and every minute he'd kissed ass, gone against his heart, had chipped away at his soul.

But Parker had a plan. Inevitably, his father wouldn't be around much longer. And he would be able to run the company the way *he* saw fit. He would be able to do right by his grandfather's vision for Wellspring Water. So, he'd bided his time, played the game, and covered his ass at all times. Now, it was his turn.

Parker Wells Sr. had suffered a massive heart attack several months earlier and was now comatose. The doctors weren't hopeful, but Senior was holding on for some reason. Maybe it was the old man's way of saying "fuck you" to all of them. As long as he was alive, the company would be his, the legacy would be one of darkness and corruption, not light and responsibility like Parker envisioned.

As the heir to the family company, Parker was next in line to take over as Chief Executive Officer when Senior finally passed away. Recently, the board had voted him in as the interim CEO while his father was incapacitated. But there was more, so much more to the story.

Apparently, his father hadn't been content to cheat unsuspecting workers, steal land, and marry strippers. He'd actually committed a serious crime, forging their mother's will. Doing so, allowed him to maintain control of a company that technically belonged to Parker and Brooklyn.

The scandal had rocked their small town of Wellspring, and he and his sister were currently working with a team of attorney's to fix the mess Senior had made of all of their lives.

A loud thump sounded from the sitting room in the front of the house. Next, he'd heard the crash of glass against the wall. Sighing, he rushed over to the room, where his sister had been arguing with Patricia for the last half an hour—about any and everything he could think of from the priceless vase Patricia felt was owed to her to the Honey Nut Cheerios she wanted to take from the kitchen.

Brooklyn. Parker sighed when he thought of his little sis. She was petite but she packed a punch. And she wasn't letting Patricia leave the house with anything that wasn't specified in the agreement they'd made her sign last week, no matter how petty and how miniscule the item was.

Pushing open the door, he scanned the room. Patricia was standing there, wig crooked and chest heaving. Brooklyn, on the other hand, was calm. There wasn't a hair out of place on his sister's head. Her clothes were pristine, liked she'd just put them on. There was glass around Brooklyn's high heeled pumps.

"What the hell is going on in here?" he asked his sister.

Brooklyn stared at him, amusement crackling in her brown eyes. "Patricia won't go quietly into the night like she agreed. She insists on breaking up all of Senior's shit. And what she fails to realize is I don't give a damn what she breaks. There is no way in hell she's going to walk out of here with anything not outlined in this agreement." His sister held up the divorce decree.

It had been their attorney's idea to offer a settlement to Patricia to divorce their father. Patricia had been happy to accept the offer, because they'd offered her a sum over and above what had been agreed upon in the Prenuptial Agreement and what would be bequeathed to her in the event of Senior's death. In fact, Patricia had been so eager to accept the terms of the agreement, Parker wondered if she'd had a boyfriend on the side somewhere.

The proceedings had gone well. There wasn't a lot of arguing, no real disputes over the terms. Ultimately, they'd come to an agreement. Which is why he was perplexed she was having so much trouble now that it was time to move out of Senior's house.

"Patricia, what is the problem?" he asked, arms out at his sides. "You knew this day was coming. You agreed to the terms."

Patricia glared at Brooklyn. "I can't stand her. I never could."

Brooklyn barked out a laugh. "Ask me if I care."

Parker cut Brooklyn a look that he hoped told her to shut up so they could get the woman out of the house. Brooklyn got the message because she stepped away, gingerly out of the glass and took a seat on one of the chairs.

Approaching Patricia, Parker said, "Is there anything I can do to make this transition better for you?" Parker ignored the muttered curse from his sister from her side of the room. "What's going on with you?"

A still seething Patricia, wouldn't look at Parker. She was still throwing Brooklyn death glares. "I won't talk as long as she's in the room."

Sighing, Parker turned to Brooklyn. "Can you give us a minute?"

His sister's mouth fell open. "Parker . . . why?"

"Because I asked you to, Brooklyn. Go have Arlene make you some lunch or something. Call Carter, I don't know. Just leave us alone for a minute."

Shaking her head, Brooklyn did as he requested and left him alone with the latest Ex-Mrs. Parker Wells Sr. When the door was closed, and they were alone, Parker motioned for Patricia to take a seat.

"What can I do for you?" he asked.

"Parker, don't play me," Patricia said with a scowl. "You're not that nice."

He blinked. Nice? He'd never pretended to like Patricia, but he was respectful of her title. Despite how she'd treated him and his sister, he'd made sure he was cordial at all times. That was something he'd learned from his mother, Marie.

Marie was kind, giving. She was all the things that no wife of Senior had been since.

"What is it, Patricia?" Parker asked, his patience dangling on a very thin thread. He didn't have time for this. He had to get to work and put out the seemingly endless fires his father had set in motion. "What do you need to say?"

"I expect to get what's owed to me."

"You'll get exactly what we agreed upon. Anything else?"

Patricia's mouth pulled in a tight line. "Yes, actually there is. I have information that's very valuable to you and that little ingrate you call a sister."

Parker was admittedly curious. It was no secret that his father was into all kinds of shady business. He wondered what Patricia had in her back pocket that would be worth something to him. Would this information affect him and his siblings? Wellspring Water?

Unwilling to show his hand yet, he sat on the chair his sister had vacated a few minutes earlier, crossing his left leg over his right. "I'm listening."

Patricia let out a humorless chuckle. "Really? Do you think I'm going to play my hand that fast and easy?"

"That would depend on a few things. One being if it has anything to do with my family. The other being if it has anything to do with my company."

"Your company? Senior isn't dead, Parker."

"Whatever he is, it's no concern of yours anymore." Parker took a deep breath. His mask was slipping, and he couldn't afford it at that moment. He'd prided himself on his ability to get the job done, and that meant being able to get to the thick of things without losing his temper.

"Oh, okay. It's like that?"

With raised eyebrows, he asked. "How should it be? You're not his wife anymore. You're free to leave with the money we gave you, money you wouldn't have seen if it had not been for me and Brooklyn. I'm not sure why you insist on dragging this out longer than it has to be. If you know something that would be of use to me and my family, why not just say it? If I feel that it's worth something, I'll act accordingly. Because I'm sure that's what this is about. Isn't it? Your bottom line? Cash."

Patricia was always after her next dollar. He knew the type, had even been fooled by a few women in the past. But he'd learned the hard way to never let his guard down, and never drop his card before his turn.

Leaning against the table, Patricia crossed her feet at her ankles and straightened her wig. "What is another sibling worth to you, Parker?"

The sneer in her tone when she said his name wasn't lost on him. "If that sibling is from you, I cry bullshit."

Patricia was younger than Senior, yes. But she wasn't young enough to be pregnant with Senior's baby.

His ex-stepmother glared at him. "Not my child."

"Whose child?"

"Senior had another child. A daughter. I only know because he slipped up one morning at breakfast."

"Why should I believe you?"

The thought of there being another Wells sibling

turned his stomach. Not that he didn't love his brother and sister. On the contrary, he loved them more than anything, anyone. He'd do anything for them, and had.

He assessed Patricia, who was watching him intently, a smirk on her augmented lips. *Fake.* She could be lying. He wouldn't put it past her to try and extort more cash from him with this long lost sister crap. But something told him she wasn't lying this time.

Senior had made no secret of his penchant for mistresses. Bryson's mother had been a long-term mistress, and most of the wives he'd brought home were former side chicks. There could very well be another sibling out there somewhere. And if there is, he needed to find out.

"Name your price," he said coolly.

A smug Patricia threw out some astronomical number that made Parker's blood boil.

"Nice try, but hell no."

Her mouth fell open. "But this information is priceless."

"If there is another sibling, I will find her with or without you." He stood up and walked to the door, swinging it open, nearly pulling Brooklyn into the room too. His sister braced herself on the door. Shaking his head, he asked, "Really?"

Brooklyn shrugged. "Sorry."

Parked turned toward Patricia. "Your moving truck is ready to leave. I suggest you follow it."

Kissing his sister on her forehead, he murmured, "I'll call you later. I have something to take care of." Then, he left.

Chapter 2

I can't believe I wasted all my pretty years on this idiot.
Kennedi Robinson shook her head as she glanced at the dollar amount on the last spousal support check she would ever write. It had been a long year, full of legal briefs, subpoenas, and surprise court dates, all designed by her ex-husband to extort as much money as he could from her.

Luckily for her, the Judge had agreed that the initial divorce decree stands and spousal support would after one year. That year was up.

Signing the check, she stuffed it in the envelope, addressed to her attorney, her colleague and friend, Paula. "Here you go," Kennedi said, hanging the envelope to Paula, who was seated across from her desk, engrossed in a file.

"You sure you don't want to deliver this yourself?"

Kennedi giggled. She knew Paula wasn't serious. The two were consummate professionals at work, and profanity while in the process of business was a no-no. "I don't want to give him anymore of my energy. He already took my money; he won't take my dignity."

Paula eyed her. "Are you sure you're okay?"

"I'm fine." Kennedi stood and made her way over to her office window. It was a beautiful late summer day in Ann Arbor, Michigan. She'd had a chance to enjoy the weather that morning on her daily run, which she rarely missed. There was nothing better than the wind in her face, the burn in her legs, as she ran her route through Gallup Park.

The park was Ann Arbor's most popular recreation area, located along the Huron River and Geddes Pond. It was a runner's dream, and Kennedi took advantage of the asphalt trails every single morning.

She heard Paula approach her from behind. Soon, her best friend was standing next to her, offering her silent strength. The two had been friends since they'd enrolled at the Michigan Law eight years ago. Since their first day of classes, they'd supported one another through everything, through the death of Kennedi's parents, through Paula's pregnancy, and now through Kennedi's failed marriage.

Eyeing her best friend out of the corner of her eyes, Kennedi said, "I need to make a change, friend."

Paula turned to her, but Kennedi refused to meet her gaze. "What change do you need to make, Kenni?"

Kennedi smiled at the nickname Paula had given

her their first year of law school. "Change of scenery, Paula. I need a vacation."

Years had passed since she'd entered the work-force, with no spas, no resorts, no time off in her plans. Kennedi worked hard in her job as a corpo-rate attorney, putting in long hours for her clients.

"Then, take a vacation, Kenni."

Kennedi folded her arms across her chest. It was almost laughable how easy Paula had made time off sound. "How am I supposed to do that when I'm pushing you down the aisle in one month."

Paula smiled, a wistful look in her eyes. "I know. I can't believe I'm getting married."

Her best friend was engaged to Mark Hoover. The two had met during a golf outing last year, and the romance had blossomed into unconditional love and acceptance. Mark was the type of man that every woman dreamed about—intelligent, polished, handsome, and a provider. Kennedi knew he was a keeper when he'd shown Paula's daughter nothing but respect and love from the very beginning. Ken-nedi's goddaughter, Lauren, was smitten with her future stepfather and that was a testament to Mark's willingness to love the three-year-old as if she were his biological daughter.

Kennedi squeezed Paula's hand. It had been years since she'd seen her friend so happy; years of tears, struggling to make ends meet, and raising her daughter alone. "You deserve to be happy, Paula. I'm so proud that I'm going to be standing up for you when you marry the love of your life. Mark is a good man. He'll be a good hubby to you and father to my Lauren."

"Kenni?"

Oh Lord. Not that she didn't love her best friend with everything in her, but she couldn't bear another *you'll find love again* conversation. Yes, Kennedi had been dragged through the longest, nightmare divorce from hell. No, Kennedi wasn't sour on love. She just wasn't looking for it at that point in her life.

She'd spent a full two years tomorrow dealing with her ex's antics. What she wanted was a little peace and quiet, away from home, away from the demands of her job.

"Paula, I know what you're going to say, but it isn't necessary. Really."

Kennedi smiled at the worried expression on Paula's face. Her friend was gorgeous every day, but she was radiant with the glow of her impending nuptials. Paula's brown skin was sun kissed and smooth. She was a natural beauty, and Mark was the lucky man who better not ever forget that he was marrying a gem.

"I'm not sad."

Paula peered at her friend with suspicious eyes. "If you were, I wouldn't blame you. We all thought Quincy was the one for you."

"Well, turns out he wasn't. And I've made my peace with that. I truly appreciate your support. You were excellent in that court room." Instead of corporate law, Paula had chosen family law as her field of choice. Her friend's long-term goal was to become one of the top divorce attorneys in the state, and she was well on her way.

"Can I just tell you that you are my shero?"

Surprised, Kennedi took a step back. "Me? Why?"

"You could have let this man break you. He put you through the ringer, with one motion after another, false accusations, going after your family business. But I watched you walk in that courtroom every day with your head held high, your shoe game fierce, and that uncanny ability you have to turn off your emotions. He tried everything he could, threw any and everything at you. But you never let him see you sweat. That's why you're my shero. I don't think I could have done it."

It wasn't an uncanny ability, Kennedi thought. It was a learned behavior she'd been able to perfect as the result of losing both of her parents at the same time to a horrible crime. Kenneth and Yolanda Robinson had been the unfortunate victims of a home invasion. The culprit, an older gentleman, high on drugs had broken into their home, in their middle-class neighborhood, and killed them for daring to be home while he stole everything they'd worked hard for.

"Kennedi, you're the strongest person I know. But even the strongest person needs time to regroup, to relax, to release. So, if you need a break, please take one."

Her bestie had given her a lot to think about. She'd spent years being strong for everyone else around her, for her sister, for her friend, for her aunt. For the past few months, she'd felt bogged down. Like her aunt used to say, "she was kicking, but not high. Flopping and can't fly." "I think I'm going to head to Wellspring."

Paula grinned then. "Good. You need to visit."

Wellspring, Michigan, nestled between Kalamazoo and Grand Rapids was Kennedi's hometown.

She'd been born in the small, mostly African American town. Although, her parents had moved away before she hit high school, she'd visited many times over the years, spent summers there with her Aunt Angelia.

It was just what she needed, time away to renew, to relax, and begin the process of rebuilding her life. "I'll talk to my boss this morning."

"Maybe Jared will take some of your workload from you."

Jared Smith was a junior partner at the firm, and her senior. He was the first African American partner, junior or otherwise, at their firm. They'd met during law school, and after a disastrous start at another firm, he'd brought her in and helped her find her footing there.

"I don't know. He's busy at home, with his family." Jared was a proof positive that attorneys could lead fulfilling lives outside of the office. He was happily married with two lovely children, and part owner of one of her favorite after-work destinations in Ypsilanti Township, Michigan.

Ypsilanti was located six miles east of Ann Arbor, and approximately forty miles west of Detroit. It was home to Eastern Michigan University, and where Kennedi currently resided. Her mom and dad had moved to the area when he'd taken a job as an attorney for an automobile manufacturer in Detroit. She'd followed in his footsteps when she'd decided to go into corporate law. Kennedi couldn't say that she'd done it because she loved the work, though. Mostly, she'd done it because that's what he'd wanted for her, what he'd groomed her for.

"It doesn't hurt to ask, Kennedi."

Paula was right. She'd ask, and hope for the best.

Later that evening, Kennedi turned down Main Street in the downtown Wellspring area. After she'd talked to Jared, he'd worked everything out with her, agreeing with Paula that a vacation was long overdue. He'd worked so efficiently that she was able to leave the office by noon. Kennedi decided it was better to get on the road right away, or she'd definitely change her mind. So, she'd sped home, tossed several things in her suitcase, picked up an ice coffee and some snacks and left town.

The drive from Ypsilanti to Wellspring took about two and half hours. It was easy driving in the middle of the day and she'd had a chance to listen to her audiobook and enjoy the beauty that was Michigan.

She glanced to her left, then her right. The town hadn't changed much. It was still the quaint little place she'd remembered. There were people walking down the street with their kids, dog walkers, elderly couple holding hands. On her left was the Bee's Knees diner, which she would definitely pay a visit to as soon as possible. Dee Clark's Western Omelets were to die for, but Kennedi preferred the catfish with lots of hot sauce. Her mouth watered in anticipation.

The downtown area had grown since her last visit a few years ago. There was a Panera Bread and a Jimmy John's on the strip. And she'd heard there was a new Walmart on the outskirts of town. But she was glad to see that the overall charm of the city hadn't changed.

Kennedi was ticking off all the things she'd like to do once she was settled. Distracted by the tranquility she'd felt as soon as she hit the city limits, she went to grab her second iced coffee and squeezed a bit too hard, spilling the drink on her brand new Chanel bag. The one she'd given herself as a divorce gift, the one that had cost a pretty penny.

She reached over and opened the glove compartment and pulled out several napkins. Dabbing her bag, she prayed it didn't leave a stain on the light colored leather. Then, she was jolted forward, her chest smacking the steering wheel.

Oh no. Through her front window, she could see the luxury truck that she'd rammed into. *Oh my God.*

Immediately, Kennedi jumped into action. The last thing she needed was to shell out another dime on a careless mistake. Putting the car into park, she hopped out and rushed forward, checking for damage on the truck. Of course, since it was a truck and she was driving her Ford Taurus, she was the one with the huge dent in her front fender.

Grumbling a curse, she resisted the urge to kick her tire. She heard the door of the truck open and footsteps heading her way.

"I'm so sorry," she said, still mentally cursing herself for distracted driving. How many times had she told people to avoid texting and driving, talking and driving . . . anything while driving? "I promise I'll pay for any damage to your truck. I was distracted." Kennedi rolled her eyes. She'd basically just told on herself. Another thing that she'd cautioned her clients against. *Way to incriminate yourself, Kennedi.*

"It's fine."

The voice was like butter, poured over fat, juicy crab legs—warm. When she finally looked up, she gasped. The man behind the voice was just as appealing, just as he'd always been. Parker Wells Jr.

Tongue-tied, she pointed to his fender then hers before finally finding her voice. "I'm so sorry," she repeated.

Parker smiled, bending low to assess the damage to her fender. He smelled like musk and woods. Perfect. "It's okay. There's not damage to my car. It's yours that is in need of a mechanic."

And he didn't remember her. Well, she hadn't expected him to. She hadn't lived in Wellspring in years. Even when she did, he was older than her and traveled in a different crowd. "Yeah, I noticed that."

"Are you okay?"

Kennedi swallowed, rubbing her chest which seemed to suddenly ache. "I-I'm good."

"Did you ram into the steering wheel?"

Nodding, she flinched when he reached out the touch her, nearly falling on her ass. Thankfully, her car was there to stop the further humiliation. "Yes," she answered once she was standing straight again.

She tugged on her shirt and smoothed her hair back. *I need a mirror.*

Parker frowned. "Do I know you?"

"No," she blurted out. *Get it together, Kennedi.* Clearing her throat, she muttered, softly this time, "No."

Parker's tongue peeked out to wet his lips. "Are you from Wellspring?"

"Yes, and no."

He searched her face, almost as if he was still trying to figure out how he knew her. "You look familiar."

Kennedi scratched her head and shrugged. "I must have that kind of face."

His gaze dropped to her mouth and she prayed her lip gloss hadn't failed her. "You're probably right. I don't know you. Because if I had, I'd remember."

Kennedi sank against her car, and smiled. There were few things she remembered about middle school at Wellspring Middle. The pizza was good and Parker Wells Jr. was fine as hell. But now she was faced with a grown up Parker and she'd say time was good to him.

Her phone rang from inside her car, and she jumped. "Oh, it's probably my aunt. Hold on." She rushed to the door, and pulled out her purse. Slipping a business card from her case, she handed it to him. "Again, I'm so sorry. If there is any damage, please call me. I have to go."

Parker peered down at her card. "Okay. I'll give you call." He handed her one of his business cards. "If you need a recommendation on a mechanic, let me know. I have a friend."

Kennedi tucked her hair behind her ear. "Thanks."

When she was tucked safely in her car, she gripped her steering wheel and watched him hop in his truck and pull off. Sighing, she leaned back in her seat. Staring down at his card, she ran her finger over the embossed letting of his name. Parker Wells Jr. Kennedi smiled at the masculine design, and thought maybe her bad luck was running out.